A SICKNESS IN TIME

by
MF Thomas & Nicholas Thurkettle

***

Edited by Katherine Jurak

Cover Art by Kevin Necessary

***

ISBN: 978-1-48357-621-3

First Edition: JUNE 2016

10 9 8 7 6 5 4 3 2 1

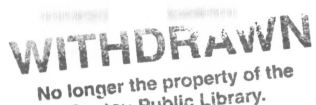

ALSO BY
MF THOMAS & NICHOLAS THURKETTLE

Seeing by Moonlight

PRAISE FOR *SEEING BY MOONLIGHT*

"*A complex thriller that offers new revelations up until the very end. The book's science-fiction element drives the major plot twists, but the most engaging scenes are those in which readers learn the real relationships and histories between the characters.*"
    -Kirkus Reviews

"*This writing team is extraordinarily gifted. Their style is smooth and lyrical and their characters are finely drawn and quickly come alive in the reader's mind...highly recommended. 5/5 Stars*"
    -Readers' Favorite

"Seeing by Moonlight *is a thoughtful and intricate story, with enough food for thought to keep the reader's brain and heart engaged from beginning to end. 4.5/5 Stars*"
    -Indie Reader

***

ALSO BY
NICHOLAS THURKETTLE

Stages of Sleep
short story collection

PRAISE FOR *STAGES OF SLEEP*

"*Nicholas Thurkettle's writing is finely tuned -- immediate, lyrical, and lean. His work has elements of various American short-story masters — Damon Runyon comes to mind. So does O. Henry. And particularly Ray Bradbury...a triumph for self-publishing.*"
    -Playwright Scott Charles

"*Thurkettle's tightly constructed stories are bursting at the seams...(he) did well to put these narratives in the context of sleep and vigilance; it's a perceptive approach to interpreting many of them. But no single theme could contain, much less exhaust, the philosophical richness and psychological acuity of the stories in* Stages of Sleep.*"
    -Author and Essayist Philip Lawton

***

To all the authors who ever excited us about the Future; and to the baristas, who fuel the maddest dreams of misfits without judgment

-PROLOGUE-

Praia, Cape Verde – 2039

Even the heat was wonderful, delirious. Laurent normally hated the heat. Brisk winds, mountains, snow: these things he knew and these things felt natural, like home. But now, as an attendant wheeled him out of the hospital into the summer air of Praia, he felt the damp swelter roll over his flesh and for a moment the sensation consumed him. *There will be a storm today,* he suddenly thought. And while this was never a bad bet to make in a Cape Verde August, the sureness was a surprise, but totally without doubt. It was as though the water droplets above were pulsing the message into his body.

Laurent was no stranger to sensual pleasures. He indulged in the vividness of drugs and the ecstasy of attentive female touch habitually and without embarrassment. This had some of those qualities but with no vulnerability. It was pure knowledge as a form of exhilaration, complete with a rush of mastery.

Already he knew that he had got more than his money's worth.

His security detail made a corridor of men leading to his car. He rose from the wheelchair unsteadily, muscles weak from two weeks' convalescence. He felt like half himself in this famished body. He brushed off the attendants and took just one moment more to bask in the air. The equatorial fire, the blazing sun, clashed with the chill waters of the Atlantic all over this little African island, making breezes or storms as the day warranted, but never ceasing. *Nature is churn,* Laurent thought. *Nature is perpetual warfare.* This was consistent with what he knew of life and how to stake a place in it.

He settled into the back of his car, and his driver greeted him with some sing-songy Creole half-gibberish. Laurent closed the shutter at once and turned his attention to Quon as the car began to hum through the Capital streets towards his hotel. She waited silently, giving him a moment to collect himself. "Water," he said finally.

She grabbed a glass from the service and poured it half-full. "Full," Laurent croaked with vehemence. "Hang social custom, we're alone here." She filled the glass, and Laurent drank. The water was chilled and clean, and now tasted better than a five-star meal. He breathed deeply between each sip, luxuriating.

"You'll acclimate to the sensory enhancement," Quon said in her usual even tone after he swallowed. She took the glass back and ran a finger around the bottom, stealing a last droplet to lick.

"I hope so," Laurent answered. "I can hardly think."

Quon snorted with the insouciance she had earned from years of discreet service. "You're thinking more than ever. That's the point."

She pushed up her sleeves and reached out to examine the bandage on his head. Laurent flinched – it seemed like no matter how long she assisted him, how much he paid her, he still had this instinct that her hands were dirty. But he submitted to her scrutiny. He wouldn't admit it to her, but he got a private thrill from the lack of awe with which Quon treated him. It was like having a low-dose dominatrix for daily use.

She lifted the bandage and saw the remnants of the surgery. He would get a hair graft as soon as possible, but for now he bore the telltale equals-sign wound, two parallel incisions above his forehead. "These look good," she said. "Good docs here."

"The best," Laurent insisted. "Just like you."

She shrugged and pulled a jackpad from her satchel. Its screen flashed on and she danced her fingers over it, searching for signs that it recognized the tiny device now embedded in Laurent's brain tissue.

She frowned, her most natural expression. She was a genius, and like the most valuable geniuses she lived to push the limits of conformity. More exciting problems existed on the outside, which was why she was now accessing the Beetle – the slang name for the implant which had been banned in all but a few nations – in order to install patches and upgrades that were banned everywhere. The early versions of the Beetle had been designed to stabilize seizures before they could begin, to treat sleep disorders, to ward off dementia. It did all these things well, but it could do other things, too.

Her jackpad was custom, clean, and stripped of everything that could connect it to rWeb. Unlike most devices on the planet, it could not talk to satellites, nodes, or any other devices. The only device it could communicate with was the one that had just switched on in Laurent's head. If rumor were believed, his life could depend on this.

The car lurched in traffic. Outside, a crowd of child-beggars had materialized around them, tapping on the windows, the press of their bodies rocking the car on its shocks. Laurent couldn't hear them through the car's heavy security windows, but their lips moved and he could imagine their weary monotone pleading.

He snorted with impatience. Patience had not been a virtue of his before, and he suspected that it was going to be even less of one now that he could access more of his mind's power. "They have no respect," he complained. "Coming to us like that."

"They respect that you're rich."

"I mean self-respect. This whole nation would be under water if it weren't for us, and how do they respond to being saved? Dependence. Like stray dogs, begging because they've forgotten how to hunt."

Quon smirked as she looked up from the jackpad. "You've never hunted in your life."

This wasn't true at all. He hunted every day: hunted for opportunities, hunted for advantage, hunted to grow his wealth. He knew he had a fighting chance to become one of the thousand richest men in the world. Already he had a True 9 Nano portfolio making him richer every second of the day; Quon had helped build the algorithms that made it return more than almost any of the other True 9s out there (which really earned more like True 6s these days with more and more people crowding into that market sector.) He might soon have the wealth to invest in True 12 access: even a trained donkey could make the initial price back in only a few years with that kind of market speed.

But if you wanted to get ahead, you had to exploit every possible advantage. In his mind, Beetles were the same as buying into True 12 access, but there were whispers even among his peers – in the private chambers at their economic forums, after the meals where they decided which nations presented the best opportunities – that there might be something different about Beetles. Something dangerous. But whispers were nothing – the studies said that Beetles were safe. The fear, Laurent knew, was that even among the people most gifted at skewing systems to their benefit, the idea of skewing *themselves*, of tinkering within their own minds, caused them to quail. It was natural, it was human...and it was a chance for Laurent to put himself beyond them.

Australia was about to pass new laws. Laurent knew the people that had helped write them, who had maneuvered the politicians into place who would pass them. These laws would commit a whole continent to a desalinization effort of an unprecedented scale, disrupting the water economy of the whole planet. There was money be made at every level in a thousand different sectors.

Laurent was decisive, nimble, and brilliant. Although his middle-aged belly sagged from plenty, in the worldwide dance of currency he was a martial artist. But for a moment with this kind of potential, he needed to be more insightful, more calculating, more responsive to the cascading interplay of transactions and influence. He needed to be more *himself*. That was the power of the Beetle, and it was worth this little medical vacation.

Quon read the movement of his lips and poured him another glass of water. Full this time. She said something in Chinese as she handed it to him.

"What was that?" Laurent asked, surprised at the idleness in his voice from the pleasurable haze of being quenched.

"Confucius," Quon answered. "The chase of gain is rich in hate."

"Something a communist would believe." Laurent spoke automatically, with a drowsy version of the same superior smile with which he'd answered so many naïve doubters and other prisoners of that peasant mentality. He knew Quon was only teasing him: she found gain plenty appealing in her own way.

He was drifting into sleep, even with the pounding hands of children and the new droplets of rainwater pattering on the car's roof.

***

Quon shook him awake as they neared the hotel. Laurent cursed losing even those few minutes. Already, he could feel his mind going to work creating the strategies, contingencies, and combinations of financial maneuvers and personal manipulations that could increase his success tenfold. This was the playing field of the future, where the planet's true elite could leave ordinary struggles beneath them and engage in new, titanic contests whose complexity would never be understood by the masses.

Laurent was ready to be among them.

"Quon," he asked. "There's a patch that lets me sleep less, correct?"

"They're out there," she answered. "Forums say they do some of the scrubbing dreams do, only in half the time. I haven't checked the code myself; it could make you whackadoodle."

Laurent grinned. Her personal pride served him well. He imagined what he could accomplish with four more hours every day to work. Who needed dreams? He was manifesting his in reality.

The hotel was the oldest and most luxurious still standing in Cape Verde. It sat right up against the ocean levee built fifteen years ago, and was in many ways symbolic. If there had not been a reason for people with money to come to Cape Verde, there would have been no cause to spend money protecting it from the ocean. This truth, that money and nature were identical and inseparable in their power and movements, was so obvious to Laurent, and yet the upheaval it had caused here demonstrated that many people still had no sense of history.

Laurent was already dreaming of five-star room service, and, finally feeling some puckish verve, smirked at Quon. "Care to come upstairs?"

"Piss off, old man," she answered. Laurent caught something in that moment, a glint in her eyes. Something behind the defiant humor of the reply. She always rejected his come-ons, which he saw as neither personal nor entirely serious. He had always assumed that she knew these ground rules and played along accordingly. But now he detected something else, real injury. Was Quon, his personal super-hacker, betraying genuine emotions? It wasn't like her. It had to be his new perceptions manifesting themselves.

Still, whatever her private struggles, she kept her show of composure, so Laurent didn't let on that anything had happened. *I know you better now,* he thought to himself as a hotel worker opened his car door. *Which means I can use you better.*

***

Laurent's stride gained strength as he crossed the lobby's fine scarlet carpet towards the elevators. He wondered if his newly-empowered brain would be more sensitive to the autonomic messages of his body, swifter to dispatch aid and heal. Perhaps Quon could even create a patch that could help him get into shape. He chuckled at the fantasy as he stepped into the elevator.

Alone, he pushed the Penthouse button and used his thumbprint to unlock access. The elevator greeted him by name in the same Creole accent of that driver, only far more polite. Laurent breathed deeply and relaxed.

He felt a funny tap, like someone had flicked their finger against his forehead, and suddenly the world slowed to almost complete stillness. He was able to think of a great deal in only a few seconds.

He felt his legs switch off. No, that wasn't right, they had simply gone silent to his perceptions. His body began to slump. He was heading for the floor, only it didn't feel like falling. The floor of the elevator was moving towards his face, gently, in a kind and gradual curve.

He felt a single heartbeat, magnified at this speed, thrum like a cold explosion in his chest, and a fascinating tingle surged through his arm. Why was the whole process so vividly interesting?

You are dying, Laurent realized. He was dying very quickly, but had the perception to really take it in as he never would have before.

A pulse not his own was cascading through his brain: he could feel it tearing away his thoughts like a tidal wave. *The Beetle is killing me.* The realization came in a moment because Laurent was so very intelligent now. Nearly as quickly he guessed that there would be no record of his surgery, and that a death that appeared as natural as this would prompt no investigation. He had just enough time to appreciate how well he had been murdered.

He had been wrong about the danger. That was obvious. Was this Quon? Despite his new understanding of the way she hated his flirtations, they weren't cause for murder. Someone else, then, someone seeking an advantage. A rival? A successor? Just an investor keenly positioned to exploit chaos?

Laurent saw his death as a seismic event in the great fabric of money. The loss of his personal authority, the dispersal of his assets and duties, the bets that would be made for and against a future in which he did not participate – they painted the most profound and beautiful sight he had ever seen.

And in it he found truth. He saw the chess piece that had put itself in striking position. He saw the cause and effect, the reason why this was the most perfect moment for him to die. He knew who had killed him.

The chase of gain is rich in hate. His head hit the carpet. His eyes drifted.

The elevator welcomed him to the Penthouse.

***

-1-

White Mountain National Forest, New Hampshire – 2015

There. There was the first. In the slowly purpling dusk, a tiny pinpoint of white had appeared. Had it switched on like a lamp? No, Maria Kerrigan knew, it had come into sight gradually, each minute making her wonder – *Are you there? Are you real?* – until finally there could be no doubt, and another night had shown its first star.

She fixed her eyes on it for a time, enjoying its singularity. She knew it would be only minutes before it had company. Out here in the clear mountains, it would have so much company.

She sipped her coffee, and her campfire popped. Down at other campsites she heard some chatter from groups and families drifting up into the air with the smoke from their fires. But she and her star were going to have a conversation all their own.

She lay back on her elbows and tilted her head towards the nearest peak; a second star had faded in right above it. The stars' light could outlive the stars themselves, so what she was looking at were just their ghostly echoes. They affected her the same either way.

Suddenly, she turned her gaze back down from the sky and frowned. She splashed the coffee into the fire pit, earning an angry hiss from the logs, and cinched a blanket up around herself. She stared into the beguiling flames and didn't look up again even as the last of the sunlight abandoned them all, purple became black, and sparkling glories revealed themselves.

***

All the colors changed with nightfall. In daytime the forests of the White Mountains were a celebration of autumnal shades, a riot of natural fireworks frozen in time. This display stood out all the more against the severe granite of the peaks beyond, as if the trees were owning and reveling in their fleeting beauty before more vast and eternal things.

At night the colors deepened, muddled together and became mysterious. The forest, to human eyes, became all dark on dark shapes. It seemed so much more a child of the mountains then, retreating into those high, shadowed backdrops.

Maria couldn't say she liked the sound of the woods at night. It didn't make her happy or peaceful. It was more that she felt compelled towards it these days. Too long at home and the restlessness would start, and then she would pack up the car and drive out of town. These days, rather than store her tent and bag in her garage, she would take them out at home, clean them, and put them right back in the car.

The wind was picking up, and she walked a circle around her tent, checking the lines and spikes. Stepping wide to avoid tripping over a line, her foot came down in the darkness on top of a rounded rock and turned. She stumbled, her ankle throbbing in complaint, and she cursed quietly to herself. Even as she turned her foot to test for injury, she felt her left hand snake down towards her leg out of old instinct, searching for a 341.

341s. It had been twelve years since her Basic Military Training with the Air Force at Lackland, and the drilling of those two months still hid in her muscles and in her mind. The 341 was a trainee report. Every day on drills you were required to keep three blank 341s, folded precisely into fourths, in the left cargo pocket of your pants. A TI or anyone else authorized could demand one if they wanted to register an official compliment or demerit against something you had done. They never registered one as a compliment. To be told to reach for a 341 became one of those ominous fears that followed a cadet everywhere, from the jogging trails to the mess hall to their own dorms as they aggressively swept away the Texas dust that returned every damn day. To go through BMT was to learn that you could fail in ways that you couldn't possibly have imagined before.

After a couple of weeks, though, Maria had started to see the point. That the stringent – even sometimes arbitrary – demands and threats had a larger purpose: to break her out of old ways, teach her how to bond with her squadron under round-the-clock stress, through overt attempts to confuse and divide them. More importantly, she learned that even a 341 filled out completely didn't count without a signature, so a lot of the so-called demerits were just scare tactics.

That knowledge didn't stop her from imagining the barks of a TI over her shoulder even years later, and didn't stop, after some especially stupid mistakes, her left arm from twitching down towards paper she no longer carried in a pocket that didn't even exist on these pants.

She pressed the leg down firmly into the ground. The ankle was fine. It was sore, but that was nothing. You could work through sore.

Her circuit complete, she slipped off her boots, entered the tent, checked her watch, set an alarm, and fell asleep almost immediately. Most people came up here to get away from alarms. Not Maria.

***

She moved through the woods as much by sound and feel as sight. The creek was somewhere ahead. During the day you could whack your way to it in probably a half-hour without much experience, even if you weren't supposed to. But night was a different story. The darkness up here could be staggering. So could the quiet; or rather, the new curtain of noises that emerged once your ears adjusted themselves to the lack of civilization. Night vision was common parlance. But not enough people talked about night hearing.

This was against the park rules. Once she woke to her alarm at 10:30 pm, she emerged from her tent, zipped on her layers and laced on her boots, and tromped off the campsite into the wilderness, which was at least three 341s' worth of trouble. It would probably merit a washout too: not the psych-out ones where they came and took you back at the last minute, but a real don't-let-it-hit-you-where-the-Lord-split-you washout.

Still, the Air Force didn't own her anymore, and she was compelled to do it. Her brain told her to seek out water in the night, and she was going to do it because her brain telling her to do anything but drink was a thing to be encouraged.

She crunched ahead, trying not to disturb the carpet of first-fallen leaves, but finding it impossible to avoid them. *Yeah,* she thought to herself, *better that you know I'm coming, critters. Maria's in the woods.*

The temperature was dropping and she couldn't move fast, but she enjoyed the brisk shivers, the palpably chilly air cupping her face. She enjoyed moving with all four limbs engaged, feeling her way around skinny tree trunks, balancing in case of a false step. And she enjoyed – loved, really – moving her legs. All the taunts and sideways whispers she had heard in high school about her full, round thighs, the time she had given up wearing dresses and skirts completely...all those weak and frightened memories had been put away the first time she out-squatted half the men at Lackland. Now, as far as Maria was concerned, anyone who wanted to joke about her legs or her butt was welcome to do so from the dust cloud behind her on the jogging trail.

Maria knew that the Appalachian Trail cut through these mountains, and for a sweet moment she speculated on how she ought to have a go at that business someday. It sounded ideal: just months and months of letting her legs pull her through mud, over mountaintops, past fat tourists with too much gear...

Finally the sound of the creek swelled enough to wash out the others. She knew she was close. Despite her caution, her steps picked up. She didn't know why the little creek excited her, or seemed to call her; only that it did, and that she would answer. It was not always her business to make sense of her orders. That much she knew.

There it was – there it had been for who knows how long, burbling its path through the woods, around rocks and reeds, housing the bugs and fish, ferrying the dead leaves, always one way from some peak to some pond.

Maria couldn't help seeing the creek as a little like an alien universe. Growing up in a desert that some folks had conquered and called a suburb, she hadn't seen water doing its business this way until she was an adult. Sometimes a hydrant blew and she had seen the water trickling in little piss rivulets down the pavement looking for a sewer grate. And of course there were the flash storms. There was nothing like a flood to make you believe that there was an Almighty and that He or She or It was ticked off.

But this, something perpetual enough to hold lifetimes in it, something that shaped the land with patience, this was very different. Maria felt strangely wary as she walked to the creek's edge.

She found a flat, craggy slab of rock and stepped onto it. Another was just two hops away, this one big and dry enough for a sit down. She sat, and immediately felt the stone's chill smack her right on the ass. She snorted, clenched her teeth defiantly, and kept on sitting.

She hugged her arms around herself in the middle of the flow and listened for whatever the hell it was she was hoping to hear.

Rustling, bubbling, the movements of air and water, the tiniest chatters and buzzes: these were all the sounds. They seemed so small in the face of the quiet. Even on Maria's perch, surrounded by the ever-carrying creek, the silence was massive. It was a funny contradiction, and Maria followed the thought. If silence was a lack of sound, if silence was emptiness, how could it seem so big and bottomless? How could it seem to hold so much? Another contradiction: what could be inside nothing?

Suddenly a violent shiver started in her. It was far beyond the shake of a cold night: the tremor started around her rib cage and rammed full-speed into the fortress wall of her composure. She was chastising herself before the first tear could even threaten to come.

No! she told herself. *Don't be weak, Kerrigan! Nothing can get you here!*

She knew that wasn't true.

Her hand started to quiver. She brought it down on the rock with a *thwack.* It hurt like a furious sumbitch. *That was stupid, Maria,* she thought. But at least it was a thought and not panic.

Whatever she was searching for, it wasn't out here. She put a foot under her and started to stand.

Her foot slipped on a wet spot on the rock.

Her body fell forward, and her head hit another rock.

She rolled over onto her back and looked up at the sky, blood welling out of her forehead, the water all around her, soaking and pulling, the night going blurry.

Stupider and stupider, Maria, she thought, and then stopped thinking for a while.

***

Pain never wakes you up politely. When Maria's brain finally plugged back in, her head was stomping mad with her, and the cold had gone beyond character-building. Whether or not she had ever experienced worse was not a question that helped at all. This whole scenario had gone from peaceful to suck PDQ.

She pulled herself to shore, and stripped off her jacket, plus the sweater, shirt, and bra underneath. She shook off the jacket, which was water-repellent, and put that back on over her bare torso, fumbling with the zippers with her tingling fingers.

She didn't fancy traipsing through the woods pantsless, so she pulled them off, wrung them out as best she could, and put them back on. If she could keep her core warm and gut out the rest, all would be well.

Now the question was which way to go.

She remembered enough to find where she had stepped into the creek, but as she tried to trace her progress back through the dark, the memories were jumbled. Landmarks were things of the imagination in darkness like this, and whereas before the sound of the creek could lure her towards it, it was useless now as a means to guide her back.

She was more annoyed than panicked. She had been through survival school, and cold as it was it was too early in the season for life-threatening temperatures. This would just be a long, irritating, uncomfortable night, and as far as Maria was concerned, she deserved no less.

As she searched for signs of her own outbound steps, she thought about impulsiveness: the number of times that she had been told she could not or should not do something and had then become bird-flipping determined to do just that thing. It probably came from her Salvadoran mother, who had raised two children on her own after her charming Irish rogue of a husband had decided that the "rogue" side of him had priority over the "husband" side. Mama had heard plenty from people who were generous with their opinions of what she couldn't do, and that's the spirit Maria had been reared in.

Had that been the reason she had left the campsite on this hike? For all she'd thought about solitude and listening to the sound of nature, was she just rebelling against some stupid warning sign she had glimpsed somewhere? *Sounds about right,* she thought, pushing a branch out of the way.

Many, many stars were out now. Maria wondered why she wasn't back in front of the campfire, looking at them. Or just sleeping, damn it. And would it really have been so bad if she had just stayed the hell home for a couple of days?

Is that regret? asked a voice in her head.

"Shut up," she mumbled audibly, and then caught her foot on a root and pitched forward again. Damn, was she ever sick of falling in the dark.

Something strange was under her fingertips as she readied to push herself back up: a hard, straight edge. Funny how a straight line could feel like an intruder in nature, but there it was, metallic and almost sharp. That was what had caught her notice. A rock could be split by water, or worn flat or rounded out, but that long, straight, sharp line was uncannily human.

Curiosity can intervene in any moment of a person's life. Maria remembered collapsing once during drill because she hadn't hydrated properly. And even as her brain spun and her body turned to noodles, there was a part of her that saw this little wisp of cloud in the sky – the tiniest cloud, the only cloud around – and finding that just so interesting.

So, cold and ticked-off, she decided that she needed to know what the thing was, even if she could only learn by touch.

The thing was a flat slab, about two feet by one, stuck in the ground and mostly covered by dirt. It reminded her of a grave marker, and on that impulse she ran her fingers over the top. She felt grooves, markings that were probably letters, gouged into the surface. She squinted and brushed at a section, but saw only numbers.

Digging down, she found the underside. The object was about four or five inches thick, and a heavy sumbitch. She wondered if it was some kind of surveying marker, or something left by the park service. She didn't know who else might leave something like this in the middle of a mountain forest, but she also didn't know why anyone would leave something of this shape and size at all. Something about the letters nagged at her; in markers she was used to, the letters were raised off the surface, not carved in. And the smoothness of it, the way it seemed to resist the elements, was also damned weird.

If nothing else, the perplexing thing had stopped her from shivering for a couple of minutes.

She sighed, mentally weighing the mystery of it against its very real heavy sumbitchness. She was pretty sure she knew which was going to win, and she wasn't happy about it.

***

Anyone still awake at the campsite would probably think Maria was a bear coming out of the trees, staggering and groaning. *Wouldn't that be the perfect ending for tonight's adventure?* she thought. *Some coward with more shot then sense decides to make a rug out of me.* She was in that miserable state of shivering and sweating all at once, still lugging her stupid find as she had done the whole winding, blind walk back.

She reached her campsite and let the thing drop in the dirt. Then, she slipped into her tent, stripped, put all her wet clothes in a bag, and slid naked into her sleeping bag.

Inside that cocoon, her circulation began to return. She groped for her big flashlight and her bag, found the first aid kit inside, and started probing herself for wounds. Anyplace she found blood she quickly wiped, spread ointment on, and slapped a bandage over. Her care probably wasn't accurate, and was definitely overkill, but she'd give herself a better once-over in the morning.

She found her clean flannel shirt in her bag and slipped that into her sleeping bag with her, which did just enough to take her from Holy Jesus Cold to A-OK. And maybe if she had thought for a few seconds more, she would have made up her mind to slip back out and drag in the mystery marker she'd gone to so much trouble to get here, but this is was it for Maria. Rack time: to hell with everything that wasn't sleep.

***

Nature and sleeping in didn't mix for Maria. The sun was just too in-charge, even on misty mornings like that one. She could have stayed in that bag three more hours with no complaint, but the light was on her and her body was just too used to being up. She pulled on warmup pants and stepped out to start making coffee.

After her first step out of the tent, she stubbed her toe on the big metal hunk that had quickly become the bane of her whole existence. She would have kicked the thing if her foot wasn't already hurting enough to remind her she'd surely break it if she tried.

So finally she sat down in the dirt to read the thing, pledging to haul it back to the creek and chuck it in if what it had to say wasn't worthwhile.

Along the top, it read "White Mountain National Park: 44°16'12.0"N 71°12'00.0"W 1/1/1999." Maria figured the coordinates for latitude and longitude, and by a quick reckoning they seemed likely to be accurate to within a few clicks of where she found the thing. If the date had been when it was placed, it seemed an odd time to be lugging big engraved markers through the woods, since the parks were closed and the mountains covered in snow.

Below the coordinates it read "Please deliver in-person to Dr. Weldon Qualls, Department of Physics, Princeton University." Then, "Send confirmation to:" and listed a P.O. Box, followed by "Next Marker" with another series of coordinates, and then a series of letters and numbers, followed by "Please Provide:" and another series of letters and numbers.

Maria couldn't stand the rudeness of the thing. *Princeton? That's a seven-hour drive!* She wanted to yell at it for being so presumptive and inscrutable at the same time.

Why couldn't it explain itself more? If the thing had been truly placed there over sixteen years ago, how likely was it that Dr. Weldon Qualls was even still at Princeton? What kind of prank involved putting it in the woods instead of just taking it to him themselves?

Maria decided she was going to really hold Dr. Qualls's feet to the fire when she got to Princeton. Then she stomped over to her camp stove to make that coffee. The day had already gone too damn long without it.

**

-2-

Daegu, Republic of Korea - 2039

"Regret," Josh Scribner said with the clarity of late hours, "is the most human emotion." Then he took a long sip from his whiskey glass and set it on the table, letting the thought breathe in the silence.

Min-Jun Dan gave a soft smile but said nothing, just sipped at his tea and waited for his friend to elaborate. Josh had really been hoping to be asked for a follow-up, but gave up the tiny battle of wills and picked up his glass to gesture with as he continued.

"Think about it," he said. "Regret is bringing the past back into the present for examination. So right there, right there is two huge concepts." He sipped again. "What the hell does an animal know about the past?"

"When a deer is born it already knows to run from the wolf. This is a past it did not even live through."

"You're talking about ancestral memory, learned behavior. I'm talking about context. The ability to summon up everything about a moment, a real moment; the images, the sounds, even what you were thinking and feeling at the exact moment you zigged when maybe you should have zagged.

"Regret," he concluded, "is a form of time travel."

He'd finished his whiskey. Within seconds, a subtle waiter placed another in front of him, along with a disposable nasal inhaler. Such a discreet signal: *maybe it's time to pace yourself.* Those inhalers, which would de-drunk his brain, weren't cheap, but in a bar like this that served such high-quality whiskey with real ice, they came compliments of the house. You could drink most of your liver away in a single night at a bar like this. But, if you came to a bar like this, a new liver was something you could afford.

Josh left the inhaler on the table. He wasn't done being drunk.

"I'm talking about vision," he continued. "Humanity takes its greatest leaps based on imagination; we see something that must be so, even if we don't know how it's so. In those moments, you sense a truth, you know what I mean? That handful of moments in your life when you really sense truth?"

"I sensed truth the moment I saw my future husband," Min-Jun remarked, still taking every opportunity to derail Josh for sport.

"We're talking about regret," Josh insisted, spilling a splash of whiskey worth a family's groceries for a week.

"I regret nothing about my husband."

"Hang your husband. Where is he, anyway?"

"At home in Paris. He didn't feel like coming to the conference this year."

"He hasn't wanted to leave Paris since you moved there."

"It is that sort of city, isn't it?"

"Well, Daegu's no pile of garbage." Josh paused for a moment, brain bumping its way up to where the conversation had gone. "Are you going to adopt?"

"We have already applied for two."

"God damn it, that's great." Josh was still young, only thirty-eight, but at hours like this he could let slip the sudden and overpowering sympathy you saw in far older people. "You two will be great parents. What was I talking about?"

Min-Jun sipped his tea. "You were speaking of regret."

"Right!" Josh wagged his finger several times at an empty spot by the wall. "There's more than just the past and the present involved in regret. You have to see the future *from the perspective of the past.* You have to see a present that's different from now, wind it back to a moment, and say, 'Here. Here is where we chose this path.' Only a human can do that. It's a mental evolution to sustain these ideas in our head."

"What is the point you make, my friend?"

"Here's my question." Josh set his glass down and put his elbows on the table, the better to use both hands to stabilize his head. "Is regret...is our capacity for regret the human race imagining the possibility of time travel?"

Min-Jun slurped his tea at a thoughtful volume, smiled again, then set the cup down and reached across the table to touch his friend at the elbow. "Have you ever been to Gatbawi?"

Josh's eyeballs fluttered for a second, a visual signal of his brain rummaging through long-unopened drawers. "Statue? Out of town? Big stone Buddha? Hat?" His hands circled his head with the final question.

"Yes." Min-Jun looked up at the ceiling and smiled, as if transporting his senses there. "You walk up a great staircase, and there you see Gatbawi. Your troubles are far below, and his smile is so peaceful and joyous. And your problems..." his fingers waggled, "they fly up into the clouds, like letters tied to balloons."

"You're ridiculous," Josh interjected.

"It has long been said that Gatbawi will grant you one wish. I sometimes wonder how hard people think about their wishes before they make them. Do they start thinking when they see him? At the bottom of the staircase? When they leave on their journey to visit him? I wonder how specific they are. Do they just wish to be wealthy, or happy, or to find love? Or do they say, 'Gatbawi, make me two inches taller!'"

"We make vague wishes," Josh countered, "because we don't want our faith shattered when specifics fail to materialize."

"Or perhaps it is because we do not care to look closely at our life to see what needs changing, because it is almost always inside."

"I didn't think wishing was a Buddhist thing."

"Not in the way that Westerners understand the word. But to your point: does the emergence of the idea that Gatbawi will grant wishes mean that we have imagined the truth of the Buddha? Or that we have infinite power to better our situation?

"Or," Min-Jun finally reclaimed his cup of tea, "is it proof that a bracing walk does wonders to clear the mind?"

Josh finally laughed. It was a rueful but honest one. "Min-Jun, you're one of the best scientific minds on Earth, so why is it I never catch you talking about science?"

"But Josh, my friend, can you not see that I am?"

Josh sat back quietly in his chair, the momentary pleasure of Min-Jun's conversation fading into the dark murmurs of the bar. Everyone in this place was a mover. There was an old Hawaiian word, *waiwai*, that meant rich. *Wai* by itself meant "water." *Waiwai*, then, was "water water." Anyone who had "water water" was wealthy by the best measure the ancient people of Hawaii knew, because water meant you could grow taro, which meant you could eat.

Josh hadn't fully defined the irony that had brought this word and its circumstances into global applicability, but there it was. Water mattered now, and being wealthy meant you could draw a lot of it. It made you *waiwai*, like the people who drank here. Like Josh.

He felt the urge to look outside, into the streets of Daegu. He knew what he would see there: struggling people, some doing better than others. Beggars and the ill, and the quietly, dutifully desperate who kept all the machinery working. Glamour and decay all joined in the singular organism of the city. This bar was remarkably cunning at hiding it all. A simple trick, whose only required instrument was human nature. All that unpleasantness drained of its urgency by a nothing more than a wall.

"You know what I'm going to say tomorrow," Josh finally said, reaching the thing he'd wanted to voice all day, but needed four glasses of whiskey to broach.

Min-Jun stayed neutral. "I have read the same leaked preview summaries of your remarks as everyone else."

"Do you think I'm softballing the problem?"

"I think you are avoiding the casting of blame with great artistry."

"You're mean when you want to be."

Min-Jun bowed his head slightly in polite apology.

Mood darkening, Josh asked experimentally, "Do you think I just shouldn't bring it up at all?"

"It seems to me that your perspective is that it has already been brought up, in that it is a problem which really exists."

"Well, what do you want me to do? If I point fingers they'll burn me at the stake."

"People of guilty conscience always imagine a finger pointing at them, and will blame you for it whether you do it or not."

"So I should just say nothing?"

Min-Jun looked at his friend with disappointment, or maybe just sympathy at the weight he carried. "Josh, I will return your compliment to say that you have one of the greatest minds for data and systems on Earth, and part of what drives you is the desire to put your answers to use. Not only am I not telling you to say nothing, I do not think you are even still deciding whether or not to say nothing."

"Giant finger," Josh said, eyes drooping. "Ever see that old movie *Yellow Submarine*? Giant finger. Worked for the Blue Meanies. Always coming to get you." He looked ready for a snooze in his chair.

"They had victory in that movie by singing, didn't they?"

Josh nodded.

Min-Jun smiled. "I like that movie."

"Min-Jun, my friend...did I ever tell you how I got rich? I mean how I actually got rich?"

"Not specifically, although I am sure some brilliance was involved."

"Oh yeah, it was genius. I did something no one else on the planet thought was possible." Finally he reached for the inhaler and shoved it up one nostril. "Ask me about it sometime."

As his brain came back to life, his first thought was that he would have to tip heavily, since the owners of bars like this did not philosophically approve of Min-Jun Dan's serene ability to nurse one pot of tea for a whole damned evening.

**

Although his reasoning centers were back online, Josh's body was still processing the finely aged, single-barrel poison he had just enjoyed, so he hailed a cab to take his wobbly muscles home. He hoped it was a smooth ride.

Josh watched his driver steer the vehicle. One hand rested atop the steering wheel, but didn't grip it. The fingers seemed to shake slightly. The diver wasn't old: probably Josh's age, but he seemed accelerated somehow. Agitated, like a bird with a fast heartbeat. His head bobbed helplessly.

"Are you alright? Headache?" Josh asked, using some of the little Korean he knew.

The driver nodded, waving around at the signs of the fashionable district where Josh had been doing his drinking. "City lights. Too much," he answered.

You're sort of right, Josh thought. *Although not in the way you think.*

He slumped back in his seat and looked at those lighted signs, many in both Korean and English. They weren't splashy come-ons like in the marketplace district, where impulse shopping found tourists along the sidewalks. Instead they radiated power, every logo a work of very classy art and branding. This was not a place for wandering; even the choice of where to drink was viewed as a strategy.

He pulled out his travel pad and opened up his speech. In the small security tab he always kept running on the screen, he immediately saw other devices in the area noticing his pad, reaching out to test it, to tap at its windows, so to speak. Some of these self-guiding hack scripts were well over a decade old, but still lived in the local network; or perhaps more like haunted it. They couldn't even penetrate your average consumer device, and Josh's was far better protected than average. It fascinated him to watch these old programs lurking and propagating without their creators, a new species of city vermin that didn't even need food, but scavenged forever, looking to spread decay and disease in the world of bytes.

He wondered how they saw time, these code strips that moved in nanoseconds. To a small bumblebee the air is so thick that to fly feels like swimming through water to us. How hard and thick was a second of human reality to these tiny invented lives?

He re-read his speech. "Honored and Distinguished Attendees, blah blah blah..." The words sounded disgusting to him.

"Driver," he suddenly spoke with force. "Changed my mind. Take me to Gatbawi."

"They are closed. Too late."

"They will open for me," Josh sighed. He hadn't encountered too many closed doors in his life that he couldn't open.

***

So many stairs. But of course, once Josh started climbing them, turning back seemed like a waste of good bribes. The air was cool and pleasant, but Josh's muscles wanted him to be supine. *Perhaps*, he thought, *I should be borne up on a couch.* It would suit his stature to be brought before a god in this way, wouldn't it? But Buddha wasn't a god. He was a man who figured something out that mystified others.

Josh glanced at his wrist, as he did every few waking minutes. The numbers on the screen there didn't tell him the time, and they hadn't changed from his last look. This didn't set him at ease; rather it allowed him to continue in his normal state of unease without interruption, neither happy nor sad, but certainly not burdened with anything like hope.

The stars were easier to see here, even just a few miles from the city center. With so many stairs behind him, Josh morbidly considered that it could well look like he was ascending into the black sky. But he didn't think puffy clouds and happiness waited for him up there.

Multiplication. In pre-school, when his peers were struggling to understand that one block and two other blocks were together three blocks, he was already learning multiplication. He devoured the processes of solving, made them the muscles he otherwise lacked. One good process could solve millions of problems. And as he got older, he learned to great reward that one good piece of code could ease millions of lives. Or commit millions of sins.

Josh wondered about the tabulation of sins, wondered how many of their echoes applied directly to the ledger of their creators. Or maybe sins weren't even a thing to think about on your walk to see a Buddha.

At last, there he was: Gatbawi, great and smiling just as advertised, with a joyous belly and his plate-like hat. Frozen in total peace, an easy thing for a statue to do. *Statues are an unrealistic standard to hold a Buddhist to,* Josh thought. He would have to say that to Min-Jun next time they spoke.

Technology now made it so simple to face what was horrible in the world. All Josh had to do was push a button or two on his wrist and he could see more of the misery and cruelty and death and folly of man than most humans throughout history would ever have seen in their whole lives. He supposed that the counter to that was that more wonder and beauty and wisdom were available from the same button. But how could that help him?

Had he ever smiled like Gatbawi at solving a math problem? Maybe what a Buddha enjoyed could not be his. Certainly not when Josh knew what he knew: about what was happening in the world, about what needed to be done. In the end, maybe they just had different missions.

Josh's wobbly, weary legs finally collapsed under him, and he puked on the ground before Gatbawi. And his artificially-cleansed brain was ever so awake and aware of the whole putrid experience.

He spat out the last driblets of whiskey and half-digested rib meat, turned and looked down at so, so many stairs, lamenting the taste of rot in his mouth.

He turned to Gatbawi and spoke resignedly. "Don't have any mouthwash, do you?"

Gatbawi only smiled.

"Didn't think so. Glad I didn't ask for anything bigger."

***

The driver was still waiting for him. Josh would be his best client all night. Or maybe it was a real human courtesy not to leave him stranded out here. Josh was too distracted to settle the question. He gave the driver the address of his hotel and then locked his gaze out the window.

He wasn't sure if he said the words "screw it" out loud. The driver didn't tell him one way or the other. He opened up his speech and starting typing and deleting, typing and deleting. He even started to giggle from a sense of giddy doom. *I'm typing a bomb,* he thought to himself. *Who ever thought you could type one of those?*

Between paragraphs, he opened up a new window and started writing a separate document, a letter. Every study he had ever read told him that multi-tasking was a myth, and counter-productive. But it was a habit he could rarely shake, and at times like this he was grateful. He didn't want to be monomaniacal. There was only one thing that ever got his absolute and full attention, and neither of these tasks was it.

As his thoughts bounced between the speech and the letter, he put words where they seemed most appropriate. There was a motivational speech he used to deliver – and for which he'd received a great deal of money every time – in which he talked about the relationship between programming languages and the true processes of the human brain. Language was a reductive delivery system, an end result of a process, and to truly understand thoughts to the extent that you could teach a machine to think, you needed to see behind the words.

So each phrase he typed was a product of emotions, triggered memories, instincts, conscious strategies, and the strange sub-logical human associations, mashed and cooked together and then run through a compression codec in the hopes that it someone else could receive it and unpack it into something like the original. The process was never perfect, rarely even close, because everyone's minds were so uniquely pre-loaded with their own triggers and biases.

Words fall so short, he thought, *but they sure were a brilliant try for cavemen.*

He knew enough of what would happen because of the speech. This was why it would be necessary to have the letter ready.

Something spiked in his security monitor. He max-sized it and watched. Someone was trying to break in. Someone specifically after Josh. And judging by the way the assault bobbed and weaved, someone with a brain in their heads.

He had a pretty good idea who was behind it. He could have tracked the attack, deployed a counter-worm, but he let the thing flit around his defenses. It wouldn't work this time: maybe working wasn't the point. Maybe someone just wanted to remind Josh they were out there. As if he needed it. As if he ever needed it.

You don't know it yet, man, Josh thought as he went back to working on his speech, *but your tomorrow just got so much worse.*

* * *

Josh entered his hotel suite, feeling a very modern blend of animated and terrible. He tapped at the master room panel, setting his alarm and starting the sleep cycle. He watched as a graph appeared, mapping the hours (too few) between now and wakeup time, and plotting gradual changes in light and ambient sound that conformed to a cloud-stored record of his sleep cycles. *The machines know when I dream,* he thought.

But he put the thought away, and went into the darkened second bedroom. The only illumination was a small power indicator on the monitor around the wrist of his daughter.

Josh approached and, with the most delicate touch, activated it, checking the numbers against those on his wrist monitor. They were aligned and identical. Cierra looked so beautiful when she slept, but she slept far too much. He wondered what kind of life she lived in her sleep. He hoped it was better than the one she had here. Maybe *you actually prefer it this way,* he thought, morosely.

He washed his mouth out, over and over, then washed his hands. Then his face. Finally he stuck his head under a cold shower and soaked it. It seemed more honest than the nasal spray.

He put himself into bed, lay his head back on the pillow, and stared at the ceiling. Modern technology could do more to see him to good sleep than had ever been possible in history. So the only thing that could be keeping him awake had to be his own spirit. *What a concept,* he thought. *If computers could do what we never could, and prove the existence of a soul.*

It didn't relax him. His thoughts almost never did.

-3-

Laconia, New Hampshire – 2015

"Where'd you find this thing?" Lia asked as Maria came through the front door. Maria hadn't expected Lia to be awake yet, but Lia wasn't much for predictability.

"Got coffee," Maria said, ducking the question and offering the cup holder and bag from Dunkin' Donuts.

Lia drifted over from their little kitchen table, took her cup and some creamer from the holder, and returned to her seat.

"Don't want your doughnut?" Maria asked, sitting down opposite her.

"I think I need to re-balance my sugar intake," Lia said quietly. "My body needs to get used to better energy sources."

Maria shrugged and started tucking into her own doughnut.

"This thing is very heavy," Lia offered. She hadn't drunk from the coffee yet, and was just staring down at the metal marker from the forest.

"That's why I left it in the car, space cadet. You didn't have to go lugging it in yourself."

"So you're going to take it to this guy? Dr. Qualls?"

"Yeah, maybe. I don't know: I don't have a lot of time for stuff like this."

"But what is it? I don't know what they're trying to do. If they know where he is, why didn't they just send it to him?"

"It's science stuff. Science people are woolly." Maria knew she shouldn't stereotype, but every science class she had ever taken, in high school or college or in the Air Force, had been taught by someone of the cuckoo clock persuasion.

"Do you think it's one of those shows where they put a camera on you to see what you'll do? I always get nervous about one of those shows happening to me." Lia slipped her hands around her coffee cup, as if she suddenly needed to warm them.

Maria said nothing. She lost patience with Lia way too easily, and had learned through experience that you couldn't just bark at her to move her ass or stop being silly like Maria was used to. It would be a lot easier if that worked, but it didn't.

"You working today?" Maria asked.

Lia gave a weary sigh and looked down again. To Maria, she always looked like a flower you could just blow right over. "I think so, I have to check. I think they said they might need me in the afternoon. I might tell them I can't. I don't know."

Maria popped the lid off her coffee so she could dip a quarter of the doughnut into it. "Got two ups today; got to head in soon."

"Oh, good. Any plans for the day beyond that?"

"Just to stay alive and sober."

"You shouldn't joke about that. It's very serious."

"Don't I look serious?"

Lia reached out and ran her hands over the marker. "It feels so cold. But also very precise. I kind of like it."

"Like it?"

"Don't you like it?"

Maria didn't know what to say. It was a big, heavy, annoying thing; whether or not to like it just hadn't seemed like a necessary question.

"If you're busy, I could take it there. To Princeton, I mean. To save you the drive." Lia offered.

Maria could see Lia's eyes flitting towards the bag, tempted by the doughnut. She felt a flare of possessiveness over the marker. "You'd drive to New Jersey and back?"

"Well, I mean, I guess I'd stay overnight somewhere. It would be like a little getaway."

"You'll call me an hour down the road with a panic attack."

"Maria, you shouldn't be mean."

Maria made a frustrated sound and pushed the bag across the table. "Eat. You'll wear yourself out fighting it." Lia's mouth screwed around in a wrestling match between guilt and surrender, then she took one side of the bag in a delicate grip and opened it to peek inside.

"You shouldn't tell me I can't do things. You should tell me I can do things," Lia insisted, still in her quiet voice, as she reached in the bag and pulled out her doughnut.

"I ain't your doctor."

"I'm just offering to help."

"No, no it has to be me. He'll probably want to know where I found it and all that. You probably shouldn't have even put your fingerprints on it."

"Oh, I'm sorry. I hadn't thought of that. Should I wash it?"

"No!"

***

Maria opted for the motorcycle. It needed more fixing than the car, and honestly she should have replaced both years ago, but she couldn't exactly afford that. And today she just wanted to hear herself growling down the road.

She walked the motorcycle out from the garage around the little house she and Lia shared, waiting until it was in the street to turn it over because Lia had told her the noise startled her. During her years in the Air Force Maria had bunked with women who gossiped, snored, stole toiletries, left hair everywhere, hogged the bathroom, and farted in bed. Not one of them ever drove her as nuts as Lia. But the two of them had each other's back, and that was that. Inside the house, she would give Lia crap. Outside, she would put down anyone who looked sideways at her.

The motorcycle coughed awake, and Maria cruised out of the neighborhood.

It was a short trip through town to the little airport. Maria watched Laconia awakening as she drove: flags going up, those old coots gathering outside the café to talk about how the world was going to hell...she could never get over how damned white New Hampshire was. Maria was half-white and usually got treated as all-white since those freckles her bastard dad had bequeathed her would peek out if she hadn't gotten much sun. But she never really felt white. She'd had her whole childhood to learn who the in-crowd was, and how she and her Mom and brother weren't part of it. She'd gone to battle against the most evil people on Earth, and still none of them could make her as angry as a judgmental look from a tastefully-dressed soccer mom.

Still with the soccer moms? the voice asked her.

Maria swore under her breath. She hadn't wanted to have this conversation this morning. Part of the reason she'd chosen the motorcycle was the irrational belief that maybe it would prevent this conversation.

Come on, you know it doesn't work that way.

Maria still ignored it.

And we both know you can hear me.

"Yeah? So what do you want?" Maria finally answered, leaning aggressively into a corner and picking up speed past the cemetery on her way to the highway.

Hadn't checked in for awhile, that's all.

"Wish I could just crack my head open and shut you up."

You tried that already, in your own way. Did it ever work?

"Maybe just one more really hard one is all it will take."

I always know when you're bluffing.

"Wish I could hit you." The trees whipped by as her agitation spurred the bike along.

Your head's not where it should be. You've got things to do. Pre-flight starts long before you get to your plane.

"Yeah, you didn't teach me that, my instructors did."

I just like to remind you.

"I don't need your help."

Who said I came around to help?

Maria gritted her teeth and found herself wondering if she could get herself arrested between here and work. Of course, that wouldn't actually get rid of the voice.

***

They were cruising over the lake, Maria and What's-his-name. What's-his-name couldn't bank for crap, and was trying to pedal his way through every maneuver. *If that's what you want to do,* she thought to herself. *You paid for the ride.*

She sold an illusion for a living, the idea that she could make someone a pilot in an hour. But she did the checks, she talked with the tower; hell, most days she towed the plane. Some men tried to be chivalrous when they saw her hooking the bar up under the nose and dragging the 152 out onto the runway, but she wouldn't let them even if she liked chivalry. Her job was to get them in the air and then let them take the stick. It was literally the easiest part of being a pilot; you just needed enough brain cells to keep the horizon steady.

The law said she couldn't train anyone under twelve, but she'd met nine-year olds who would be able to handle a 152 in the air with supervision. They were so simple people used to call them Land-o-Matics. Still, some days Maria felt like she'd be safer with the auto-pilot.

What's-his-name was having a good time, his face a mix of concentration and bliss. Maria zoned out, as she sometimes did listening to the drone of the propeller and the rush of air around the cabin. The world turned beneath them at a gentle pace. At the velocity they were going, Maria could probably race them on her bike and win on a straight road. She had a strong, strong urge to be doing just that.

Suddenly, What's-his-name's voice buzzed in her ears. She snapped out of her daze. "Say again?"

"So, uh, how long have you been doing this?"

"Three years as a trainer."

"Three years? Didn't the website say you were in the Air Force?"

"That's correct. Didn't fly planes while I was in. Did some flight training after my commission but got assigned somewhere else. Finished training as a civvie."

"Oh, why not?"

"Watch your altitude." Maria put some edge into her voice, trying to emphasize that this was not get-to-know-Maria time, even in one of the easiest machines to fly short of a balloon.

**

"Realize you kicking my wall?"

Maria looked up from the magazine she wasn't reading, then realized that Albert was right. "Sorry, man."

"Your next up's not two hours. Isn't somewhere yoush rather be?"

Hell yes, she thought. *I want to be at Finnegan's with a dark pint and some darts.* But she didn't say anything, just shook her head and reached for her rotten Styrofoam coffee.

"Doing okay?" Albert asked.

Maria liked Albert; his old doughy face and all those red vein-trails coming off his nose, the way he was too old to give a good damn about speaking in coherent sentences. He had a little patch of white-red hair that looked like a carpet square someone had slapped on top of his head on his way out the door, and he always looked like he ought to be wearing a rain slicker and holding a fishing rod rather than running a small airport. She put up with his concerns as a means of liking him. "Didn't sleep well. Fucked my ankle up in the mountains two days ago."

"Ought learn to relax, little lady."

"It's overrated."

"I buy you a burger? Cheeshburger?"

Maria looked at the boring wall, listened to the buzzing lights, and decided a cheeshburger was at least better than this.

***

The sun was setting when Maria came home. She saw the porch light was on but all the house lights were off, which meant Lia was home.

She entered, and heard a low, confident male voice. It was one of Lia's audiobooks. Maria took off her boots in the doorway and walked quietly, following the sound to her roommate.

She was in her bedroom. Maria pushed the door open with a creak and saw Lia, wearing her big bathrobe and laying under her comforter. She had a stick of that freaking incense burning in the windowsill.

"Hey champ," Maria said.

Lia picked up a small remote from her bedside table and paused the book. "Hello Maria. How was work?"

"Went up twice, came down twice. Can't complain."

"That's good. I'm glad to see you."

"Yeah. Did you work?" Maria knew she hadn't.

"It wasn't a good day. But they said they could use me on Friday. I need to wash my work blouse anyway. It looks terrible."

"Shut up, kid, nothing looks terrible on you."

"Thank you." Lia pulled off the covers and sat up; she seemed to be gathering herself to stand. "I made some tea.

It's downstairs. I don't know if it's cold. I don't know what time it is."

"It's okay. Hey, you got everything you need around here? Your food and everything?"

"I think so. I'll be fine. Are you going camping again?"

"Nah, gonna take the thing to the guy. Tomorrow morning."

"Oh. That's nice of you. I'm sure they'll be glad you did, whoever they are."

Maria shrugged and turned to head out.

"Maria?" Lia's voice stopped her. "Thank you for living with me."

Maria turned. "Thank me? I should thank you, weirdo. Nobody else can stand me."

***

Maria sat on the porch in the dark. The last of the fireflies had stopped glowing about a month ago, so now it was just her and the sky and the house lights of the neighborhood. Her hand wanted so badly to assume the shape of holding a bottle of beer. Not to drink, the wicked part of her promised. Just to look like she was doing something, so she didn't look like some creepy staring zombie. That part of her had so many lies to whisper.

She got up and jogged six miles. Five for the exercise, and one just to not stop moving yet.

***

She was up not long after the sun and made some proper eggs on toast instead of doughnuts. Lia floated through the kitchen and absentmindedly chewed a piece of toast. She came back in and said, "I'd like to show you something."

Maria shrugged and followed Lia into the little den, taking her plate with her and munching while standing.

Lia stood over by the empty mantel and gestured to it.

"Yeah?" said Maria, shaking her head uncomprehendingly.

"I dusted it. I found that thing with your medals and I thought we could put them up here."

Maria made a growling sound and almost choked on her eggs. "You went through my shit?"

"No! I just saw it sitting there, you know. We don't really have much, I thought I'd put it there, and then like maybe a little flower pot next to it or something. I saw one last week that was very cheap."

Maria looked at Lia's face; it was already contorting into her trademark expression of fear and confusion and guilt that she'd done something she wasn't supposed to do despite all her intentions. She'd voluntarily crawl in a hole and never do anything again if Maria said to. So Maria swallowed the eggs, cleared her throat, and said, "Sounds good. Sorry I snapped; didn't mean anything."

"Oh good. I thought I might have upset you."

"Nah, Princess. I'll see you tomorrow, okay?"

Lia, big stupid robe and all, came over and hugged her. Maria took it.

***

For a trip this long, Maria took the car. She didn't trust the bike for this many miles in a day. She headed south and soon enough was passing through Concord and Manchester, quaint and leafy and so very white. Just like Laconia, only bigger. For a while she found herself trapped behind a line of buses, the motorcade of some asshole governor who wanted to be President and so was parading all over the state shaking hands in diners and putting up flag bunting in every empty field he could find. When she pulled off the road for lunch, she did a slow perimeter check of the joint to make sure no politicians were anywhere near it. They all loved that she was a veteran, and she hated the conversations that always followed when they learned it.

Eventually, as she guessed it would, the voice spoke to her again.

Strange responsibility you're taking on.

"Could be twenty years before someone else tripped over that thing. It had been there long enough."

Still, it's good that you're keeping busy.

"If you had an ass I'd be busy kicking it."

You handled that business with Lia and the medals really well.

"Like I care about your approval."

I think she's doing you good. Even more good than you do her.

"I ain't marrying her, if that's what you're getting at."

Why would you go there? I'm just talking about being a good friend.

"We're as good friends as we have to be."

But not completely?

"Cut the therapist bullshit. I've had those."

Oh, I don't have to play therapist. I already know what's in your head. You'll give her a lot of friendship as long as she respects the deal.

"What deal?"

That she never makes you tell her about me.

"There is no you. You're a voice in my head."

That's so true. So why do you hear me?

Maria turned up the stereo, refusing to continue the conversation.

***

After she crossed from Connecticut into New York, she stayed on 84 so she could vector around New York City and all the surrounding nonsense. Of course, her luck being her luck, she ended up in a wretched single-file traffic crawl. It took over a half-hour to even find out what was causing it: some massive earth-moving equipment digging a trench that looked like it was going to pass right under the highway. So much expensive bullshit and none of it ever seemed to help.

It's not that there weren't traffic jams in the sky – she'd circled a few runways waiting her turn – but provided everyone did the required communicating, you had a clear track between points A and B, and you never had to do this stop-and-start lurching along. It was already much later in the afternoon than she had planned, and she wondered if Dr. Qualls would even be there, or if she should have called ahead to make sure. She had entertained the fantasy that she could be home that night, but now it looked like she would need a hotel after all, which was an expense that didn't thrill her.

She looked over her shoulder, imagining the thing that was sitting in her car trunk. "Maybe there's a reward for finding you, huh? At least the Professor ought to have some gas money for me, don't you think?

***

Princeton was a fancy campus. Maria hadn't spent much time on any other than her own, but this one breathed money and history from every brick. She left the thing in the trunk so she could find a map before she had to start toting it around. The pause gave her a moment to appreciate the place.

The kids looked so damn young. Of course, they'd already looked young to her when she'd attended college. Since she had already done a full term as an NCO before taking Air Force money to finish her degree and re-enlist as an officer, in her first year on campus she'd been a twenty-three year-old combat vet in classes alongside eighteen-year olds flailing around trying to find an identity out of Mommy and Daddy's house. Now, they looked even more like babies. As unmarked and shapeless as Play-Dough in the can.

She located Dr. Qualls's office, then went back to her car and grabbed the marker, which she had covered in a blanket to fend off the curious. Of course his office was on the third floor. Not able to get a hand free, she knocked on the door with her foot.

"Come in!" a cheery voice said from within.

"I don't have a hand free for the doorknob."

"Alright, just a moment." She heard a great deal of shuffling and creaking. Finally, the door opened and she felt rotten all over. Dr. Weldon Qualls was in a wheelchair.

"Aw, crap, I'm sorry, I didn't know."

"Know what?" Dr. Qualls smirked. He was thin, with brushed gray hair and big round glasses that screamed 1980s, as if he'd seen himself in the mirror one day thirty years ago and thought to himself, *Yep, this is what we're going with.*

"You're Dr. Qualls, right?"

"That's right, Ms...?"

"Maria. Kerrigan. Just use Maria." Maria found herself uncomfortable between the weight of the thing she was carrying, the way Qualls' condition had thrown her off-balance, and the sudden memory of how being in a Professor's office was, weirdly, so much more intimidating than the loudest T.I. at Lackland.

"What can I do for you, Maria?"

"I, uh...okay if I use that table?" she brushed awkwardly by him and dropped the marker onto a round table strewn with magazines. It made an impressive *clank* on impact.

Dr. Qualls seemed to spark at this sound, and he turned his chair to wheel over to the table.

"Now what have we here?"

Maria reached out to pull off the blanket, but Dr. Qualls raised his arm first. "Wait...before you do this...how far did you travel to get here?"

"About 400 miles, thanks for asking. And you know gas ain't cheap these days, right?"

"I do. We'll see to that, don't worry. Now, go ahead."

Maria pulled off the blanket. Qualls looked at the marker with a kind of sad marvel, a strange, humbled joy that Maria had seen in some church folk. He touched it lightly, reverently, and read the markings along the top. "1999; you have waited a long time, haven't you?"

"Yeah, so, what is it?"

Qualls looked keenly at her. "Just a little game some friends of mine and I play. Have you ever heard of geocaching? We stash things hither and yon. It helps us meet interesting people, like sending out a message in a bottle."

Maria glared silently at him. "Really? So, what, I have to fill out a questionnaire or something?"

Qualls waved off the question and chuckled. "Nothing like that. Tell me, what do you do?"

"Pilot trainer. Up in New Hampshire. Laconia."

"You carry yourself very confidently. You've had military training?"

"Air Force. Two stints, one as an enlisted, the second as an officer."

"Forgive me," Dr. Qualls adjusted his glasses, then pressed his fingers together, giving her an appraising look usually reserved for specimens in Petri dishes. "The details of how those things work are outside my experience. But you saw...action?"

"Yeah."

"And have you killed anyone?"

"As part of my duties, I participated in the blowing up of some dirty bastards who wanted to blow you up. That bother you?"

Qualls smiled at the challenge. "All violence bothers me, but let's say yours bothers me less than other violence might."

"Boy oh boy do you speak Egghead fluently."

"It takes all kinds. Now, forgive what must seem like a drastic shift in topic, but what are your ambitions?"

"Ambitions?"

"Sure: we're all trying to chart a course somewhere into the future. Where would you like yours to go?"

"Why does this feel like a job interview?"

Qualls chuckled again. His laugh got more unsettling each time Maria heard it. "That's what it is. A job interview is exactly what it is, and for a very unique job. Are you looking for a job?"

Maria shrugged, deflecting instinctively. "What's the job?"

"A-ha! This is part of what makes this job special. Everything happens in the wrong order. First, I will interview you. Then, you will make a great deal of money. Then, I will tell you if you are hired or not. And then, only then, I will tell you what the job is."

"But I keep the money either way?"

"Absolutely."

Maria tilted her head and was silent for only two seconds. "Okay, that's the most ridiculous thing I ever heard. Your school has too much money to play with. How do we start?"

***

-4-

"I have done that, says my memory. I cannot have done that, says my pride, and remains adamant. At last, memory yields. This is what Nietzsche said.

"Shakespeare said it with less brutality: to thine own self be true, and it must follow, as the night the day, thou canst not then be false to any man. The insight is the same," Josh said, keeping his cadence even and non-threatening. "All lies start from within, and so we almost never consciously tell lies to someone else, because what we say is what we have already convinced ourselves is true. Or perhaps we simply think of it as a small lie worth telling in service of a greater truth.

"But let's come back to something else from Nietzcshe. All things, he said, are subject to interpretation. Whichever interpretation prevails at a given time is a function of power and not truth.

"Power." Josh paused for a moment. He heard the amplified word echo back at him as it struck the rear wall of the hall and rebounded. He knew he had the audience's absolute attention. He even imagined he could sense people leaning closer to the screens on which they were watching the livefeed of his speech. Since it had been announced that billionaire computer language visionary Josh Scribner would be coming out of seclusion to give the keynote speech at this conference, there had been buzz about whether or not he would say Something, with a capital "S." That he would say Nothing was the safe bet, was expected. A good keynote speech was ideally a dazzlingly-crafted performance of Nothing-saying.

Those who whispered, though, who suspected that there was Something he could say, had already been speculating. Not because the result of him saying Something would be positive; it would probably be horrible. But at least it wouldn't be boring. *Drama,* Josh thought in his brief pause, *is a response to boredom.*

And the preamble to this portion of the speech, drowning as it was in the kind of epigrams that were so often abused by acts of Nothing-saying, nevertheless teased, hinted, suggested that a very dramatic Something might be said. The audience picked up on the cue better than Pavlov's dog.

He had to continue now. Josh didn't speak off-the-cuff well in public. And if he didn't get to the juicy stuff, he didn't know how he'd be able to veer back into the pablum of his old draft. Funny that his aversion to appearing clumsy in a speech would be the final prod to saying the words that would radically change his whole future.

Josh cleared his throat. "Let me start with a truth about myself, a very well-known truth. I first made my fortune in school when I helped codify what became known as the 'bridge alphabet' that allowed human-made programs to interface with, read, and directly influence the electrical impulses of the human brain. In layman's terms, I helped computers and minds to speak directly to each other in real-time, with no barriers of consciousness between them.

"This caused incredible excitement, and incredible panic. Because a mind that could be accessed by a machine could be healed like never before, preserved like never before, even enhanced like never before. But it could also be manipulated like never before."

Josh glanced compulsively at his wrist monitor, at the numbers which gave him a snapshot of his daughter's condition. Then he continued. "These fears are well founded because they show us knocking at some very profound doors;

doors that conceal things we cannot yet conceive. We have long accepted that there is a virtual 'us,' made of all the things we share on the rWeb: jokes, memories, images...timelines of our lives. But we know these things are not fully us; we always hold things back. The network, the virtual organism we have built that wants to consume everything, share everything, never gets all of us, and I think that trepidation is very human; we suspect that in giving too much we are rushing towards the brink of losing something which defines us.

"That's why the devices we made, what we call Beetles today, were heavily-regulated, allowed only for the gravest needs of medicine and research, and, most importantly of all, built as closed systems. In a world defined by connectivity, they were made so that it would be impossible for them to interface with a network. They could not be hacked, could not be corrupted. They became part of the same closed system inside our skulls as our own most private thoughts.

"This is the public story of how I first made my fortune. And it is true. It is, however, incomplete.

"I want you, just for a moment, to imagine. Last night I was telling a friend that imagining is how we glimpse things that can be real, although we don't yet know the path to making them real. It is the great blessing of our species, but one that has also been used to bring nightmares into our world.

"One night, when I was only nineteen-years old and working on the Beetle project, I imagined something. But I lost faith in what I had imagined. I dismissed it as too outrageous to be possible. When someone else wanted to pay me an obscene amount of money for this theory, I cashed his check and laughed all the way to the bank. And I forgot. I forgot what I had seen.

"Power can corrupt truth because it corrupts minds. From pride or fear or simple inertia, we let power have its say about what truth is; we let its interpretations so deep inside us that eventually we mouth their own rationalizations without even being told to. We become perpetuators of power's designs. This is all too similar to some virus codes I've written." The audience, which recognized even a small laugh line such as this, responded appropriately, although the agonizing proximity to substance in Josh's speech made it a very nervous laughter.

Josh continued. "We have all heard the stories about the rich and reckless having black market surgery, having Beetles implanted in countries that have held out against signing the treaty bans, in order to accelerate their minds to make them better traders, better deal-makers. They widen the gap ever further between themselves and those who cannot access such advantages.

"We hear these stories, and do nothing about them. Why is that? Do we feel powerless to stop them from having what they want? Are they right that – possessing the virtues and values that they flatter themselves earned them their wealth – it automatically follows that they will only use these abilities in virtuous ways? Do we look on with envy, and allow this to carry on because we cling to a dream that one day we will be able to buy into such an elite category, the first true example of Humanity Plus?

"Perhaps what finally stops us from acting is this: that even if the worst rumors are true, that Beetles are dangerous to their owners in ways that have yet to be documented, that they are only doing it to themselves, that it is not our problem.

"But what I imagined all those years ago, and what I ask you to imagine today, is that Beetles are dangerous, dangerous in ways that your rational mind will tell you is impossible, and that they are hurting all of us; not just their users, but every human being on the planet Earth."

Now the crowd was starting to murmur. Clearly they'd wanted to murmur for several minutes now, and had only been held back by social custom. *Finally,* Josh thought. *I've poked you enough that you'll be rude.*

They got ruder as the speech went on, as Josh started to lay out the story of what was happening, what was going to happen, and what had to be done to stop it. He knew, even as he spoke, that he sounded crazy. Not just crazy in premise, but crazy in style. That was the problem with explaining something that sounded crazy: the very act of trying to convince someone of it inevitably involved so many foreign concepts, so much strain to weave disparate data into a coherent web, that you couldn't help but to look fevered and demented and totally untrustworthy. Josh had a new empathy for people who yelled on sidewalks.

As he left the podium to tepid and baffled applause, he was already pulling out his pocket screen and tapping a couple of buttons, because he knew the first face he would see. And yes, there she was, Analuiza Gil, looking at him with a face of horrified sympathy. Poor Analuiza. She was a fearless businesswoman, one of his strongest allies and staunchest defenders, and someone who, henceforth, would by totally understandable necessity never be seen in public with him again.

"Check your inbox," he told Analuiza. "You and the others have letters of resignation for every board I'm on."

She barely seemed able to find words before he was surrounded by a crush of reporters, power brokers, and people who just wanted to be near the source of the excitement. "Good luck," was all she managed to say.

***

It was an hour before Josh made it out of the hotel hosting the conference, and another hour back to his own. Every device he had was chirping and quivering with messages from all over the world, and a couple from people on space stations, too. Many, many people had opinions, encouragements, and threats to share. The established media companies were putting their money on the "Josh Scribner went insane" storyline, with only the feisty antiestablishment sources dipping their toes in the "Josh Scribner sounded crazy but his claims merit study" waters. The nuttiest fringes were popping champagne.

The security wall in his pad was getting an incredible workout too. For a while Josh watched the battle in close detail as a worthy distraction. He wanted to see what hackers were trying these days, if there was anything genuinely new out there, or just the idiot's version of new: the old tried with more brute force.

Humanity is an interesting ecosystem, he thought. The people with the skill to break into his research, if it could even be done, were almost certainly not the people who could understand it. And the people who could afford to pay for others to do the hacking and understanding were third parties entirely. But everyone acted on faith that if they did their part, the people with those disparate abilities would find one another. This was why no trace of the research was on his pad. Josh had high confidence in his abilities, but there were eleven billion other people on Earth. Enough of them working together could absolutely overcome his defenses. If not by skill, then by simple relentless pressure, like a carpet of swarming ants leveling a field.

***

He muted everything in his hotel suite save the ambient sound of forest leaves and creatures that Cierra enjoyed most. Cierra was awake and reading a book to her nurse Lamar, who was doing a tremendous job of being surprised and entertained by it.

Josh hugged her delicately, checked all her monitors. "How you feeling, nugget?" he asked.

"Tired," Cierra replied, burrowing her head into Josh's side. Her hair needed to be washed.

And just like that, everything else was outside the room. The billions of dollars Josh had probably just lit on fire in his own portfolio, the giant crosshairs he had painted on his back in questioning the virtues of the planet's elite, the possible doom spiral of the whole species: they were suspended completely while Josh held his daughter. Lamar kept his distance, understanding and respecting the moment.

"Well," Josh said softly, "Daddy's all done with his big speech for the day, so how about we have some dinner?" Cierra nodded, and put her arms around his neck to be carried out into the kitchen.

"Did they like your speech?" she asked in a drowsy voice.

Josh wondered how he could possibly summarize the reaction to his daughter. If you could chart the whole mix of shock, passion, indignation, righteousness, tribalism, apoplexy, cynical ambivalence, belief, skepticism, horror, and determination he had just stirred into existence as competing vectors on a chart, could you cancel some out, reduce them down like an equation until you got a simple dot on a spectrum that said either "like" or "dislike"? And could you reverse the process, unpack the noise hiding inside that simple dot to reveal and understand the broadening rainbow of emotions that defined the ever-growing world of every child? In its own way it was such a wonderful question: did they like his speech?

"I think they did," he said.

***

Josh let Cierra use the small spray bottle at the table to mist the salad. She invested the process with great seriousness, putting both her little hands around the bottle and directing a focused frown at the bowl, spraying in slow, thorough passes. Josh knew that look: he had seen it reflected back on him in screens since he was younger than Cierra. He also appreciated that the spray bottles had come a long way in aesthetics and efficiency since they had become as ubiquitous to the table as salt shakers. "Is that enough?" she asked, in her usual whisper.

Josh speared a big leaf, shoved it all in his mouth at once, and crunched away. "Mmmm, just right. You brought these veggies to life!" She smiled with great pride, but still refused to eat any veggies herself. *Little do you know,* Josh thought to himself, *what's inside your beloved hot dogs these days.*

Josh and Cierra and Lamar had a quiet dinner, and it was the best thing Josh could imagine doing at that moment.

***

Once Cierra was back in bed, Josh and Lamar whispered in the hallway outside Lamar's room.

"The headaches have been less severe," Lamar shared. "Either the new medications are working or she's just getting used to them."

"I don't want her getting used to them," Josh said with a defeated sigh.

"What you said today..." Lamar let that dangle for a moment.

"You heard about it, huh?"

"Well, I've got a big family, and all of them wanted to let me know I was working for a lunatic."

"Yeah, but you knew that already, didn't you?"

Lamar smiled. "Craziest man I've ever known."

Josh had wondered if today would cost him the services of someone who had long ago ceased to feel like an employee and begun to feel like part of the family. It sounded like, for the moment at least, he didn't have to worry. "So what about what I said today?"

"Is that the reason? Why you never got a Beetle for Cierra? She would certainly qualify for a legal one, even in America."

It had been a different kind of release when Josh had made the drastic public confession earlier; this was much more intimate. It brought shudders of emotion out of him.

"Partially, yeah. Did that stuff make sense to you?"

"Well, when you really got into the weeds with stuff like telepathic fields and the crazy brain plague that we were all going to get, it sounded pretty scary. But, Beetles can't talk to each other, right? I mean, you designed them that way. So I didn't get how it was going to work."

There in the hall, Josh chuckled to himself. "I should have tried the speech out on you first. Because that's exactly the idea I needed to flip in people. Beetles can't talk to each other, but brains *want* to talk to each other. They use every tool they're given to try to connect, to communicate, because those connections are how we evolve and reproduce. You give something as powerful as a human brain a new tool, it's going to find ways to use it – ingenious ways – that just happen to have terrible possibilities."

"So that's why? Keeping a Beetle out of her will keep her safe?"

"It won't keep any of us safe, Lamar. But it will keep her safe from something much worse, the thing I couldn't even say in that bit of hellraising I did today."

"What's scarier than that?"

Josh clapped Lamar on the shoulder, almost as if checking it to see if he could put some of this burden off on his friend. But he couldn't yet, and he didn't know if this was a favor or he was just too tried. "Another time. Sleep well."

Lamar returned the touch on Josh's arm affectionately. "There is no other time. There's this one. I'm glad you're doing what feels right."

"Hopefully it's not too late."

***

Josh lay in bed, eyes wide open, staring at the ceiling. It carried a projection of a brilliant field of stars, the sky as seen on a clear night in Yosemite, half a world away. But the sounds were of the ocean's lapping waves. Somehow Josh's brain saw no contradiction, perhaps because the orientation of the stars was knowledge, but what the sound of the waves did to him preceded knowledge.

Josh realized that a truly smart hacker would try to get at him through the hotel room. The hotel, despite its luxury reputation, would not have his quality of security. It could be accessed. His room could be found. They could probably wire right into the environmental controls and talk to him through the speakers, over the lapping waves. Biometric data would be on the room pads. Maybe they could even speak in low, hypnotic tones with the waves, trying to get him to write down one or two of his encryption keys' addresses as he slept. *The best hacks,* Josh mused, *incorporate the elements outside the system.*

But he wasn't worried about the ones that wanted access, or just contact. The one he was afraid of, if he decided to come, wouldn't come knocking. And all the virtual shields Josh could throw up might not be enough.

Today, Josh had made it more likely that he would die soon. The only blessing was that he had also seen to it that the death would now look highly suspicious.

***

Josh's pad chimed with a voice request at three in the morning. He knew who was calling, because he had set the pad to block every other incoming request. He rolled over and tapped the pad to approve contact. "What time is it where you are, Min-Jun?"

"The same as it is for you, my notorious friend." Min-Jun's normal tone of gentle kidding was layered with something else. A coating of gravity, something troubled. It was understandable given the hour, but Josh wasn't used to hearing it from his friend.

"So you're still in town? You saw the speech?"

"I did. Josh, you know I have always trusted and admired your genius. But I must ask...is it true? Everything you said?"

Josh understood now how deeply he had rattled his own best friend. Despite how compelled he had been to give the speech, it pierced his heart to feel responsible for affecting someone close to him this way. "It is."

"Do you think it is...too late to stop it?"

"I don't know. I wanted to sound an alarm, encourage more research. But there's a lot of human nature working against us. People won't want to believe."

"Josh, I have not slept because I have been thinking. Sometimes one must stop everything else and think for a very long time. The irony is that usually the answer to what we are thinking about is simple and comes to us right away, but we need to spend this time accepting that it is the answer."

Josh didn't think he had ever heard his friend need so much warm up to get to a point. "Min-Jun, what is it you want to say to me?"

"What you said at the bar, about regret. What if I told you there really was a way to change the past?"

***

-5-

"**A**nd that was it?" Lia asked. "He asked you some questions and then told you to leave?"

"Yeah," Maria said, throwing up her arms as she paced around the little living room. "He sets me up like he's interviewing me for this job, and then he just says, 'that's all, see ya.' And then he gives me this yard sale in, like, Maine that I'm supposed to go to next month."

"Maine? Why?"

"He said I have to buy this painting there before 10:30am; only, to get there before 10:30 I'd have to leave here at 6:00."

"What's so special about the painting?" Lia was watching TV; a colorful cartoon, with the sound off.

"He wouldn't tell me that either! Just said to buy it and bring it to him."

"How does he know about a yard sale happening in Maine next month? Is it, like, a really big yard sale? I didn't think people announced those far in advance."

"You know what I think?" Maria planted her feet by the window, looking out through the glass. The lamps had just come on and kids were being called in from the street. "I think it's some relative of his. The painting is some stupid heirloom some stupid cousin got in a will or something, and now Doctor Weldon Qualls is using me as an errand girl because he thinks I've got nothing but time on my hands."

"You think maybe it's a test?" Lia asked.

"What do you mean?"

"Well, you always read about professors doing weird tests on people, where you think you're interviewing for a normal job, but instead something strange happens and it's just to test how you react to it."

"Lia, that doesn't make any sense. Everything about this is strange!"

Lia sunk further into the couch. "I'm just saying. Those tests creep me out."

"I'm going for a run." Maria announced. And she did. Eight miles.

It was excruciating. It was great.

***

Maria didn't talk about the trip to Princeton or the yard sale for several days after that. Life took on a little of its old rhythm. Lia worked two days in a row, and Maria took her to her counseling when she was available to. Maria didn't drink, and didn't crash her plane.

She didn't go camping, either. That urge seemed to be temporarily on hold, like the marker owned her camping habit now. This struck a spark of irritation inside her that seemed to grow each time she thought about it.

Of all the things he could have asked me to do, she thought, *why did he have to ask me to do nothing and wait?*

***

On a Tuesday night she went to a strip mall Italian place that had become a regular stop. It wasn't classy, just six tables with clear plastic over the tablecloths for easy cleaning. And it was New Hampshire, so how much could they seriously know about real Italian food? But Maria wasn't particular about cuisine; she liked the pizza well enough, the only alcohol around was those carafes of cheap wine that didn't tempt her at all, and the TV seemed to show soccer games twenty-four hours a day. Maria wasn't especially excited about soccer, but seeing how excited it made the other people there comforted her.

She had her pizza and her soda, doing the nearest thing to relaxing she could.

"Lot of pizza for one little lady..." The hard, flat vowels smacked of generations in New England. Maria looked to the source of the voice, a not-really handsome, not-really trim man in a windbreaker over a polo shirt. He looked like a kids' soccer coach, not to mention extremely married, and had a lot of teeth he was flashing at her.

She just shrugged, not giving him anything.

"You ah, you know how to work up an appetite then?" His grin seemed to pulse like a throbbing vein.

There had been times for men in her life; lately hadn't seemed like one of them. The price of fraternizing was way too high while she was in. "Don't even *look* at your brother flight," she remembered hearing during training. And since she gave up the booze, it just hadn't seemed like any fun. Still, nothing she did was enough to get herself left alone. Walking out her front door in possession of a vagina was enough for some guys.

"I bring the rest home to my roommate," she said, which was true. Lia would peel the toppings off and throw them away, and then peel the cheese off and eat it separately. It was a habit that annoyed Maria to a degree that was livable.

"Couple of girls living together, huh? You two like to have a good time?"

Oh Jesus, Maria thought. *This guy will make something out of everything.* It was as subtle as slapping his wang on the tabletop. His eyes sparkled about two beers' worth. *He probably wrote a real good e-mail today at work and feels like a stud.* She looked over his shoulder; he had about three guy friends in the booth watching him and yukking it up. Which made him the bravest of them, which was pretty sad.

"You should go home to your kids," Maria turned back to her soda and hoped for the best.

The toothy guy stood there for a second, face flushing. Then he leaned down and spoke in a whisper. "I can see what you are. You're a *puta*."

A sudden fire slammed Maria's fist into the table and she stared at him with fury. He just laughed and backed up to his table, singing "Ba bla bla bla La Bamba!"

She didn't storm out. The urge to was strong, but stronger at this moment was the urge to not show this asshole her back. She finished her soda, paid, packed up her leftovers, and took her sweet time going out the door, ignoring their calls.

***

"We need to get a new pizza place," Maria said as she dropped the leftover box on the table. "Can we please turn the damn light on?"

Lia flipped the switch, and her other hand lingered on the door frame for a moment, gripping it as if she feared a tornado would blow her out of the house. "Why? What happened?"

"Saw a cockroach running around." Maria opened the refrigerator out of habit, knew what she wanted wasn't there, slammed it shut again, and stalked back and forth in the four feet of space between walls. "You can get pizza anywhere, anyway."

"Okay," Lia said with one of those despairing sighs. "Does my hair look pretty today?"

"Kid, it looks outstanding. You're beautiful."

"Thank you. I like the length it's getting to. Jarrod never liked it long."

That stopped Maria's pacing. "Hey, what did I say about that asshole? You've got no reason to say his name."

"Dr. Morgan said I shouldn't give him more power over me by falsely denying his existence."

"Yeah, well he's 500 miles away from you and your hair and it's a good thing too because I'll kill him if I see him, so it doesn't matter what he liked or didn't like because it's your damn hair and you should make it a mohawk if you feel like."

Lia seemed to flatten back against the wall. "You've never even met him. How could you kill him?"

Maria watched Lia's face, the keen caution that was all over it, the way she was poised like a small animal getting ready to run. "Ah, I'm sorry for popping off; this jerk was hitting on me today and it just made me crazy."

Drops appeared at the corner of Lia's eyes. "That's not my fault. You shouldn't be mean."

"I know! I know. Christ, Princess, you know that I would blow myself up before I'd hurt you, right?"

Lia nodded. She seemed so exhausted from sticking up for herself for five damn seconds. Maria approached slowly and reached out to hug her. Lia returned it with a sniffle.

"Shit, girl," Maria said. "You want to play cards?"

Lia said, "Okay."

They walked into the living room. Maria added "You want to come to Maine with me?"

"What? For the thing in a few weeks?"

"Ah, let's just go tomorrow and get it done. I don't have work."

"But if they're not having the yard sale yet, will they sell it? Won't it seem weird if we just show up at their door?"

"We'll just pretend we're dykes out antiquing. Dykes do antiquing, right?"

"That's a rude word. And I would be bad at lying about that."

"I know; you're way too sweet. You're the sweetest lady I ever met."

They busted out the cards and that was their evening in.

***

They left not long after sunrise. Lia had that cheap as hell little overnight wheely bag with the faded floral print that

Maria had seen her with the very first time they had met. She also had a tall thermos of tea. Her mouth was in that prim straight line that was sort of like a smile on her face, and she had brought out the casual blouse she almost never wore. Maria felt underdressed in her tank top and bike jacket.

Lia spent a lot of her time looking out the window, sometimes up to the sky if she saw birds. Maria couldn't help but wonder what went on inside her head. She was pretty sure Lia was the sharper of the two of them, but Lia was so messed up and scared that she barely spoke to anyone but Maria, so whatever good thoughts she had just bounced around in there.

The bends in the road kept the trip from ever being too repetitive, and the colors were impressive. The sky wasn't so great: gray and wind-whipping. Lia seemed to like it.

Did you think having her here would keep me away? The voice sounded really damn smug today.

"Hey, you got some of that tea?" Maria said to Lia. Lia happily poured a small cup full. Maria steered with one hand as she sipped.

***

The Hackenmiller family up in Maine seemed surprised to have visitors. They did confess, though, that they had been setting things aside for a yard sale. The Dad was filled out, like a high school lineman who'd let himself go, and there were a couple of chubby pre-teen boys with buzz cuts crashing around the backyard. The Mom was the smallest of them, and in charge. Her clothes looked like she had learned how to mend them and make them last.

"I'd like a house like this," Lia said, as they creaked up the stairs to the spare room. "Just a nice little house."

"If it's little you want, we've got littler than this." Maria teased. It seemed like a rare moment where Lia could take some kidding.

There were three paintings set aside for sale in the spare room. Of course there were. Exasperated, Maria tried to remember the balance in her checking account as she offered to take all of them.

"Why do you want to get rid of them, anyway?"

The Mom cleared her throat, hesitated, and then finally spoke, her head jutting nervously as she did. "Oh ahhh, we just wanted to unload a few things. Money's been a little tight. Our youngest, Jeanie, she was hurt pretty bad in an accident and the bills have been hard."

Lia didn't catch that this was not a nice road to go down, but bless her, she tried to make conversation. "Oh, you have a daughter? I didn't see her."

"Oh, she's, uh, she's at Southern Beacon. That's the care center, you know. They keep better watch of her there." The Mom was beginning to make manically friendly gestures, trying agonizingly hard to downplay the clearly open wound. "The people there are really lovely; have you ever been there?"

Maria shook her head and decided to get the hell out of there before she couldn't keep silent and asked what kind of accident it was.

***

"I think this one's the one," Lia said. She had decided to sit in the back and peruse the paintings for the first stretch of the drive home. "They're all nice, but this one's really nice. It's too bad the Professor wants it. Do you think we could hang up these other two, though?"

"Why did you ask about the daughter?" Maria demanded. "We should have just got out of there." Lia didn't respond, just kept looking at the three paintings.

"Can we pull over?" Lia asked a minute later.

"All right, yeah," Maria replied, remembering that one of the Turnpike Plazas was just a few miles ahead. "You want a snack? I can get you something while you're in there."

"That's okay, thank you."

* * *

The plaza building, long and low, reminded Maria of a train station. She munched some dried fruit while she leaned against the car, sometimes bumping her body restlessly against it.

Accidents happen to everyone, the Voice said.

"Yeah, don't I know it," Maria mumbled back, looking down at the concrete.

Not all accidents are terrible, though.

Maria turned and stared through the car window at the paintings in the back seat. None of them seemed like a big deal. "Yeah, some people are lucky that way. So what?"

She's been a long time. Do you think she's in trouble?

Maria stuffed the dried fruit in her pocket and ran into the building.

One stall in the ladies' room was locked. Maria looked underneath and recognized Lia's little flat shoes that looked like bowling shoes.

Waiting until the last other person left, Maria tapped lightly on the stall door. "Hey kid, you in there?"

"I'm okay," Lia answered.

"I know you're okay. You're great. Just wanted to see if you're in there."

There was a long stretch of silence. "I don't want to go yet."

Maria sighed and leaned against the wall. "It's okay Princess. We can hang. I got some snacks here, you want some?"

"I really really don't want to go."

"Nobody's saying you have to go!"

Maria heard a quiet, keening sound coming from the stall. Swearing to herself, she took a deep breath, got down on her belly and crawled under the stall door.

Lia was in there, sitting fully dressed on the toilet seat, squinting and hugging herself and making that sound, that quietly piercing noise. One fist had strands of her hair clenched in it.

Maria got up into a squatting position on the floor and looked at Lia for a moment. They'd met in a group therapy session for survivors of trauma. Lia's bastard husband had knocked her around pretty bad, but even worse was the way he'd taken apart everything that could let her stand on her own two feet emotionally. She'd finally run away to a shelter and had been in therapy for over a year. They'd been treating her like a baby, giving her macaroni and paste to make things out of. Maria had pulled her into a card game, they talked, it became a habit, and soon they were housemates. It was then that Maria had stopped drinking.

She reached out and hugged Lia. "Ah, champ, it's okay. It's been a long day, huh?"

Lia sniffled. "I don't know what happened. I'm sorry. Someone was walking out and the door slammed and it was so loud all of a sudden." She was shivering in Maria's arms.

"You don't have to apologize, space case. You didn't do anything to anybody."

"I wish I was like you," Lia said.

No you don't, kid, Maria thought to herself. *You don't know what you're asking for.*

***

"So I got the thing for you," Maria said hastily into the phone.

Dr. Qualls sounded surprised. "The painting? But the yard sale isn't for two weeks."

"Yeah, I had the day free so we just went up and asked to see what they had."

"We? You and whom else?" Dr. Qualls sounded agitated, which bothered Maria. He had also used the word "whom," which had mostly been used by assholes in her life.

"Lia, my roommate. She helped with the driving. So what do we do with it?"

"Maria, you were given specific instructions–"

"Yeah, you told me to get the painting and I got the painting! I bought two others, too, just because I didn't know which one for sure was the one you wanted; they all kind of look the same to me. I had them give me a receipt, which made them feel weird because it was just a Mom and she wrote it on a Post-it, so I don't know if that'll be enough for you, but that was a lot out of pocket."

Dr. Qualls took a long, deep, dusty-sounding breath. "Maria, I don't think this is going to work out."

"Wait, what? What the hell did I do wrong? What about the money?"

"Take the paintings to an art appraiser. You won't have to worry about money again for a long time."

"Excuse me? You're telling me these are worth something?"

"One is. The landscape. It will sell at auction for $1.2 million."

"A million? I paid thirty bucks for it! How do you know about this?"

"Maria, I cannot tell you and I shouldn't have even told you that much. Hopefully that will be more than enough for your time and the inconvenience, and you can go back to your life and forget any of this ever happened."

The conversation ended soon after. Maria stared at the phone, and probably would have hurled it against the wall if she wasn't so constantly aware of how little money she had.

***

Maria had never looked for an art appraiser before. There was a guy in town named McGroarty who ran an antique shop: townspeople said he showed up at estate sales, always in a neat, sober suit, like the final confirmation of death. His thinning hair was slicked tight against his skull and he wore three chunky rings.

Maria lugged the painting in, said a friend had asked to get an estimate on it. McGroarty looked at it, smooching his lips out with doubt and disdain. He ran a finger carefully around the frame. "I'll give you fifty for it right now," he said, shrugging as if fifty dollars were nothing to him.

As little as Maria knew about art, she did know poker, and a fifty dollar play sounded like a lot more than he would offer for something worthless, but enough that he hoped she would take it and not ask questions. So, without a word, she started stalking out. This got the jerkoff moving, and he ran after her to the door. "Wait, wait! Where did you find it?"

She kept moving. He kept offering. "A hundred dollars. A thousand. Cash, right now, please!"

Of course, once you'd been caught in a bluff you could never buy your way out of it. Maria left McGroarty with the quiet, sad tinkle of the door chime, and the memories of the fortune he might have shared in if he hadn't been such a greedy liar.

**

The curving roads looked familiar now, far more so than just one trip should have made them. Maria drove them alone this time, antsy to be at her destination. The burden on her conscience wouldn't ease until she'd made things right.

She arrived back at the Hackenmiller house at nightfall. As she approached the front door on the little gravel path, she thought about what Lia said about wanting a little house like this. They could have had one. They could have had this one. Oh well: you never got everything you wanted in life.

She rapped on the door, knowing from the faint sliding and clinking sounds of a family around the dinner table that they were home. Pretty nice if that Mom could still wrangle all those animals to the same table at night. She was the one to answer the door, and she seemed pleasantly surprised to see Maria again.

"Hiya," Maria said, unsure how much to say. "Look, uh, this painting here...we figured out that it's worth a lot more than we paid for it. So, uh, you should have it back."

The Mom instinctively shook her head, tried to push away Maria's concerns with a fervent, almost self-annihilating politeness. "That's lovely to hear, but we don't need it. What you gave us was very helpful."

What I gave you was a pittance, Maria thought, feeling the weight of guilt almost physically pulling at her. She set her feet firmly and said, "Ma'am, I insist. We like the other two and we're happy with the price we paid, but you need to take this to a professional and have it appraised. I looked up a couple and here are their phone numbers."

The Mom took the painting and the numbers, unwilling to push back further against Maria's firmness. "Thank you; isn't it funny, this was in the attic when we bought the place. How much do you think it's worth?"

"I'm not an expert, but my understanding is that you shouldn't let it go for less than a million. Really, stand your ground on this one. No less than a million."

And with that, Maria spun and walked away, leaving Mrs. Hackenmiller alone and agog.

***

Maria didn't drive home. She headed south, hugging the Atlantic Ocean most of the way, driving right through the night for New Jersey. She was too ticked off to be sleepy.

She arrived before sunrise, and found a bakery to stew at, jacking herself up on coffee and thudding her feet against the floor as she watched the rest of the world wake up. At 7:30 she was pacing around in front of the building where Dr. Qualls's office was, and glared at the alarmed secretary who unlocked the main doors.

She was sitting in the lobby, staring at the door, her mind beginning to stretch and twist with fatigue, when Dr. Qualls finally arrived, punching the big square button on the all-access door and waiting patiently for it to grind open before rolling in. He had a little leather satchel in his lap and his hair was already going awry, like it just assumed this shape upon reaching the campus.

"What kind of crazy-ass test is this?" she demanded, rising and stomping towards him. He stopped rolling and froze, looking alarmed. Finally he made kind of demented "ShsshshhHHH!" sound, and gestured for her to follow him to the elevator.

He wouldn't speak again until they reached his office. "Maria, I told you that we were finished. Was the painting not enough to compensate you for your troubles?"

"How could you send me out there to take a million dollars out of that poor family's pocket? What kind of asshole does that?"

Dr. Qualls choked on the first word of his reply. He seemed even more unprepared for her question than he had been for her appearance. "They were never going to get the money. They were going to sell the painting at the yard sale two weeks from today at 11 a.m., and the buyer was going to get the million dollars. This way you were going to get it instead, so what's the harm?"

"What's the harm? They've got a sick daughter, their house is falling apart, and you know they've got the answer to all their troubles and you didn't tell them?"

"They were not the priority. Finding out if you could follow directions was, something you are clearly terrible at."

"Hey, quack, I can follow orders. But I'm out now, so I don't have to do it blindly anymore, especially if someone orders me to do something terrible."

"What did you do?" Dr. Qualls finally was raising his voice in consternation.

"What do you think I did? I gave it back to them, told them it was worth a lot. Jesus Christ, if you'd been in their house you would have done it too."

Dr. Qualls pressed his fingers together for a long time, looking at her. Finally, she couldn't take his gaze anymore. "I don't care what the job is, I don't want it. Enjoy your games, Professor."

She headed for the door, but Dr. Qualls asked "Wait, Maria. Wait." She turned back and looked at him. "Forgive me, I can be a little programmatic at times. What I was just considering is that you have accidentally proven that you are even better for this job than I knew. And the truth is, I don't think I can risk the time it would take to find anyone else. We lost the chance to give you the financial freedom to do the job, but perhaps we will find some other way. Whether you realize it or not, you have already started doing the job; now what I want to know is will you let me tell you what it is, and ask if you will see it through?"

"What is it?"

"Why, to save the future!"

***

-6-

Villigen, Switzerland

Josh watched the seconds pass on the clock on the wall panel. Far more exciting things were available for him to view there: headlines from around the world; weather reports; water prices and exchange rates and quality reports; a celebrity gossip show. His own name flashed by once or twice; his notoriety was still cycling out of immediacy. Still, his fascination remained with the clock, ticking steadily away with no judgment or agenda. It was soothing, in its way.

Finally, a door opened and Min-Jun Dan entered, head already pitched forward in apology. Two badged security officials flanked him, shuffling nervously, not sure where to stand.

"Josh, my friend, thank you for your patience. It was a peculiar problem we faced; you see, you are the first outside visitor we have ever had. So there is no procedure for how to bring you into the building in a way that satisfies all the...important paranoias." As if to punctuate this, one of the guards raised his palm and, using the lens mounted there connected to a basic wrist device, took a picture of Josh, then asked for his finger print, which Josh provided by pressing his thumb onto the face of the wrist device.

"Your security must have about five million images of me just from while I was sitting here."

"Is it not strange that we try to make security so predictable, but constantly want it to have a human touch?"

Josh scratched unconsciously at his neck as he followed Min-Jun into a sterile corridor. "I've cashed so many checks over that problem. People would hire my firm to design better talkbot software. A lot of my competitors focused on the timbre of the simulated voice, trying to lick that Uncanny Valley issue and make it sound more human, but that's not really the problem. The problem is that we're spoiled by human shorthand in conversation. We convey so much with tone that even when we have terrible grammar, we have some hope of being understood. The guys who want these talkbots want conversation trees that can direct people to the exact solution, but the most efficient ones in the world still leave people feeling cold and unsatisfied because computers are terrible guessers and they don't feel what we're going through. So they ask more and absorb less.

"Most of the time what makes people happy is just feeling like they've been heard and understood. It's not talking to a machine that makes them feel alone, it's that the machine always seems to be across from them, rather than at their side. We've gotten better at that but we've never licked it."

Min-Jun smiled as they stopped outside a lab door. "Very profound. We do want people by our side." The door scanned his retinas, then a projected number pad appeared on the door's surface and Min-Jun typed in a quick sequence. The door opened into Min-Jun's lab.

***

"Look at my desk. What do you see on it?" Min-Jun asked.

Josh sighed. "If you have another lesson for me about the philosophy of simplicity, you've brought me a long way to hear it."

Min-Jun replied evenly. "Someday I will resume that argument with great pleasure. For now, just look and tell me what you see."

"On the screen or the surface?"

"On the surface: on top of the desk."

"Okay, I see your little teapot and cup, and a potted orchid. That's it."

"Alright, now turn around and look at the shelf behind you. What do you see?"

"Two more orchids. You like orchids a lot."

"I truly do. And you can see that the door has closed behind us, and was very secure and hard to enter?"

"Jesus, Min-Jun, you sound like you're setting up a magic trick."

"In a way I am, but one that's far more real than any magic trick ever performed. Also, far more expensive. Now, this next part is very important. I am going to create a reaction in the accelerator chamber. You will be able to watch it from here, and I insist you follow along.

"Min-Jun, what I understand about particle physics could fit on the palm of my hand."

"I know many particle physicists who would find the makings of a very funny joke in that remark. Nonetheless, I insist: everything depends on you watching the screens with me as I work on them."

Josh shrugged. "How much leeway do you get to do expensive nonsense here?"

Min-Jun began to play the keys projected across his desk surface like a pianist. "Over the last year, more leeway than anyone should be trusted with."

Josh couldn't decipher the impact of what Min-Jun was doing, but he saw readouts for two different particle accelerators, and that Min-Jun was most definitely accelerating something in them, while preparing a beam of some kind. Josh knew that the Villigen facility was one of the most advanced in the world, but what that actually translated into, he had no idea. For all Josh had unburdened his work woes – which seemed inseparable from his life woes – on his good friend, Min-Jun had, in turn, hardly ever talked about work and seemed to consider it an act of friendship for Josh not to ask.

"See how I start the timer here," Min-Jun said, tapping one virtual button which started a countdown. "We are two minutes away from something very exciting. Or rather, something exciting has already begun, and in two minutes it will be done! Now, my good friend, keep looking."

Josh remembered a test he had taken as a child. He had been left alone in a room with a marshmallow, and been told that if he could wait for ten minutes and not eat the marshmallow, he would be rewarded with a second. His understanding was that just about every child of his age failed this test miserably, being unable to see beyond their immediate desires, unable to conquer impulse with reasoning. Five-year old Josh, however, had stared fixedly at the marshmallow, disappearing into a private mental zone of contemplation. And when his parents and the doctor entered to congratulate him, he had only asked how many he would get for ten more minutes.

Staring and waiting was not a problem, provided he had faith it was worth it.

The real-time monitors displaying the accelerators flashed. Josh heard nothing: the speakers were off and he didn't imagine that the sub-sub-sub-atomic particles in play made a lot of noise to begin with. Still, he was sure if he were there in the flesh he would hear some powerful magnetic thrumming or the like. It was rather like being in space. Josh had done that, once. At his level of wealth you could experience just about anything.

Then, the countdown hit zero, the screens flooded completely with white light, and all the readouts went haywire for a moment. Min-Jun powered everything down, tapped a few buttons, and typed out a report which, using the automated syntax of hundreds of similar reports, took him only six key strokes.

"We have had a successful launch! Of course, I knew it would be successful before we started; that's the marvel of it."

"Okay, Min-Jun, now you're just being cute. What did you do?"

"Turn around and look at the shelf."

Josh did. There was a small, rectangular plate of metal there now, a solid lump with some letters etched into the surface. Josh took a couple of steps towards it to see more clearly. The letters in the surface simply read, "Hello, my friend Josh."

Josh smiled, because it was just like his friend to want to pair a cosmic marvel with something impish. "Okay, so we work from the assumption that you're not bullshitting me or using mirrors, right? Is this MEM?" He used the initialism for "Matter-Energy-Matter" that had entered into common parlance once speculation had begun in earnest that such a thing might be possible on the subatomic scale. "If so, congratulations; you've leapfrogged everyone and got us right to *Star Trek* about two centuries early."

"A good guess, but you leave out an important detail."

Josh caught up before Min-Jun's sentence was done. "There's nothing here to reassemble it. It can't be just beam delivered. Is it safe to touch? I mean, it's not radioactive?"

"It is slightly radioactive, but no worse than going to the dentist."

Josh picked it up; it was cold. He had guessed hot, but it had been a pure mental coin toss. "Okay, Min-Jun, I give up. What the hell did you do here?"

"What I did was not MEM. For all I can tell, the object never ceased to be matter."

"For all you can tell? Wow: so you're in some oogy-boogy territory now."

"The key question is not how it arrived, but when it arrived."

Josh paused for a moment. "Wow, yeah, that happened incredibly quickly; I mean, as fast as I could turn around. Wait, is that why you kept me staring at the screens? So I wouldn't see it arrive?"

"Yes, although there is more complexity in that answer than you yet see. Come, sit down and look at the monitors with me."

Josh complied, his head still spinning with the desire to consider practical applications for whatever Min-Jun was showing him. It was a fulfilling distraction, if nothing else;

one of the most truly novel situations to which he had ever been asked to task his brain.

Min-Jun searched through a menu on the monitor. "Our security system demands that we always have a monitor pointing out from our desks. Our archives know every face I make when looking at a problem. Watch us from a few minutes ago."

And, just like that, their faces from before the experiment stared back at them. Josh grimaced to see his own expression of dull hyperfocus. Once again, he heard Min-Jun say, "See how I start the timer here. We are two minutes away from something very exciting."

"Wait a minute!" Josh interrupted. "Back that up!"

"So you see?"

"You're damn right I see." Josh instinctively reached for the controls, and Min-Jun released them with grace. Josh backed the video footage up. As the recorded Min-Jun pressed the button to start the two-minute timer, the little metal plate just appeared on the shelf behind them. No fizzle of energy, nothing to announce it at all: it was simply not there in one frame, and then there, whole, in the next. Actually, it seemed to appear in the air a half-inch above the shelf, then drop and settle with a noise so slight he hadn't registered it at the moment.

"It arrived before the countdown finished. But you said the countdown led to the launch." Min-Jun was pointedly silent, allowing Josh the seconds needed to make the leap to the truly radical thought.

"Did you send it back in time?"

* * *

"The real problem with time travel turned out to be space," Min-Jun confessed as he peeled an orange. The cafeteria had been vacated so they could converse in private. Josh had coffee in front of him, and a stunning view of the Alps to his right. "We are perpetually traveling in space, though we do not think about it. If you picked, say, the center of the galaxy as a reference point, we have moved countless miles just since you and I sat down."

"In essence," he said, pulling out a wedge of orange and biting into it with great pleasure, "We stumbled onto time travel at least three years ago, but weren't aware of it for some time. Because of space. The particles we were sending through time were ending up somewhere out in the cosmos, far from our detection."

"You said the plate was delivered by gravity?" Josh was trying his best to catch up with something barely five people on the planet understood.

"It is more accurate to say it was delivered by a weakness of gravity. Gravity is a very elastic, susceptible force, and there are good reasons for this to be so. But it is also something we can manipulate.

"What we discovered was that certain particles – Higgs singlets, we call them – have the capacity to pass outside of the four dimensions of ordinary space and time and then re-enter them. This has made the string theory boosters quite smug. As we accelerate them closer to the speed of light, they gain mass under the ordinary principles of relativity. And they drag a kind of distortion field behind them. A gravity wake, we call it. We found that ordinary matter could be grabbed by this wake – literally, towed – on the same parabolic path out of space-time, and then re-enter."

This began to resemble an equation Josh could understand. "So this really is navigation? You create the particle, and you chart a path for it so that once it accelerates out of time, it re-enters when and where you want it to, dragging the package with it? The calculations for that, I mean..."

"It is why we have started so simple and so small. To move something of that size two minutes back in time and a few hundred feet is the height of our sophistication after many experiments."

"But it's just a Moore's Law situation, right? I mean, your range will increase as the years pass and the calculating power of computers increases."

Min-Jun set down the orange and wiped his fingers with a damp napkin. "Josh, this is why I wanted to show this to you. Your speech alarmed me so deeply. I wonder if we really have the time. I wanted you to see this so I could ask you that if we could reach back, actually send a message into the past to change the direction we have come, would that increase our chances?"

Josh was already several steps down this road. He was speculating on ways to increase the Institute's calculating power, possibilities of using processes already in place to shorten steps in the navigation plotting, the articulation of a margin of error that accounted for increasing spatial distortion and rogue gravitational influence...

And in that brew of consideration a simple question emerged. "Why didn't you let me look directly at the shelf? Why just show me a video after?"

Min-Jun looked out at the mountains. The snow on their peaks looked like a great pile of gold in their thirsty world. "Because I think that would not have worked."

"You think?"

Min-Jun chuckled with nervous humility, as if apologizing for his failure to master the universe. "Yes. You see, I cannot ever remember directly observing the arrival of an object. It occurs to me that, seeing it, we somehow adjust ourselves mentally to a reality where the object is simply there."

"Are you suggesting that we get selective amnesia if we look directly at an object that's traveled through time?"

"I am saying that there is something about the process which is fundamentally outside the capacity of human consciousness. It is something that, I think, we are not supposed to be doing."

"According to whom?"

"That is the question we have always asked, isn't it?"

Josh let Min-Jun have his spiritual moment; it was not an actionable answer to the problem. The idea of minimal invasiveness, though, was a compelling one. It was the beginning principle of design and programming. K.I.S.S.: Keep It Simple, Stupid.

Josh was ready to start already. "So," he declared, "the two operative questions are how far back do we go, and what do we change?"

***

Josh hoisted the box through the door and into Cierra's new room. He had already configured all the screens to her private profile, locked their access to the full network (she was too young for that stuff), and set the environment the way she liked it. Even though she had never been to Switzerland, the room would be the one she knew in every way but its physical dimensions from the moment she walked in.

Children always needed an extra tactile familiarity, though, so Josh set down the box filled with her puzzles and toys and dolls in the middle of the floor for her to organize as she liked.

"Come on in, nugget!" he called out.

Cierra walked in cautiously, holding Lamar's hand. She had a thoughtful look on her face, and examined the room from the doorway, looking from floor to ceiling. Then she walked past the box to the window. She looked out into the courtyard and beyond, to the curve of the hill leading down into the village.

"What was this place before it was a house?" she asked.

Josh felt an incredible swell of pride. She was already going three moves ahead in her mind; it might make it tricky to talk to her peers, but Josh followed perfectly. "It was a hotel, a small one. People would come here to stay when they were going skiing."

"Are we going to have time to ski?"

Josh underlined the question in his mind. The project with Min-Jun was now his only pursuit in life. They would live here until they either failed, were stopped, or, against all odds, succeeded.

He remembered a time when he was just fourteen years old and had his first brilliant idea. He had been grounded from the old internet for downloading movies – such a ridiculously quaint crime – and he had snuck out of the house, craving access. He had been so feverishly committed to getting back online: mentally mapping the neighborhood to find nearby friends, guessing the walking distance to the library and trying to remember its closing time. All that mattered to him was re-entering the unceasing virtual stream.

He had passed the high school, heard sounds of whispering and sneakers scraping against pavement. He had thought about hopping the fence to see who it was and what they were up to. Instead, shy and self-conscious, he had walked towards the track field.

There he had stopped and watched as, under the lights, a woman jogged around the track. Her huffing breaths traveled across the night air to his ears as she rounded the dirt oval, not hurried, but never slowing. She had seemed so focused, so privately determined, and to young Josh that looked like the only form of peace he had ever sought. And so, even in his street clothes, never having cared about exercise in his life, Josh had gone out on the track and started running too.

Less than a single lap reduced him to wheezing exhaustion. But as he had strained for air, he had an idea. He had taken that idea home and written his first software app. It made him half a million dollars. His parents never took his phone away again.

Josh made a half-joking deal with a higher power he was pretty sure he didn't believe in: that if they found time to ski, he might get another bolt of insight. This time, the one the whole world really needed.

-7-

"You're insane."

Dr. Qualls patiently absorbed the accusation.

Finally Maria spoke again. "The future? The thing came from the future?"

"It did. The year 2039. It was sent back forty years, to 1999. And then it took sixteen years to be found."

"If they wanted to deliver it to you, why didn't they just pop it into your office? Then you could have got it back then instead of having to wait."

Dr. Qualls topped off their coffee from the cheap little electric percolator he kept on a credenza. "The truth is, I don't completely know. I have some speculations. You see, these markers are the only communications I receive from them. I can post them letters – which then sit unopened in a P.O. box for a quarter-century – but if they have something to say to me, for some reason it must go on one of these. My guess is that they don't want to put them in populated areas just in case they miss the mark. One of these appearing out of thin air and falling on someone's head would be too conspicuous. But, of course, I am not the most mobile, so they put each one somewhere where they hope it will be stumbled upon, and they hope whomever does the stumbling will be good enough, or even just curious enough, to deliver it."

Maria realized that she sounded dumb and repetitive, but she found she just couldn't move forward in the conversation yet. "But it's from the *future?*"

"Yes."

"How can you know that for sure?"

"I had a sample examined privately, and this metal does not technically exist yet. That, and the tendency of the messages to know about things like that painting."

Maria's brain was engaged in some crazy off-road racing, knocked askew by fatigue and the mad possibilities Dr. Qualls was grinning about so stupidly and fuel-boosted by way too much coffee. Finally she grabbed a key fact. "So you've seen other markers?"

"Yes. The first one found its way to me about twelve years ago. I went through very much the same process you're going through now."

"Why do they send things to you?"

"Again, unfortunately, the conversation has not advanced enough for me to know that, but my hypothesis is that, well, it's because I had a hypothesis!" He chuckled. Maria didn't. He coughed and continued. "My field is particle physics. I admit I'm not one of the leaders in that field, but what I am is, for lack of a better term, extremely nerdy about the possibility of time travel. I have published a few essays in magazines speculating on how particle accelerators might make it possible to send objects back in time. This may be someone in the future letting me know that my theory was correct, which truly does make every day like my birthday!"

"Okay, so what do they want us to do?"

"Oh, they haven't told me yet."

"Really? Twelve years of talking back and forth and they haven't said why they're doing this?"

"Well, twelve years from my perspective. We're dealing with a much shorter window there. I might mail them a letter, then mail another five years later, and they probably open them both on the same day in the future. It's very funny to think about!"

Maria shook her head. "If it's funny to you, that's fine. But what's the hold up?"

"The hold up is that I've needed a partner. Someone here in our present able to retrieve the markers they send. I don't know how many of my questions they've answered! And someone must undertake the tasks they need done. Someone able..."

"...to follow instructions exactly," Maria finished the thought. She stared at the floor, feeling her brain throb. She'd never trafficked in science fiction, except maybe some of the technology she'd got her hands on in the Air Force, which was certainly more advanced than she had imagined but was nowhere near this level.

"So other people who have brought you these things, they got interviewed and tested like I did?"

"Yes. One thought the markers were some sort of communist plot; he'd run a Geiger counter over the thing, found a harmless level of trace radiation and decided it had something to do with water fluoridation. I pity the man's unhappiness that he had to live his life with his own Geiger counter.

"Another posted a bunch of pictures online about the thing, which caused all sorts of problems, although thankfully it was before picture sharing became too ubiquitous; I bribed him to take it down. He wanted to know more but I got a bad impression of his motivations. So we've been through a few false starts."

Maria made a dubious face. "You think I measure up?"

Dr. Qualls chuckled again. "I think you're temperamental, rude, and uncooperative. However," he said, tracing his fingers over the surface of the marker, "I think you also have a sense of duty, and believe strongly in doing what's right."

He took off his glasses, rubbed the bridge of his nose, then stared at her with prominent and unshielded eyes. "I don't know what happens in the future. I don't know what we're supposed to change. We may never know if it's for the better or for the worse. Apparently it's my choice who carries out this mission." He laughed with just a touch of despair as he waved around his small, plain office. "You might not take this as the most ringing endorsement, but, having seen the competition, I don't think I'm going to find anyone better than you."

Maria dug in her pocket and found a stick of gum. With deliberate care, she unwrapped it, stuck it in her mouth, and chewed, feeling the burst of mint start to wash away all the acid and bitterness she'd been swallowing. "It's okay," she finally said. "If you had told me how awesome I was, I wouldn't have believed you."

"Two things," she continued, rubbing her hands together. "I don't know how to stop global warming or anything. If they give me something to do, it's got to be specific."

Dr. Qualls nodded assent. "Second," she continued, her eyes hardening perceptibly, "I'm not killing anybody. Do not ask me to do it. I don't care if it's baby Hitler junior. If the job is to kill baby Hitler junior, you do it yourself."

***

Her passenger was arrogant, and he was screwing around. She was trying to teach him how to do controlled turns using a landmark on the ground, and he kept banking left and right like it was a goddamn amusement park ride. He would chuckle at her chiding and then go right back to it.

"Sir, if you don't follow my instructions I'm taking us down."

"Hey, I paid for the full experience; I'm just getting my money's worth."

Finally, Maria had had her fill of him. "You want to know what being a pilot's really about?" she asked.

He looked over, interested. Keeping her voice even, she said, "To recover from a spiral dive, throttle to idle, level to the horizon using both your rudder and aileron together, pressure back, pull the carb heat, and cruise. Got it?"

He looked blankly at her, so she repeated it. "Throttle idle, level horizon, pressure back, carb heat, cruise."

He shrugged at her. "Okay, so what are we..."

And she grabbed her stick and yanked it hard to the right.

At her command, the 152's nose pitched down and the plane started to scream towards the ground, exactly in the spiral shape she'd described. The man in the other seat yelped and threw up his hands, eyes wide in panic. Releasing the controls, she started hitting him and screaming, "We're crashing! We're crashing! Do something! We're crashing!"

He shut his eyes and screamed obscenely. Shaking her head with disgust, Maria turned back to the controls and executed the recovery sequence. Within seconds they were cruising at 1,000 feet, smooth and dandy. 152s were so easy.

She could hear Albert's panicked voice in her headset. She'd settle him down soon enough. She turned to the man who had paid for the "full experience." "Being a pilot," she said, "means you spend 1,000 nice, quiet hours in this seat, always ready to handle that twenty seconds of hell immediately if it starts. I don't even think my heartbeat went up. How'd you do?"

It was a silly question. She was pretty sure the idiot had pissed himself.

***

"So I got suspended from work," Maria announced on her way in. Lia was chopping vegetables very slowly and carefully in the kitchen. It took her something like an hour to get through a damn onion.

She stopped chopping. "Oh no! What happened?"

Maria settled in a chair and pushed around the newspapers and mail cluttering it. "Ah, I yanked a guy's chain. Albert's not really mad, but he had to do something. Hey, do you want to go camping with me?"

"What? You've never asked me before."

"Well, I've got to go out. It's actually the other job. The Jersey thing. I have to find another one of those metal things."

"Oh. That seems very unlikely. The last one was so random."

"They gave me directions, brainiac. This one's in New York, the Adirondacks. It's beautiful, you'd love it."

Lia rubbed her forehead and looked worried. "I don't, I mean, I've never really...is it safe?"

"Well there's some moose." Maria saw Lia start to look very alarmed. "It's not a big deal. They're mostly out fighting other moose for girlfriends this time of year. If we keep the junky people-food locked up they'll leave us alone."

"I want to, I really do, I just don't know how it works. I don't even have a sleeping bag."

"We'll get you fixed up, kid. The Doc's going to get us some money for the job. We just pitch the tent, bundle up, and then hang out listening to the wind. It's pretty awesome, you'll see."

"Can we play cards?"

"We'll play so much cards you'll hate cards."

Lia was quiet and still for a very long moment. Then she threw her arms around Maria and hugged her. "Thank you! Yes, it will be fun."

"Whoah, kid, watch that big knife you're holding!"

* * *

Maria was grateful that Lia was so far not too interested in the details of her job for Dr. Qualls. The sheer craziness of it all wouldn't stop dancing around in Maria's head, and she had a hard enough time not blurting out to the guy at the doughnut shop that she was going into the woods on a mission given to her from the future. Lately, she'd had a lot of sympathy for that nut down by the gas station who was always rambling about death satellites.

Lia volunteered to take the first leg of the drive, up through Rutland where they would stop for brunch. Maria watched her as she navigated the woody highway; she seemed about as happy as Maria had ever seen her. Maria felt safe enough to let her mind drift for a while.

After lunch, she took over and Lia napped contentedly beside her. The kid looked really peaceful.

I'm surprised you agreed to this, the Voice said, catching her off-guard and puncturing the illusory respite of their little scenic trip. *Not that you don't have it in you, Maria, you definitely do. I just thought you were done with it all.*

"Not now," Maria mumbled.

Why not? Don't you like our conversations?

"Who wants to talk to the dead?"

You do, apparently.

"Got me there." Maria shook her head.

Lia opened her eyes. "Did you say something?"

"Just talking to the voices in my head," Maria grinned awkwardly, curving around a beaver in the road.

Lia frowned, trying to decide whether or not to take Maria seriously. Lia had a really hard time knowing when Maria was bullshitting her. Of course, Maria had told the truth, but she had wanted it to come off as bullshitting. So now she didn't know whether to laugh it off or just pretend it had never happened.

This is about as awkward as it gets, she thought to herself as she stared ahead, gripping the wheel and just trying to forget she'd opened her goofy mouth.

***

Maria wasn't used to having help making camp. At first she told Lia to just hang back and relax, but she kept catching Lia peering over at the tent pieces, so finally Maria called her over to help.

Before too long everything was set up. Maria usually opted for the further in, more sparse campsites, but for Lia's sake she'd taken one with real showers, which made it a luxury hotel by Maria's standards. "Is this it?" Lia asked. "Are we camping?"

"Yep. This is what we do."

Lia looked around. A couple of kids were pitching horseshoes, some dads were cracking their first beers of the day. "It's very quiet."

"Nice, huh?"

Lia frowned. "I don't know." She crawled into the tent.

Maria let her be for a moment and unrolled the map she had purchased. She found the coordinates Dr. Qualls had provided her. They were back country, all right. She would have to hike several hours on the trail, and then spend several more hacking through the forest to reach them. Getting the thing out in a day, even assuming she found it right away, would be a push, and it would be very, very cold at night.

There was a primitive, pack-in campsite along the route. Maria could break the trip up into two days and have all the time she needed. But that would mean either 1) convincing Lia to pack in with her, 2) putting Lia in a cabin or hotel for the night and taking the one tent, or 3) leaving the tent with Lia and bundling the hell up somehow. Of the three options, the second looked best, and maybe Lia wouldn't mind not having to "rough it" even to this extent.

Maria ducked her head in the tent. "Knock knock. You okay, kid?"

Lia was lying naked on the tent floor.

Maria jerked her head out. "Ah! Uh, sorry, sorry. I didn't see anything."

"It's okay, Maria," Lia answered.

Nonetheless, Maria kept the tent flap in the middle of the conversation. "You just surprised me, is all. You feeling okay?"

"Yes. I'm sorry, I just...the air felt really nice."

"Hey, no apologies needed, it is pretty fresh up here, huh?

"I think I like it."

"Great. Awesome. So I'm uh, just going to take a walk around, see who our neighbors are, okay?"

"That sounds good."

Maria turned to walk away, but Lia called out after her. "I don't want you to get the wrong idea. I still like boys."

"Yeah, Princess, me too. But you're still hot stuff."

"Thank you, Maria."

***

Maria handled cooking dinner – pan steaks, primally satisfying. They drank root beers, and just holding the glass bottle felt slightly forbidden, a graze against danger. Maria wasn't so much a binger as she was a bad drunk; in the last couple of years especially, she'd been a howling live-wire of a drunk who might bawl-cry or headbutt a pint glass depending on the phase of the moon. She didn't know if that made her an alcoholic, but she did know she couldn't afford it these days. And honestly, she didn't know when "these days" would be over. What she had been calling a troubled phase was beginning to bear an awful resemblance to normalcy.

Lia held her bottle close to her chest with both hands between sips. The sun was starting to set, and she squinted contentedly into it. "How long have you been doing this?" she asked.

"Ah, I did a couple years of Girl Scouts," Maria admitted, using a stick to poke at some sand in the fire pit.

"Was it fun?"

"Sometimes. Girls can be nasty, but I liked camping. Desert camping can be pretty awesome. Ain't nothing like that sky."

"But you stopped?"

"Yeah...." Maria lingered on the word, and then the heavy silence became too much to ignore. "My uh...my brother got hit by a car. After that Mom wanted to keep me close."

"What!" Lia's whole body crumpled a little, the shock touching her physically.

Maria shook her head; there was no avoiding this one now. "Yeah, he was thirteen, just walking back from McDonald's where he'd been with his buddies. It was dark, he was walking on the road shoulder, they swerved suddenly and psshl..." she glanced one hand off the other with a clap. "They clipped him, freaked out, and drove away. Thirteen. I was watching TV while he bled to death." She scratched a boot awkwardly in the dirt, looked down, and nodded to herself as if to acknowledge reaching the end of the story.

Lia shivered, hugged herself, then ran over and embraced Maria, who felt awkward getting a bent-over hug while she was slumped in the camping chair. "Yeah, yeah, it's a big suck. Biggest suck of my life. He was going to be the one flying planes. Air Force was all he talked about."

Lia backed up, sniffling, and sat on the edge of the fire pit. "Is that why you joined? For his memory?"

"I guess...I don't know. He doesn't even feel like a memory. He's still kind of with me." Lia nodded fiercely, suddenly investing great importance in this idea.

"What's his name?"

"Sean. Dad got to name him, and he was browner than I've ever been. Mom gets to name me Maria and I pop out looking all gringo. That's life, right?"

"Can we...drink a toast to Sean? A root beer toast?"

Maria managed a smile, impressed by Lia's reaction to the story she almost never shared. "Why the hell not? To Sean!"

They clinked bottles. *Yeah, here's to you, you big jerk,* Maria thought. But no one answered.

* * *

They played cards in the tent for a couple of hours until the cold got to be too heavy and they stuffed themselves in their sleeping bags for the night. Maria switched on a heater and set a big flashlight by Lia. "You're going to hear sounds you're not used to, but it's mostly pretty okay. This will help you find your way if you've got to take a piss."

Lia had her knit hat pulled far down over her ears so only her face was visible. "I think I'll hold it. I still have my socks on. Isn't that funny?"

"It's a great way to go up here. By the time we're through, they'll be all stinky."

Lia wrinkled up her nose and seemed delighted by this. "So far I like camping."

Maria shut her eyes and thought for a while. Tomorrow wouldn't be the day to set out; one extra day of acclimation would make a world of difference on a big hike, and she still wasn't sure what to do about Lia. They were the same age by years, and the space case seemed so capable sometimes, but Lia could go back to being wobbly and uncertain in a fingersnap. It wasn't her fault, but it made it harder to judge what was okay with her.

Maria wondered how an extra day might affect the urgency of her "mission," whatever the hell that was. Was the thing already there, waiting? Had it only just appeared? Weirder still: did they know when she was going to go get it and it would just appear five minutes before she arrived? Did they know if she was going to leave Lia here or hike her deeper into the woods before Maria had even made up her mind?

She would never know. The thing would just be there, or it wouldn't.

Going around and around that cost her some sleep.

***

The next day started easy. Maria took a jog in the foggy morning that left her gasping but happy. Lia found the trail to the small lake's shore and spent a long time with a little mug of cocoa just watching the water. For a while it was okay to treat this all as it exactly what it appeared to be: a getaway for two friends and roommates who had badly needed one.

Around mid-afternoon, Maria was prepping her pack for the next day when she heard the car door open and shut. She instinctively checked her pocket for the keys, which she still had. Curious, she walked over to the car and saw Lia sitting in the back seat, crying.

Moving very slowly, Maria opened the opposite door and sat down beside Lia, then put her arm across her friend's shoulder and held her.

"It's just so quiet," Lia sobbed. "I can't...it's so quiet."

Maria kissed the top of Lia's head and rubbed her arms. "I know. Quiet ain't always easy."

Sometimes hearing a scream would be better, wouldn't it? The Voice asked. Maria grimaced, feeling a desperately unwanted tear form in her own eye.

***

The cabin was up a hill a little away from the main drag of Chestertown, which was a map dot of a couple hundred people about ten miles outside the park. It had two bedrooms, a solid porch, and a lake view. Plus it had a little TV. Lia had bundled herself up on the couch to watch some cooking show.

Maria was on the phone with some computer run by her bank, trying to figure out where her credit card was. This little indulgence was an extra $300+ whack she hadn't been planning on, and whatever scheme the future had for paying her bills it sure hadn't played out yet. She also had a voice-mail from Dr. Qualls, who obviously had no idea that there could be a place in the woods in America that could actually take a long time to walk to.

Finally she sat in the soft, saggy old chair by the couch. "Feeling cozy, Princess?"

"Yes. I'm sorry I made us leave. I really did like it."

"Don't you dare apologize. You made it over twenty-four hours without a solid ceiling over your head. You know how many worker bees would freak out about that?"

"Thank you. That's very nice."

"So listen, I've got to leave you here alone tomorrow to find the thing. We've got some food, and there's a restaurant down the hill and about a half-mile up the main road if you get cabin fever." She knew that Lia knew no animal called cabin fever. "Just have a good time, but I want you to have the car, so you're going to have to do me a favor and drop me off at the trail and be there for me after."

Lia nodded. "What time will you be done?"

"That part I don't know. It's a long day and a lot can happen. If you don't mind, bring a book and a blanket and something hot to drink and park around 5:00 pm. If I'm not out by 8:00, it's because the sun was going down and I decided to camp. So I'm at a campsite back there and I'll be fine, and you can just come back at 8:00 the next morning and wait for me then. Sound good?"

Lia nodded. Then, after a minute of silence, she asked, "Do you like me, Maria?"

"Shut up. Of course I like you."

"Could I ask you a really big favor?"

"You can always ask, Princess."

"If we start getting more money because of this other job, do you think we could find a doctor for me?"

Maria shifted in the chair, suddenly uncomfortable. "What, you don't think we're doing okay?"

"It's been very nice. But I want to be the way I used to be. Like, I want it a lot now. The group and you and the shelter have all been so nice; I think a doctor should be next." She looked down and mumbled, already uncertain. "I think I could try. I'll help you on these trips so I can earn the money."

Maria looked at her friend, and sympathy finally drilled through whatever part of the idea was gripping her with discomfort. "Of course, kid. If it's what you want, we'll get you a doctor."

"Thank you. I mean it about helping. I want to help."

"You're going to help me tomorrow. So you're already earning it."

Maria took a last walk for the night and found a couple of jigsaw puzzles in the main cabin for them to pass the time with before bed. They were far from finished when the lights went out, but Maria knew Lia would finish them all by the time she came back.

***

Layers. It was all going to be about layers. Layers to keep out the freezing morning. Layers to shed as the hiked miles got her sweating, layers to keep out moisture, layers she worried about keeping dry, layers that were inconvenient to carry when she wasn't wearing them. When Maria left Lia at the trailhead and marched into the woods, she was wearing a lot. Hours later, most of it was stuffed away, and she hiked in a long-sleeve flannel and jeans without even a thermal underneath.

She passed the pack-in campsite, which was sensibly empty at this time of year. In fact, Maria hadn't seen another hiker the whole day. This trail wasn't especially scenic for the area, and it was hard to reach. Maybe there was some deep woods treasure if you went far enough in, but no one at this time of year was going to invest the days to reach it.

She could use her phone's GPS to find the new marker's coordinates, but she had also done a fairly careful study of the trail map and was tracking how far her steps took her. Hopefully the two measures would line up. Of course, the Voice wanted to weigh in now. *You picked the way to do this that was hardest on you.*

"That's where you're wrong. Trying to get her to hack this walk would have been harder."

But you could have taken your time, shared the load. You're going as hard as you did at Lackland.

"God gave me legs, I'm using them."

Haven't heard you say His name in a while.

"Like He doesn't know I know He's out there."

It's good that you know He hasn't forgotten you.

"Hey, I just thought of something. If you're dead, you can tell me what it's all about. Any clouds where you're at?"

I don't think you believe I'm really a ghost.

"Yeah, you're not, are you?"

Nope. Just a reminder.

"Like I'll ever forget you."

Forgetting me isn't the point.

"And what is?" Suddenly all she could hear was the soft crunch of damp leaves under her feet and her sucking breath. Just like the obnoxious Voice to clam up at a moment like that.

There was a sharp crook in the trail: it bent over ninety degrees and backtracked up a slope. In front of her was a massive, flat face of rock. To the other side was an iffy downward slope, and her intended goal.

She carefully sidestepped her way down, moving from one tree trunk to the next to hold or brace herself. With every step she scanned the ground all around. Her GPS told her she was at the coordinates, but it was a wide field of dirt to cover. The best way to work would be to sweep outward from a central point, and on a slope that promised to be annoying and dangerous as hell. Instead she just paced off about a hundred steps along the trail above, then moved about twenty feet down the hill and started pacing back.

It was past one in the afternoon and Maria's stomach was roaring with hunger. She thought about animals she could kill and eat if given the chance. Big ones. Of course, it wouldn't matter a damn if she didn't get out of here.

Then, almost an hour after she stepped off the trail, she saw it: a corner poking up under a carpet of leaves. It looked like it had dropped to the ground and slid a ways down the hill, one of those stupid little realities the geniuses of the future probably hadn't considered.

Remembering from last time how annoying it was to limp along with the thing weighing her down, she stepped slowly as she approached, then finally knelt down and swiped the leaves off it.

"Hello, Maria," it said along the top in those carved, precise letters.

**

-8-

Josh had become paranoid about everything concerning time. He didn't know if they had changed anything yet. Min-Jun was so accepting of the idea that, if any of the messages they flung out of the universe and back into the past were actually changing their present, they would never be aware of it. In fact, the more he talked about it, the more cheerful he seemed to become, and the battier it drove Josh. Their meal breaks in the cafeteria, they always promised, would be a work-free time. They never kept their promise.

"We're continuous, aren't we?" Josh wondered aloud. "We go forward unbroken, just transposed into a changed present on our way to a new future."

Min-Jun chuckled and shook his head. "This calls into question the very nature of our identity. It is just as possible that the moment we interfere, we annihilate ourselves utterly, like an eraser scrubbing everything back to the moment our interference manifests, and a new us is created, and this is the us which is speaking to one another now. Or perhaps I am in an entirely new body but my spirit leapt across the dimensional chasm. Perhaps we have murdered ourselves a dozen times already."

Josh stared out the window. Appropriately, dark clouds were rolling over the mountains. "Do you think we've done this more times than we're aware of?"

"We? I think we can account for all we have done. What others with our names did...?" He shrugged.

Josh could never acclimate to Min-Jun's cheerful personification and acceptance of Time as some inscrutable living entity. Now that they had cracked it open, Josh saw only vectors of force, mapable coordinates, things he could decode and put to work for him. The mystery, to Josh, was no longer how to cross time, but how to make the necessary change with minimal collateral impact.

"But okay, say that you're right, then maybe we've already changed things and we don't know. Have we made things better? Have we made them worse?"

"Whatever we have done, the people we are have arrived at this moment still with this power and still believing something should be done."

"This is what I'm afraid of," Josh said, turning away from the window and trying desperately to tug his brain out of the abstract, if abstract was even a sufficient label for the territory they were dwelling in. "This woman's name is Maria Kerrigan, right? So the first thing I want to do is a full records sweep on her. Birth, career, death...hell, wedding pictures. I want to know everything about her so we know what she's capable of.

"But that life's already got our fingerprints on it, right? She found a marker. Qualls told her what it was about – or, anyway, as much as we've told him – so right now the Maria Kerrigan that exists is the one that got the mission and then never received any follow-up instructions. She was promised the chance to save the future and then got nothing. Cosmic crickets. That's already a massive, personal-level piece of weird we've just...I don't know...*installed* in her for the rest of her days. Statistically, there's a non-zero chance she's alive right now. And if we send the follow-up, give her the assignment, do we obliterate that Maria and make another one? Or...Jesus...what if we get her killed in this version of things? What right do we have to say that the life Maria ends up getting is the right one?"

"A strange sense of justice is awakened when we know how powerfully we can affect another person's life."

"This isn't about philosophy!"

"It very much is. You worry about one while you still believe that far more lives are at stake, don't you?"

Josh brooded on how correct this was. They had been at this for nine months now: refining the launch procedure, boosting their geographical and temporal range thousands of times over, obsessing over the most minimally-invasive means to meddle; then, finally, sending forth their messages and receiving the – from their perspective – instantaneous responses. Meanwhile, outside their experimental haven, the world was getting uglier. Sicker.

Early on they had decided to include numbers on the markers, snapshots of various index funds dating from the target arrival date of the marker to their own reality. Min-Jun's theory was that, as a relic of their specific present, the numbers on it would persist in the past even if the future changed, and by asking Dr. Qualls to include them in his return messages, and then measuring those numbers against that of their own reality, they could confirm the presence and extremity of changes.

So far all this had provided was noise. *Something* had changed, but whether this was some butterfly effect of their own actions, or simply a few billion daily acts by the human race that zigged instead of zagged in this new version of reality, there was no way to track. Josh had no filter for the effect of free will, or even the existence of free will, which seemed to be an even bigger mystery behind time. If they had a bigger impact, it might be possible to see. But bigger impacts were worrisome things.

"Do you think life on other planets has changed?" Josh asked, indulging in a rare bout of absurdity.

Min-Jun seemed delighted. "That is a very revealing question. I think probably not. And that helps us picture time, does it not? Things are very active near the center of the manipulation, and recede with increasing distance from the point of the surgery."

"Surgery...like we've cut into time and what's happening is...some kind of infection?"

"It is a most provocative way of looking at the situation. Although I think we presume much to consider ourselves surgeons. I don't know that I would promote us past the level of white blood cells."

"You made the discovery, Min-Jun. Don't sell that short. You did what no one else has ever done: you discovered time travel."

He shrugged. "This version of me did; perhaps another me didn't need to." This was how their conversations tended to go.

**

"You can talk to her now," the doctor said.

Josh stepped into the darkened bedroom. "I thought we were going skiing today, nugget."

Cierra lay in her bed, head shaved and covered with conductors for the external neural pacemaker she was hooked up to. The hair had needed to go a month ago, and Josh helplessly wondered sometimes if she would ever get to grow it back. She kept a hairbrush on her bedside table, investing it with that beyond-rational value only children are able to grant things.

"Daddy, I got tired. I'm sorry."

Josh pulled up the little chair that lived near the bed and sat down next to her. He poked her nose affectionately and she gave a sleepy smile. "Never apologize," he urged her. "You need your rest."

"Daddy, I have to tell you something. It's important."

"Okay, what is it?"

"The milkman didn't come today, and I drank an extra lot of milk, so you might not have enough milk tomorrow."

Josh touched her warm cheek. Her whole body was cocooned under blankets. "Milk is better for daughters than daddies, so if we're short on it I always want you to have it, okay?"

"Are you sure?"

"Absotively posilutely."

"Those aren't words, Daddy."

"I'll tell you a secret, nugget. Words become words because people agree that they are. So if you agree with me, and we can get some other people to agree, then maybe in the future they will be words."

"Okay, we can do that. But right now it's just you and me, right?"

"Right."

"Okay."

Her eyes closed and her chest rose and fell in slow, deep rhythm. The doctor came into the room and checked the readings on the pacemaker, which was essentially an over-the-counter, low-grade coma inducer.

"This is a good window," she said, fingers hovering over her pad. "I can trigger it now, with your consent."

"I give consent," Josh said in the cold monotone of repetition.

The doctor nodded and gradually calibrated the pacemaker to the deep resting state that would stabilize and soothe Cierra's chaotic brain waves. "If you would let me network this I could do it remotely. It would save me time and you a lot of money."

"Money's not an issue," Josh said, realizing that he sounded like a high-handed asshole, but that this was as safe a persona as any to be stubborn with. "I won't network it."

The doctor nodded and began to pack up her instruments. "In three days we'll review whether we can bring her out."

"Three days?" It was longer than usual.

"She's in rough shape," the doctor admitted. "She's very resilient, even more so than people her age usually are, but things are getting worse. She's safer like this."

Safe, but not living, Josh thought.

He followed her into the hallway. Lamar slipped in the door behind them to watch Cierra for a few hours. As Josh showed the doctor to the door, she said quietly, "I know we've had this conversation before, but I could get her a Beetle."

"No."

"The restrictions are loosening, if it's a question of legality."

"It isn't," Josh sighed, wondering how far he could trust this doctor.

They stopped at the door and she lingered, not ready to exit yet. "I know you have some...investment...in your feelings about them." Which was as delicate a way as any to point out that she was aware of the infamously nutty speech he had given. "I just want you to consider your priorities in this situation."

Josh treaded carefully. "Beetles are more available now because of the outbreak, right? New categories of neurological malfunctions, inexplicable seizures, symptoms showing up in more and more people each day. I haven't kept up with the latest figures, but it's on the brink of being classified an epidemic, right?" The doctor nodded soberly. "So Beetles seem like the perfect cure, don't they?"

"We're not talking about those people," she retorted. "We're talking about your daughter."

"What if I say to you what I said in my speech: that Beetles aren't solving the problem, they're causing it, and every one that gets implanted makes things worse?"

"I would say that it defies common sense, that it's totally backwards, and that it has no basis in any of the scientific literature about the brain and how it operates."

Josh smiled politely, resigned to not being believed. "Then your advice comes from a place of the best intentions, and I'm sorry, but I won't be following it."

The doctor finally walked out the door, then turned for one last thought. "That's your right as her father. I just don't see why a man as smart as you would...." She couldn't finish the thought, and instead walked away, shoes clicking on the old stones.

***

Josh stood outside and pressed his wristpad, powering down the house to night mode. Everything faded out except the soft glow of a nightlight leaking out Cierra's bedroom window. He looked down the hill into the heart of the village, which was similarly dark but for the beckoning glow of a few all-night cafes.

He liked Urban Dark. He had been a major financial booster of it, had nurtured the technology that made it self-managing in most of the cities of the world. Somehow the choice to turn off a light was daunting to a person, but if it turns itself off, many will just let it be. It saved energy and more stars came out at night. On holidays, cities sometimes still threw the switches to light their skylines in a blaze of celebration. That was welcome too.

But Josh enjoyed the deep late blue that turned to black over the hours, enjoyed the feeling of people better synched up with an Earth they had resisted for so disastrously long. He enjoyed the silhouettes of houses.

He entered his front door, and the motion sensors lit his path up the stairs into his office before darkening again. There he logged into the house and studied the systems; it was a brain in a hive mind, connected to hundreds of millions of other houses on Earth, reporting their conditions, their energy usage, and whatever else their inhabitants elected to share.

He ran a packet profile routine to categorize the billions of pieces of information flowing into and out of the house by their behavior and destination. Most were automatic and easy to classify; Josh had set this house's security up well before he had considered moving into it.

But here was something new: a tiny stream reporting on a very slow time cycle. It was coming out of the house. It appeared as a single discolored thread in the vast, rippling weave of data. Josh flagged it at once, broke it open, then jumped from his chair and ran into the bedroom.

**

"I gave you specific instructions not to network it," Josh growled to the doctor on their call. She was sight-shielding, so he imagined she was at home. It was late, but the issue couldn't wait.

"I didn't network the controls at all. I just created a simple reporting function so I could get advance warning if her numbers went out of range. You have the same function on your watch, I've seen it." Her tone was assured and slightly patronizing in the way that doctors could get when they weren't accustomed to being questioned. Most of the time Josh would have been on her side. Not this time.

"I programmed my watch myself," he answered. "That machine is another matter."

"If you're worried about security, it works entirely one-way," she promised. "There's no control over the device involved."

Josh's tone was cold. "This isn't a discussion; I've switched it off and removed it. Now I'm reminding you not to take any action like that without my consent again."

He could hear how it came across; he didn't exactly sound like Father of the Year. And that was exactly how the doctor took it. She managed a diplomatic "It's your call." And then Josh wished her goodnight.

He turned his attention to the record of what the machine fed out. Cierra's vitals, her brain waves, the current configuration of her stasis...

And there it was. Josh saw it in a snapshot: it had lasted a billionth of a second, but there was the evidence. Someone had drilled into the stream. Someone had stolen away with an exact picture of his daughter's mind. Someone who saw that it was there for the taking.

He shivered to himself and rang Min-Jun. His friend answered from his bed, where Josh saw the sleeping shape of his husband behind him.

"Yes, my friend?"

Josh's tone was grim. "I need to move Cierra. When can we send the next marker for Maria?"

***

-9-

"With the Power Play Option. Do you do that or do I do it?"

The cashier muttered unintelligibly and waved with vague impatience at the Powerball machine in front of her, as if to say, "Don't hassle me, all your answers are here."

Maria went back to the screen. She had never bought a lottery ticket in her life. According to her mother, her father had played every week before he left. "Sombody's gotta win!" was a kind of motto of his.

The Power Play Option was important. So was only matching the five regular numbers, not the Powerball number. She had the Powerball number; it was an impossibly weird thing to know that she had the instructions to win $200 million scribbled on a Post-it, but wasn't supposed to use them. By matching five with the Power Play and deliberately not matching the Powerball, she would only win $2 million, but she could also remain anonymous. $200 million was a lot more than $2 million, but fending off "financial advisers" and "long-lost relatives" who had the legal right to request Maria's name as a jackpot winner would become the worst full-time job on Earth. And really, it was unnecessary; even after taxes and all, neither she nor Lia would ever have to work again as long as they weren't dumb.

"Three dollars," droned the clerk. Maria added a pack of gum and handed over a five. The Powerball drawing was the following night. She had twenty-four hours to decide whether to hide the victory from Lia, or just practice sounding really, really surprised.

**

In the third mile of her jog Maria finally spoke. "You know, for once in my life I've got something to talk about and you're staying nice and quiet."

Oh, you wanted to have a conversation?

"Not really, but I'll lose my mind if I don't get some of this out and I don't want to lay it on Lia."

I'm glad I can help you not lose your mind.

"Ha ha, you're a riot."

So, what's happening Maria?

The road sloped up and Maria huffed and pushed into it, thighs driving. "So there's this super plague in the future, and it's caused by these little computers people put in their brains. Only when people get afraid of the plague, even more people put in the computers, thinking it will save them. Which just makes more people even more sick and everything just goes to shit, I guess."

Sounds very serious.

"Sounds just like us. Everybody stepping on everybody else trying to get one extra inch."

So what can you do about it?

"Qualls is still looking into that part. Something about some guy and a pipe. I don't like it."

Why?

"Because it sounds like I'm going to have to do something heavy."

You told them you wouldn't kill anybody.

"Yeah, but they didn't mention if they heard that part or not."

Well, you and I both know that's not ultimately a problem for you.

Maria stumbled to a stop, shocked, and cried out in rage. The Voice didn't respond, and this felt like mockery. Feeling trapped, a dark spiral of nausea and self-hate grabbing to drag her into the depths, she cut off the whole thought cycle by slamming her head into the nearest tree.

***

"You're bleeding!" Lia jumped up from the couch and ran towards Maria as soon as she opened the door.

"I know, I know," Maria said, stomping towards the bathroom. Her head was killing her.

Lia followed and waited outside the door as Maria studied her wounds in the mirror. "What can I do?"

Maria wiped most of the blood from her face and stepped back out again. "Does my nose look broken?"

Lia started crying. "Who did this to you?" she pleaded.

"Nobody did this. I fell, that's all. Come on, is it broken?" Not getting anything from Lia, Maria turned back and studied it in the mirror. It hurt like a mother and it was purple, but she didn't see any kind of bump or break.

Only then, with Lia still crying behind her, did Maria replay in her mind the exchange they had just had. *Fell? What a lie. What a dumb, horrible, insensitive lie.*

Maria grabbed four Advil, ran a towel under some cold water, and turned back to her housemate. "Kid...Princess...hey. Nobody did this; I did it to myself. Scout's honor."

"Why?"

"Because I'm fruit loops and I hurt myself sometimes. You know that."

Lia silently turned and glided down the hall. Maria heard a sound of wood sliding on wood, took a moment to compose herself, and followed.

Lia had shut herself up in their little cupboard with the sliding door. Maria had no doubt she could muscle it open if she wanted, but decided that would just dig the hole deeper.

"Hey listen, I'm sorry I fibbed. I lost my head while I was jogging and I ran into a tree. I didn't hurt anybody else, so it's okay, right?"

Lia didn't respond. Maria took a deep breath and tried again.

"I just have shit I'm going through, okay? Bad memories, and the new job, and...and just trying to keep this thing we've got going. Christ, you know I would never hurt you."

Still nothing. Maria went for the easiest bribe. "Hey, how about I just put an ice pack on and we play cards? I can't even see out of one eye, you'll whoop my ass."

"Stop that!" Lia's voice resonated through the door with vehemence.

Maria backed away from the door instinctively. "Hey, kid, what did I say?"

"I know you won't hurt me."

"Then why are you hiding in there?"

"Because I can't take you hurting yourself. I don't know anything about what you're going through so I can't help you and I just never know when you're going to do something awful to yourself and I can't take it." Maria heard hard sniffs between Lia's words as she fought for composure.

Maria slumped down to the ground with her back against the door. Lia was so goddamned right. Maria touched her tender face and found fresh blood leaking from a cut on her forehead. Her jogging clothes were a mess out of some horror movie. Some fighter for the future. Some millionaire-to-be.

Lia deserved to know more, but Maria didn't know where to start. So instead she just started singing the craziest song she knew:

"They're selling postcards of the hanging,
They're painting the passports brown.
The beauty parlor is full of sailors,
The circus is in town."

Damn Lia. No one got to hear Maria sing.

***

"You've got to speak up, there's traffic!" Maria stood in the berm of the turnpike as cars whizzed and trucks growled by and her stupid car lay dead alongside it all.

"This is not the best way to give you this information!" Dr. Qualls shouted into his phone.

"Well, it's either now or you wait until I can get my ass down there, Doc."

"Why don't you replace that car already?"

"Yeah, I'm gonna, but I only won the lottery yesterday and I won't have the check for a few weeks. Hell, I just stuck the ticket in the mail on my way out this morning, and now I'm going to go bust on a tow truck and a bus ticket so I don't know how we're making rent next week."

"Can't you take extra shifts at work or something?"

"I work when they ask me. I can't make more people spontaneously want to take flying lessons. Jesus!"

Qualls's already loud voice took on a flustered edge. "We don't have time to deal with these sorts of problems. You have to complete your assignment in the next two weeks or else it will get much, much more difficult."

"Well, tell me what it is and let's find out if I need a car to do it or not!"

"There's a pipeline being built between Philadelphia and New York. You need to damage it badly enough that it will take an extra year to finish."

Maria absorbed this as a loud angry honk dopplered past her ear. "Jesus Christ, you're making a terrorist out of me!"

"It's not going to hurt anybody. All it's going to do is prevent some very rich people from becoming disgustingly rich." She could almost hear him tugging at his hair in exasperation.

"Well what does the pipe carry, oil?"

"Cable. It's for fiber-optic cable."

"What? How the hell...I don't understand."

"Well, do you want me to explain it, or do you just want to know where it is?"

This was a new moment for Maria. Like she had told Qualls, she was glad to be out of the Air Force to the extent that she didn't have to just follow orders anymore. And the mission at least sounded as if it wouldn't harm anybody, so weird as it sounded, maybe she could just go through with it and...

Black smoke began to spiral up from under the hood of her car. She kicked the door and growled, then finally answered Qualls. "No, no. I want to know what I'm doing. I'll see if I can borrow Albert's car and drive in tomorrow."

"Who is Albert? You can't tell him what we're doing!"

"Yeah, no shit, Doc," Maria answered. "Now you're all science-y, so what's the best way to blow something up?"

***

"Yoush work Thurshday?" Albert asked, pushing some papers uselessly around on his desk.

"Yeah, sure, I'll be back," Maria answered.

"What happened your nose?" He waved towards it.

"Ran into a tree."

"Hope you taught the tree whoshe boss." He unclipped a massive ring of keys from his belt and separated his car key from it. "Needsh oil. You do that?"

"Yeah, fair deal. See you Thursday."

Maria was grateful for short conversations like the ones Albert preferred. Any longer and she might start really saying things.

***

Maria was sliding a pan under Albert's car when Lia ventured out onto the front stoop in her bathrobe.

"Hey kid," Maria said. "We can eat in like a half-hour, okay?"

"Okay." Lia sat down, pulled up a piece of dead grass and fiddled conspicuously with it.

"Something on your mind?" Maria started draining the oil.

"I wanted to ask if you would tell me what's wrong." Lia was careful with every word.

"What, with the car?" Maria joked, trying to put off what was coming.

"I mean, you talk about how bad stuff happened and you're messed up now. And you know what bad stuff happened to me. I mean, most of it. But I don't know what happened to you, and I think I should. So, like, I know what you're going through."

Maria stared silently at the uncovered car engine for almost a full minute. Then her body took over, replacing the gasket and oil plug down below, dropping in the funnel up top, filling the oil, finishing the whole process from memory as she talked. "I got my commission and wanted to go into pilot training. Instead they said they had a new program they needed people for, and that they thought I'd be great for it. So they made me a Predator pilot. Drones. Sweet gig, right? Stay on base, and nobody's ever shooting back.

"Only it starts to make you woolly-brained. You're sitting there in a comfy chair all day looking at this picture of a house, and you get to know the people inside, watch them come and go, how they dress, little stuff you don't even realize you can learn just from watching. And you don't know why, you just know that one of these shifts, someone's going to walk in and give the order and you're going to push a button and blow up that house and kill everybody inside it.

"I'd jog at night, just run until I couldn't think about it anymore. I had to jog further and further. Then I would drink and jog. Or jog then drink. Or drink then drink some more. Whatever combination got me to sleep."

Maria paused for a second, listened to the quiet glug of the oil pouring in. "One day the order comes in. I painted the house – that's when you put the targeting laser on it – and my other chair, he launched the missile.

"After a missile's been launched there's this countdown until it hits, and my job in those seconds was to keep my hand as steady as possible. Surgeon steady, so that dot didn't move off that roof and send the shot into the dirt.

"With three seconds left I see movement, someone coming out of the shed up in the corner. Someone little." Maria's breath caught for a second, remembering the image, wondering if she could say anything more about it.

"Then boom. Screen goes white. Everything and everyone is gone. And I ask the other chair, 'Did you see that? Was that a kid?' And he doesn't know what to say. We've always got a chat window open with Command, so I type in to them: 'Was that a kid there?'

"And for a few seconds I get nothing back. Then this message pops up – I don't know from who – and it says, 'It was not a kid. It was a dog.'

"Like dogs walk on two fucking legs..."

***

Albert's car ran a little bit better than Maria's. A little bit. She left in the early afternoon, after taking a long and awkward time talking Lia out of coming along. The Princess had poured out sympathy and support, and Maria hadn't really known how to take it.

It wasn't her fault; that was what Lia kept stressing. Hadn't been Maria's fault that her hand had been so steady, that she had said yes to playing pilot on a base instead of pushing to really go up in the air. Maria wondered how she could have kicked down so many doors to get through college, to get her wings, to gun so hard for this dream and then pass up on it so close to the finish.

It hadn't been as easy and casual as all that. The lean from on high had been pretty strong; at that point Maria had been blindly following orders for almost a decade, so words like *there's a war and we need you here* were pretty hard to deny.

Still, she had wanted to fly. She had done all that so she could fly.

It's good that you're talking to other people about it, the Voice said.

"This is your fault, you know," Maria answered.

Is that right?

"Of course it is. If you hadn't died, you would have been the one to go in. You would have made pilot, and I would have gone on to be a volleyball coach or something."

Oh...you think I'm Sean.

"Of course you are: who else would hang around and bug me like he did?"

I'm not your brother.

I'm that boy you killed.

Maria wanted to jerk the wheel, steer off the road, crash into the barricade; better yet, fly off a cliff. Instead, she tightened her grip on the steering wheel and stayed steady. Perfectly steady. And she refused to answer.

***

"Come in!" Dr. Qualls announced. Maria opened the door and entered the Doc's little ranch-style suburban house. It looked like an extension of his brain, cluttered with open magazines and books on every flat surface. He was in the kitchen.

"You keep your door unlocked?" Maria asked as she walked down the hallway.

"This is a very nice neighborhood. My odds of being robbed are one in ten thousand. Every time I turn the lock, that's a daily gesture reinforcing fear. Why bother with it?"

Maria shrugged. "Your funeral. What am I smelling?"

"Oh, I thought we would be talking for a while, so I'm making soup."

Maria entered the kitchen and saw him, in a robe and natty striped pajamas, stirring something in a saucepan.

"If it came out of a can, you're not making it," she ribbed. "You're heating it."

"Willie!" he shouted suddenly. "I bought some of that bread yesterday, do we still have any?"

A full-bodied alto voice responded from somewhere in the house. "Why are you asking me? I'm in here. Check the box."

"She's never easy on me," Dr. Qualls murmured to Maria. "Not for a minute."

Suddenly an exceedingly tall, solidly framed middle-aged woman walked in, wearing a robe of her own and a bemused look on her face. Her arms were folder over her chest, and Maria pegged her at 6'2, easy. Maria suddenly understood why Qualls wasn't worried about locking his door.

"So you're the flying ace," Willie said, a splotch of half rubbed-in cream on one cheek. "Weldon told me you'd be dropping by."

"Willie knows about everything," Dr. Qualls assured Maria, rummaging behind a regular loaf in the breadbox and holding up the precious half a baguette he'd sought. "It's safe to talk around her."

"She knows about all the crazy stuff?"

Willie shrugged. "I knew I was signing up for crazy when I married him."

Maria looked again between the towering woman and the sheepishly grinning Professor. "This is your wife?" she asked Qualls.

"Used to be his nurse," Willie said, turning to exit. "But the son of a bitch wouldn't stop making me laugh."

***

"So what is this cable pipe, and why is it so important?"

Qualls ate from a soup bowl perched on his lap, which made him look grandfatherly. "The cable pipe is being laid by a private group of hedge fund managers. It will transmit trade orders from Philadelphia to New York five milliseconds faster than the current fiber optic cables allow."

"Five milliseconds? Like, thousandths of a second?"

"Yes."

Maria frowned uncomprehendingly from the couch. Her soup sat untouched on the table next to her, under a lamp. "Why would they build a whole new pipe just for five milliseconds? That's got to cost millions of dollars."

"Somewhere around half a billion is my understanding."

"Okay, just lay this out for me, Doc, because this doesn't make sense at all."

"Alright, imagine you're standing on a road on a hot day with a big group of people. Someone says there's a stand about a mile down the path that sells ice cream for a dollar. So everyone sets off down the path. Only you, Maria, you know a secret path through the woods that will get you to the ice cream stand more quickly. You take this path, and you buy out the ice cream stand – everything they've got – for a dollar apiece. Your friends arrive, and you say that the ice cream is for sale for $1.01. And this isn't what they expected, but they set out determined to buy and the difference is so small that you sell everything you bought. You didn't make the ice cream, didn't market it, didn't invest in building the cart or securing the location: all you did was have the knowledge that a purchase was going to be made and the ability to move faster than the purchasers, so you make a penny from every person in the crowd."

"Okay, so I make pennies off a group of people. Great, I just made a quarter. Why spend a half-billion to get that?"

"Well, imagine that you had that same path to every ice cream business in America, every day. You're not getting a jump on twenty-five transactions, you're getting a jump on two hundred million. Every day. With no risk. You don't even have to actively monitor it, because you've devised a program that will buy the ice cream automatically on any signal that someone else wants it, and you'll always beat them to the purchase."

"Okay, that sounds like some skunk shit. Who's doing this?"

"It's called flash trading, and the answer is everyone who can afford to. People think of the stock market as traders on a floor barking out orders, but that's theater. The real action in the market is happening faster than human hands and eyes; algorithms pitted against algorithms, all lurking in the subatomic structures of the economy making billions and billions of transactions every day, automatically, owning massive chunks of our economy for less than an eyeblink and skimming pennies off the top of every transaction we mere mortals might make."

Maria felt the chip on her shoulder itching. "How the fuck is that even legal?"

"It's legal because the law doesn't adapt to technology quickly enough to stop it from happening. People who own these pipelines can not only make incalculable fortunes for themselves with minimal risk, but they can rent access for tens of millions of dollars more to others who want the same power."

"Okay, screw the future; now I kind of want to blow it up just on principle."

Qualls chuckled as he dunked a hunk of bread into his bowl. "Remember, all we need to do is delay its completion by a year."

"Why's that?"

"From what I gather, when the man sending us these messages was younger, he sold something to a very wealthy person which that very wealthy person then used to cause a lot of misery. He hopes that if that very wealthy person doesn't have as much money, he won't sell."

"And this guy got rich using this pipe?"

"So I understand it."

Maria mulled this over. She wasn't used to having to consider all the costs and benefits, the truly big picture of where to act in a world where nothing happened without consequences. She had never risen far enough in the ranks to be the one choosing what trigger to pull and where.

"How much do we know about the guy sending this stuff?"

Dr. Qualls nodded in approval at the question. "Distressingly little, I'm afraid. I don't even know his name. He says it's because his younger self is alive in our time and he doesn't want to risk what might happen if we knew how to find him. The idea is to interfere as minimally as possible."

"But you believe he's one of the good guys?"

Qualls paused for a moment, then looked off to the side with a smile, as if he could look right through the walls to where his wife slept. "I believe that there are people who just instinctively make the world more chaotic, with no conscious consideration. And then there are people scheming to rig the world to their advantage. They work patiently and unrelentingly, and they assume the worst of others because that's all they know in themselves.

"And then, I think, there are the ones who task themselves with the never-ending, ever-futile mission to fight the chaos and do a little something good, fed only by the hope that this effort – when joined with that of others – will take us somewhere better. They can't promise success or a reward, but, human to human, you somehow recognize the way that they try, and somehow you find yourself wanting to take a try with them.

"Either he's doing a remarkable job of imitating the third type of person, or he's genuinely trying to do some good. But I feel like I recognize his uncertainty, and his hope, and it moves me to act in the same way that I was moved to write crazy theories about time travel."

Maria sighed to herself. "Interfere minimally? This explosion won't be minimal."

***

-10-

In another time they might have traveled in the dark, leaving under the secretive shadow of the night sky. Maybe they would have waited for a new moon, or a night where the clouds sheathed the light of the stars. They would have huddled close against both the cold and their fears, and made every step light to protect the precious silence.

But now they were not hiding from eyes that depended on light, but on waves that rode the air regardless of the hour or the weather. The old accoutrements of stealth were meaningless when what you wanted to hide from was around you at all times.

So Josh, Cierra, and Lamar departed in the day, when the journey would be safer. Josh had the means and reputation to make eccentric purchases, and he bought a vintage car with no navigation system, no proximity ping, no auto-drive; a car he would drive himself. He knew that anyone who wanted to see and track him badly enough could still do it. But maybe these steps would blunt their reach, which Josh feared more and more.

When they reached the airfield, he made his daughter comfortable in the back of the jet. She was awake but sluggish and moody, and wanted nothing but to lie down. Josh secured her in a reclined seat, and then stopped for a moment just to listen to her breathe.

Then he made for the cockpit. Plugging into the control system, he disabled every networked component; fortunately, it was still legal to fly with old-fashioned equipment like radar beacons. Sometimes it was a lucky thing that the law couldn't catch up with technology.

"You're sure you're alright handling it like this?" Josh asked the pilot, a fit middle-aged woman.

She nodded. "It's all stick and rudder at the end of the day."

Josh found that her confidence, even though totally unrelated to his crisis, was nonetheless a comfort. He thanked her and returned to the back.

It was an exotic novelty, figuring out how to pass the time without the network. No screen, no pad, just three people in the back of a jet, one deep in sleep.

"Do you remember when they used to have magazines on these things?" Lamar asked, with gentle good humor.

Josh chuckled. "I took my first flight on a private jet when I was sixteen. They had a whole different set of magazines."

"*Rich Asshole Monthly*?" Lamar asked.

"Yeah, I think that was one of them."

Lamar leaned forward and clasped his hands together, his face worried. "So how far do we have to go?"

"I've got us a place. Very few people, no network penetration at all."

"But we'll have electricity? Things like that?"

Josh looked over at Cierra. Some fuzzy patches of hair were re-emerging on her head, but the little circles where the conductors of the pacemaker spent so much time these days were still bald. Was their light but persistent current frying her hair follicles? He longed to be in some parallel world where his biggest worry was that she wanted to do something awful to her hair because all her schoolmates were doing it. She hadn't even had schoolmates long enough for them to become bad influences.

"Yeah. Everything we need will be there."

Lamar was silent for a few more beats. The engines of the jet started to crescendo into a high whine. Finally, he spoke again. "So can you tell me, straight out, what you meant by your speech? About the Beetles and all this KG stuff? That's what you were talking about, right? That this was going to start happening?"

KG was the new shorthand for Ketron-Garry Syndrome, the catchall for the still barely-defined plague of neurological disruptions occurring all over the world, named for the first two scientists who managed to publish a coherent argument for grouping them all together. And while Josh had conjectured something like it, it was in no way any kind of preparation for witnessing it over the past few months.

Josh leaned back in his chair and closed his eyes. Talking about it in the abstract could be a distraction. "People are right that it has to do with technology and the network. But they're looking at the problem the wrong way.

"Do you remember when we were growing up and people kept saying that cell phones would give us brain tumors? They're only looking at what technology projects. But our brains have always done their own projecting. All our thoughts and feelings are real – physically real – sparks of energy leaping through our minds. They can be observed, recorded, measured, studied. But, for our entire existence as a species, the system has been closed.

"We changed all that with Beetles. Even though they had no active network connection, they were designed to speak the network language so we could program them. And we connected them with peoples' brains so that the network language became a permanent part of the brain's infrastructure. Signals flowed in and out, waking and sleeping.

"When I created the bridge alphabet, it was to translate our programming language into the pure sublingual impulses that exist in the brain. They're like the primordial soup that we build thoughts and ideas out of. What I didn't imagine, what nobody imagined, is that the translation might work both ways; that in communicating with the Beetle, the human brain could learn, well, a foreign language."

The jet rolled forward, moving into position for takeoff. Josh realized his language was getting arcane, as it often did, and so he took a beat and brought it back to basics. "Basically, we gave the mind a tool; a tool it could use to evolve. One of the strongest impulses we have as a social species is the desire to make connections and communicate. In the Beetle, our mind discovered a new way to do that, and started adapting to use it."

Lamar considered this for a long time. "So people with Beetles became, what, psychic?"

"Not in the traditional way. They weren't reading other peoples' thoughts, they were becoming conduits for the network itself. Imagine if, instead of sending an e-mail through a satellite, it passed from sender to receiver through peoples' brains. Not all of it – the connection isn't clean and we haven't advanced that far – but the tiniest fragments, bytes of data that normally would have passed through us like subatomic particles, now detected, experienced by new receptors in the brain."

"But, like, only people with the Beetles in them."

"Oh no, that's where it gets dangerous." Josh's face darkened. "Like I said, our minds want to connect. We communicate in a million wordless ways each day. A twitch of the face, a hand rubbing an arm, a hug. When a brain starts to receive data it recognizes but doesn't fully understand, it builds up as unprocessed noise that finds its way out in, say, a weird dream, a strange new tic in your body. Other people respond to that energy in their own ways; unconscious echoes, the power of empathy, the kind of low-level mind-reading we already do. Even brains that can't comprehend the signals are still hearing the noise; because it's not coming from a cell tower anymore, it's coming from something it recognizes."

"So everyone gets sick?"

The engines roared now, and Josh could feel their gathering power even though the jet was still parked in takeoff position on the runway. It was like an undertow, anticipation and potential predicting the existence of something awesome to follow. "Yes," he said to Lamar, looking again at his daughter. "Every new Beetle that gets put in –even if it helps its host resolve some naturally-occurring problem in their own head – amplifies the corruption for the whole human race. The noise is growing, our sense for it is sharpening. And at this rate, it will decimate more of us than any meteor, probably in less than three years."

Lamar followed Josh's gaze as the jet shot down the runway, building to a screaming speed. "That's why you want to get her away."

Josh watched the land recede below them, watched Switzerland – its people, its buildings, its natural wonders – shrink into a faraway thing. "There's another reason, and I can't keep it secret from you any longer."

He took a deep breath and considered Lamar. Josh had burned most of the bridges in his professional life with his speech. He had isolated himself from all his friends but Min-Jun. In time Min-Jun would know; hell, maybe Josh had told him already in some other version of now. But he didn't remember doing it, and Lamar was here now to receive Josh's confession. In a way, he was the only appropriate listener.

"One night, when I was nineteen years old, I was working on the bridge alphabet and I put on some music and got stoned. It didn't stop me from working; I was just bored with brute coding and wanted to zone out. That was the first time I imagined the possibility that I described to you, that the brain might use the alphabet. At the time, what I cared about most was hacking systems, gaining access, causing trouble just to prove my superiority, and so in the midst of that flight of imagination I wrote the basic design for a virus. Not a computer virus: a brain virus, one that could be transmitted through the Beetle. It would enter your mind without you even being aware of it, like a commercial jingle or a face in the crowd. And it could lay there, for years, completely dormant, until...who knows? Somebody plays a certain melody on a flute. You see a flash of three specific colors in succession. Whatever it is, it happens and *pop*: something bursts up there and you're dead, and it can't be undone, can't be traced.

"At the time it was so wicked, so exciting. But when I woke up it looked more like just some wank-off hacker fantasy. I bragged about it to a couple of friends and thought that was it. But one of them told somebody, who told somebody else. Then a buyer approached me; not himself, but through a middleman. He wanted to buy my design. Offered me a half-billion dollars. I was already a multimillionaire, but this would make me a much, much higher class of asshole. And what did I care? It was a sketch of a theory on top of vapor, and people were throwing stupid money at guys like me all the time back then. It was Silicon Valley, man, just a mad bazaar for venture capitalist money. So I took it.

"A few years ago, I started noticing that certain people were dropping dead. Not guys in the same government or guys in the same industry, but people who are...positioned, you know? At the junction points of influence. Always wealthy. I spent about a year thinking I was just being paranoid; pattern-building is a mother of a double-edged sword in a brain. But they were dying in the exact same way my paper said they would, at moments that were awfully convenient. I dug in and found out that all of them had made trips to countries that didn't sign the Beetle surgery ban within the previous three years. By then I was good enough that I could get just about any data that I wanted. And so I finally answered the question I didn't have the moral fiber to ask when I was nineteen: who was my buyer?

"His name was Spartak Khaslik; he was one of the more plugged-in thugs to become pretty rich in industry when Russia went into full-bore crook capitalism. But unlike most of those guys, who just liked being king of the mountain inside their borders, Spartak was thinking globally. He funneled money into hedge funds on Wall Street that were pioneering flash trading, back when it was milliseconds and not nanoseconds like now, and multiplied his fortune a few times over. Surrounded by guys who wanted reputations, he used anonymity. His network of hackers was better than China's. When the offer came to me I thought it was just some Wall Street cokehead overpaying to try to get one over on the rest. But for Spartak it was a bargain.

"Think about it: the people who have been buying Beetles on the black market for the last few years have been traders, speculators, and politicians hoping to use the extra brainpower to increase their returns or gain influence. Instead, Spartak owns them from then on and they don't even know it. The moment their work interferes with his desires, he can assassinate them at the touch of a button and no one will ever know it was him.

"Up until now, since Beetles aren't connected to rWeb, you had to access them directly – usually not a problem since they're so black market. The virus is probably in before they're even installed. But once one Beetle can start hearing another, the virus can jump. And that's just the start of the trouble." His voice got quieter. "I think that we're not far from the point where any brain on Earth could receive it, store it, transmit it. It could never be deleted; the human race itself would be its cloud backup. The old saying is that power derives from a monopoly on violence. Spartak Khaslik, one single man, will have the ultimate monopoly: the power to murder any person on Earth with absolute impunity. And even if he doesn't bother to, his weapon may take Ketron-Garry and turn it into a plague we don't come back from."

Neither of them spoke for a long time. Lamar finally broke the silence. "You think he's after her? Because you're a threat to him now?"

Josh looked at his ever-sleeping daughter. "I know he is."

***

They landed on a small airstrip in the Faroe Islands, in the sea west of Norway. The only man to meet them at the bottom of the steps was Aillig Taylor, with his thinning red-white hair and a face sculpted by hard Scottish wind. He was one of the few people left who didn't think Josh was crazy; or perhaps he simply thought Josh was crazy in an acceptable way. He ran a non-profit that Josh heavily supported that was trying to help coastal and island nations fight the rising oceans without having to give away all their land to resort developers and their government to people friendly to resort developers.

"Did you do as I asked?" Josh asked from the top of the stairway. He had the means to shield the interior of the jet from the network, but the insidious possibilities of the open air were here once again.

"Aye!" Aillig shouted, his hands still stuffed in his pockets in a stoutly grumpy gesture. "I left all my toys at home. I've been alone with my thoughts here. It's awful."

Josh allowed himself to relax a little, and with Lamar's help carried Cierra down the steps. For a moment he wondered if he should go back and thank the pilot for taking on such an odd flight without asking questions, but the impression he had of her was that she didn't need such niceties. So he let it pass, and they loaded both their cargo and Josh's daughter into the truck and trailer Aillig had brought with him.

**

"She's beautiful, a little dreamer," Aillig said, stealing glances back at Cierra. "You can see it on her face. She might be asleep but that mind is still clicking. Maybe she's slaying dragons in there."

Josh had found himself increasingly unable to talk about Cierra directly. But he made an appreciative mumble and watched the streets glide by around them. He thought about the dimensions, how some people prior to the age of technology might have lived their whole lives without ever even knowing what the place they lived in looked like from the sky. If you couldn't climb a tall tree or a mountain, you lived in two dimensions. Even the best maps were indirectly created, guesses made based on measurements from the ground. They were shadowplays of the overhead view, not the real thing.

They were doing much the same thing with time. He and Min-Jun were daring to try to chart it, and had even succeeded well enough to send those message markers back and have most of them arrive at their destinations. The metal had to be completely clean, measured to the microgram. A single speck of unmeasured dust and the thing would spiral off into the void and never be found. Josh wondered if that problem could ever be overcome, if their packages could take control of their own delivery. The evolutionary step from catapult to smart missile.

But he hadn't seen time. Not really. And that made him arrogant. He had always been arrogant, and now he felt the weight of the misery that he had contributed to, sometimes unwittingly, sometimes from studied ignorance and greed. Was it possible to right the consequences of his arrogance with more arrogance? It didn't sound promising, but Josh didn't know how to be anyone other than himself.

The truck reached the harbor. Cierra hadn't woken at all during the drive. It was a pity; it looked like a charming little place, the village, preserved inside sea walls built for people instead of profit.

**

It seemed to plunge upward from the water rather than to sit on top of it. Lítla Dímun – a volcano-shaped island of green with sheer, rocky sides, all circled by grey clouds. Too small for a plane, too windy and unsteady for a helicopter, from a distance it looked like just to get up onto its grass you would need to be good sailor and an even better rock climber.

But as they cruised around the perimeter in Aillig's boat, they found a small notch chiseled into the rock with a pontoon platform floating in the churning water at its base. A track ran up the notch, supporting a funicular car shielded from the wind and large enough for a few passengers and some cargo.

Josh felt a painful desire to have Cierra be awake. Maybe he could have shielded her from his paranoia and the weighty conversations with Lamar about death and power, all the terror of the journey. If he could have, what an adventure it might have seemed like in her eyes: crossing the skies to a faraway land, and now fording dark, freezing waters to arrive at a place that defied reason.

They loaded their supplies into the funicular car and settled in for the trip up. "What is this place?" Lamar asked.

"Some of the world's wildest grazing land," Aillig answered. "Used to be, shepherds would leave their sheep here year-round, and each autumn they'd come in, climb up the mountain on ropes, and sweep across the whole island, driving the sheep into a great pen. Then they'd tie them up in nets and lower them to the boats below to take back to the mainland. Wool business hasn't been so good lately, though, has it?" he said with rueful humor.

"These days it's just you and the birds. The birds will make quite a squawk. Breeding, you know. It's a puffin orgy site, which is why it was so damn hard to build a house here. Not enough sun for solar and the windmills would kill more puffins than any decent person could abide, eh?"

"So how did you solve the problem?" Lamar looked at the lights in the funicular as the motor cranked them slowly up through the steep notch.

"Water," Josh answered. "There are tidal generators on every side of the island. Not enough power to really populate the place, but enough for one little house."

***

"House" was a generous name for the place by the standards Josh was used to. The squat cabin looked like the sort of thing you'd see adjoining a lighthouse, or a fire watch tower deep in the woods. It was mostly stone on the outside, and wildly splattered by white streaks that Josh had to surmise were puffin droppings.

The inside was better. The sparseness had a warm quality, and the walls were thick to stop the pummeling winds and cries of bird joy.

Josh looked at the walls. "Aillig, thank you."

There were shelves and shelves of real books. Handsome and hardbound, some illustrated. He ran his fingers across the bindings, the tactile thrill transporting him. In his youth, Josh would have found a place like this to be the functional equivalent of a prison. Now it represented the ideal escape; or rather, a place that represented everything Josh wished he could be happy with. Family, peace, books. Food in the pantry.

"Lamar," he said, turning to see Lamar already setting up the pacemaker by Cierra's little single bed. "Make sure that any day she's up, she's reading. And don't be afraid to show her the hard stuff."

Lamar turned with a queer expression. "What do you mean? You're staying, aren't you?"

Josh looked his friend right in the eyes. "Lamar, the reason I told you everything I did is so there would be a chance you could understand this. I can't come back. If Spartak finds a way to get me, he will. But if he got to her through me..." A surge of feeling broke his voice, and he let the sentence trail off. He was almost grateful to know he could still suffer like this.

"I can't see her again. Not until my work is done."

***

-11-

Maria was hiking through the woods once again. Only this time there was no marked trail. She was an intruder, a criminal anarchist carrying a bomb. The jostling of her backpack put her on edge, as if any random bump might be the last sound she would ever hear.

Somewhere ahead was a hole in the ground where a section of pipe was being run through these woods in a small New Jersey neighborhood outside Princeton. Maria was less than a quarter-mile from the road, and could hear the occasional car despite the late hour. She had stashed her motorcycle at a church near the airport. No one lived close enough to the proposed blast site to be hurt, but hopefully the ones just beyond, who owned good property, would be angry enough at the threat to their homes that construction would be snarled up for a long time in community protests, and the investors who had sought to do their work quietly and unobtrusively would find a harsh spotlight shining on them.

In seven more days, give or take, this section would be complete; the hole would be filled; and the safest, cleanest chance to stop it all would be gone.

She found the fence, and behind it the big diggers, the temporary supervisor buildings, and a lot of stacked concrete pipe. The space looked wide open and obscenely conspicuous. Maria's heart rate doubled. She had left behind her I.D., had her hair under one of those shower baggies inside her cap, and had her riding gloves on. Every detail about her screamed "crooked." How could she have possibly been so willing to come this far?

Her breath sounded as loud as roaring waves. She waited in a crouch in the shadows for fifteen minutes, watching for movement. There was nothing. What reason did they have to suspect anyone would interfere?

She cut through the fence and moved swiftly for the hole. It was deep enough to leap into, more of a trench section than a straight-down hole. The open end of the laid-in pipe was there, and Maria went to work. She had a small remote-controlled car from a cheap electronics store, and she tied the explosive to it, Essentially, the car was now a mobile, homemade concussion grenade which had been way too simple to construct.

She drove the car into the pipe, listening to the childish little growl of its motor, and watching her wire unspool. It was attached to the pull-ring for the grenade.

Her ears were hyper-tuned. Every snapping twig and gust of wind could be the end of all this. Her only consolation, she realized, was that she could get a bed in the psycho ward instead of a prison cell just by telling them the truth.

Finally the wire reached its limit. She stuffed the car controller back into the backpack, took a deep breath, and pulled the wire.

She scrambled out of the hole, counting to herself, not knowing exactly how accurate her home chemistry was going to be.

The boom was muffled and low, shaking her enough to throw her to the ground. But she was clear of it, and alive.

Then, there was a second, much larger boom, and Maria felt a scorching wave of heat blast her face as all the sounds of the world collapsed into a piercing ring. The night turned orange, and hell itself seemed to be birthing out of the New Jersey dirt. Flames, there were flames everywhere.

This wasn't supposed to be happening.

Maria wasn't sure if her body would run or not. She rose to her feet. She looked at the inferno. She ran.

***

She drove hard through the night, not caring what direction, no destination in mind, just looking for any road without red lights. She put the fire in her rear-view mirror. And the sirens. And the gawkers in the street. So many curves in the roads out here. So seemingly easy to leave something behind.

Sometimes a fire truck or a police car would wail down the road towards her, coming in from some neighboring town to help contain the disaster. Every time she wondered if one would turn, follow her, accuse her. None ever did. She steered far over in the lane, let them pass, and kept on riding steady. So steady.

She didn't want to go home. She didn't want to go to Qualls' house. She felt like she was trailing the fire that she'd started, that a line of it traced all the way back to the construction site and that she would bring it anywhere she went.

And so she drove.

You ought to be smarter than this, the Voice said.

"Shut up," she answered.

The gear in your backpack, your clothes: you ought to get rid of them.

"What do you know about it?"

I know you're on a mission that's gone sideways and you need to lock your shit down.

"You're just a boy, you shouldn't talk like this."

I was a boy. I'm something much different now.

Finally Maria let the bike slow down and looked around for a sign. She was in farm country, over the river in Pennsylvania. A sign said "Ottsville" with nothing in sight to claim to be a town called Ottsville. She saw a park road leading to a small lake, and dumped her gloves and backpack in it. The leathers would have to wait until she could find some clothes. The cold would be bad enough, but a girl motorcycling through the night in her skivvies would get more attention than she wanted.

The way home was past the accident. So was Dr. Qualls' place. She had almost no money beyond what she would need to tank up. She needed time, shelter, and someone who wouldn't ask questions.

Damn it.

***

Albany, New York

Maria stood awkwardly on the front porch, feeling like she might just tip over and fall asleep with her face on the door knocker. She had waited in the grass for a couple of hours until the sun came up, just to be decent. It had meant a lot of bugs crawling all over her. The desert runt in her had never adjusted from snakes to these little bugs that lurked in the wet.

The door opened and it was his wife. That was okay; Maria was relieved to be transitioning from horrific to just awkward. What was her name...

"Jennifer, hi."

"Morning," Jennifer replied in a tone that contained a lot of "Oh Christ, what are *you* doing on my porch?" Jennifer was in sweats and a little t-shirt, with an old mug full of new coffee.

"Look, I'm sorry to be on your porch right now, but I was passing through and needed to rest for a couple of hours and thought I'd check in on you."

"Motel's two miles down the road."

Maria composed herself. "You know I wouldn't come around just asking."

Jennifer stared for a moment, then turned and walked into the house, leaving the door open. "If I'd had my coffee in me when I opened that door I probably would have slugged you."

Maria stepped carefully across the threshold.

***

Maria was at the kitchen table when he walked in. She wasn't sure whether to stand or what. So she just sat, staring awkwardly. Brian looked older but better, healthier, like he had grown into himself. There was a touch of gray in his hair and he wore it well. Jennifer retreated past him into the hallway; he brushed her hand with his fingers and mumbled something to her. Jennifer nodded coldly and left the two of them alone, not looking back.

Brian sat opposite Maria and rested his chin on his interlaced fingers, looking her over.

"Been drinking?" were his first words.

They landed like a fist in the gut. She shook her head.

"You look like you've been in a wreck," he said next. She took the offered explanation and nodded. "You hurt?" he followed up. She did something between a shrug and a headshake.

"I'm glad you're not talking for a minute," Brian admitted, rubbing at his forehead with the palm of one hand. "Gives me a second to accommodate seeing you."

"I was going to stay away," Maria finally said.

Brian nodded, a sharp inhale flaring out his nostrils as he laced his fingers together tightly. He squeezed his eyes shut and answered. "What do you need?"

"I just need to crash for a few hours, clean up. Change clothes. Borrow a couple bucks. I'm good for it, I've got a new job, I just..."

Brian shook his head quickly, cutting her off. "Just stop talking, okay?" He rose from the table. "I've got to go to work. Jennifer too. You can help yourself in the kitchen. She's got a bag of clothes for Goodwill; you aren't the same size but maybe there's something that'll work in a pinch."

He reached into his pocket and pulled out his wallet. "I think I've got about a hundred here. Will that do?" Maria nodded. "Okay. She comes home for lunch, usually about

12:30. It'd be best if you're gone by then, okay?" She nodded again.

He walked out of the room. "Towels are in the closet. You know where the shower is."

***

Maria did something like sleep for about two hours. It was hard to tell when she was unconscious in a bad dream or just dwelling in bad thoughts with her eyes closed. Nothing would settle in her brain. When she woke up she didn't feel rested but just numb, floating in some dead space outside good and bad.

She washed up and picked out some clothes that must have been great for Jennifer's skinny butt but made little tearing complaints as Maria put them on. They only needed to last a couple of hours. She put a couple of eggs on toast and chewed robotically. There was plenty of coffee there but Maria didn't touch it. She felt like if she gave her brain any more whacks from any direction it might just go over the ledge completely.

The kitchen looked like she remembered it, not that she had ever spent much time there. The differences were subtle, mostly decorations that had accumulated over time. A little whiteboard on the fridge with shopping items written on it in two different kinds of handwriting. A perky round cookie jar.

If Maria had just a couple more minutes to talk she might have told Brian that he seemed happy, and she was glad for that. But maybe that was just one pick too many at the scab for either of them.

She turned on the T.V., looked for the news. No mention of the explosion; the major networks were just jawing at each other over something the President said and whether it meant he was a tyrant or not. She had better luck online, on the site for Princeton's local paper.

No fatalities. A shuddering sob broke through at last. No fatalities. Two firemen treated for smoke inhalation. Acres of forest scorched. Some homes got a new soot paint job. But no fatalities. Maria burned the words into her retinas. She realized then what she might have done to herself if she had seen any other words.

***

She spent the day as nobody, stopping nowhere familiar, paying in cash. New clothes, a sandwich in one of those homespun highway traps for families. She spent such long stretches on the bike that the world without its motor started to sound strange and empty. Laconia got ever closer.

Was it home? Maria thought back on the path of bad choices, blackouts, and dumb luck that had made the little town in New Hampshire the place she slept. She had a job there, and that was something. There were a few friends, but Maria could never shake the feeling that they were just friendly folk on principle, and that it might not leave much of a hole in their lives if she just up and roared out of town someday.

There was Lia. Jesus, Lia. Maria didn't even know what to say to her about why she had been gone, about why the bills would all soon get handled and never be a problem again. About how any given day in the near future the F.B.I. might knock at their door because of some dumb clue or other that Maria hadn't considered.

Lia. There was a lot that needed to be said there.

***

Maria saw her on the front porch, waiting. Lia stood slowly, working out muscles that must not have moved for a while. Maria said nothing, just walked up and gave her a warm, gentle hug that Maria had to admit was more for her than for her friend.

"Is this the new job keeping you away?" Lia asked.

"Yeah, kid," Maria answered, holding on to the embrace.

"What are you doing?"

Maria felt the decision in her body more than her mind: a surrender of muscles, some dissolution of steel that she couldn't consciously stop. "Let's go in, Princess. I'll tell you all about it. And once and for all, you'll know I'm the crazy one in this house."

**

Maria kept waiting to be stopped, to be told to back up, say that again. She kept expecting to be asked if she was joking, for Lia to accuse her of messing with her head. She itched at the total lack of challenge to anything she said.

But Lia just listened, hands clasped around her mug of tea. The first time she even spoke was when Maria shared that there had been no casualties in the fire. "Oh, thank goodness," she said, though it seemed to come from impulse more than anything else.

Finally the story reached the moment when Maria had pulled up on the old bike in her crappy new clothes and seen Lia on the porch. Maria slapped the table a couple of times to punctuate it all, then leaned back and waited.

"So..." Lia looked down, focusing on some crumb on the tabletop, and then back up again. "We should get rid of the bike, right? So there aren't any loose ends?"

Maria remembered a time back at Lackland when a cadet had cracked completely. It had been building for weeks, fatigue leading to little screw-ups and then a good jawing-at by the T.I.s, and finally to waves of anxiety. The cadet would pinch her own arms at the elbow, compulsively, pinch-pinch-pinch. Maria and the others in their flight were told straight-up that she was their responsibility; that her failure was their failure. Well, they all failed hard, because no matter how hard they reassured, encouraged, cajoled, or threatened her to straighten up, the spiral kept heading down until one morning Maria saw her jamming the bed sheets tight under the corners of her mattress, over and over, like she was trying to make them more than perfect, random words dribbling out of her mouth. No more than a few words at a time were connected to anything. They were like a shattered window falling: no piece would ever belong to any other again, they would just break further and further apart until they hit the ground.

That was the last day Maria saw that cadet. In a way it had set her expectations for people. It seemed inevitable that everyone only moved closer to broken, closer to washing out. It felt right by everything going on inside her. It was only a matter of how long you could hold on.

But here the opposite was happening before her eyes. Lia seemed...steady in a way she had never previously been. The distracted air, the eyes that had always seemed to be confirming where the exits in the room were, the fragility and uneasiness that defined her demeanor: they were suddenly gone, like a shell that had fallen off. It was the absolute last thing Maria had expected.

"So do you...you think I'm crazy, right? I mean all of it?"

Lia thought for a moment, then answered "No." That was all.

"How can you not? I mean, it's the nuttiest thing in the world."

Lia frowned, wrinkled her brow, and then found the words. "I've lived with liars. And I know when you're lying: think of how many card games we've played. So, whatever is going on, I know *you* believe it. And I'll believe it too, because it would be nice to have that lottery money."

Maria looked incredulous. "Was that a joke?"

Something like a little smile twitched at Lia's lips. "Yeah. A bit."

Maria slept the rest of the day.

***

Qualls and Maria didn't talk about the accident. It would have been a foolish thing to discuss by phone, and they could both read the news. The fiber optic cable was being laid underneath an oil pipeline, and the explosion below had punctured that and led to some accidental ignition that only by some miracle hadn't left all of New Jersey burning underground. It had, however, made it nearly impossible to determine just what caused the initial blast, and the secretiveness of the people laying the new cable was enough to draw a distracting amount of suspicion. It sounded as if, by everything they had been told, Maria had successfully carried out her mission.

"So what now?" she asked.

Qualls' response was quiet. He had been talking quietly throughout the whole conversation, and Maria couldn't decide whether to interpret that as real, unconscious paranoia on his part, or some kind of impish pleasure in taking part in revolutionary subterfuge. It was getting on her nerves, though. "Well, we have the next pickup site for a marker. I think they're leaving them closer to you now, so you won't need to travel quite so far. We have to wait at least a month while I record the market information they want, and then they say that the next marker will arrive on the day that I postmark the letter to them. It will tell us what your next mission is, if any."

"Yeah, but, did we change the future? If so, do the guys we're sending it to even know what we did? Or why they're even talking to us? How do they keep track?"

"You're delving into fundamental questions about how time works, and I'm afraid I can only guess at answers. We'll just have to see."

"Wow, thanks, brilliant."

**

Life was quiet for a few days. Maria didn't work, although Lia did a couple of consecutive days in the little shop where she helped out, and that was unusual and good. The biggest worry became how to handle the rent, since their fortune had yet to arrive and Maria still owed Brian a hundred bucks besides.

She scrounged restlessly through her room, looking for salable trinkets that she knew weren't there. There was something to be said for a lean life, but Maria just thought hers looked empty. She had an album of photos other people had taken, back when she was surrounded by people in school and the Air Force. None of them were recent. She had yearbooks, and she didn't know why she still lugged those things around; she didn't know anybody in them anymore, and didn't really want to. She couldn't sell them, but burning them seemed like an option.

Her clothes were utilitarian; the most expensive items she had owned were her motorcycle leathers, and they were in a trash compactor somewhere in New York now.

She went to the living room, where Lia had, as promised, cleaned up the mantel and put up Maria's Air Force medals. She took them all, went to the computer, and looked on eBay to see what they were going for these days.

She sold them in a bundle, and made about seventy-five bucks. It would help.

* * *

-12-

"And we told her to blow it up?"

"Unless the past is lying to us." It was another of Min-Jun's patented cute answers.

Once again they were enjoying one of their private teas in the massive cafeteria at the lab. It was one most the most confusing conversations Josh had ever had. Or rather, that he could recall having had. They had entered truly bizarre territory, where they had undeniably had a drastic impact on their present, but didn't know precisely why because they couldn't remember all of what their present used to be.

"What were we trying to do?"

"I don't think we will ever know. It was to prevent someone from becoming rich. Apparently, the other us didn't give them any more information. They were very cautious, those other us-es."

Josh's head hurt. He didn't understand how this could all seem so amusing to Min-Jun. They were trying to stop the spread of a world-wide plague and disempower a mad tycoon with an assassination virus at his fingertips. And it seemed like they were always going to be in the dark about their work, even when it came to their own previous strategies.

"Maybe before, Khaslik actually bought the virus from me instead of just stealing it?"

"Do you think the younger Josh would have sold it?"

"For a stupid enough pile of money, probably. I didn't see much potential in it. Yeah. Shit, I wonder if I was a richer man than I am now."

"You're still well-off enough."

Josh hadn't told Min-Jun about the expense he had undertaken to spirit Cierra and Lamar away to Lítla Dímun; not because he didn't trust Min-Jun's character, but because he could no longer trust the flow of information under any circumstances. However much money the other Josh had enjoyed, this Josh, between ruining his reputation and hiding his daughter, was quickly running out. He had moved into the lab and was living off the cafeteria food. Which was okay, because he didn't want anywhere else to go, or any downtime either. He had put himself in the dark about his own daughter's condition, and the less time he had to consider that, the better.

"Our methods are off. We need to do something different the next time we send a marker. Some of the knowledge of the future we're in now needs to pass through their past and come back to us, somehow, like the market data."

"We still must deal with the crude medium that we have."

"I've been meaning to ask about that. I want to look at the records of every launch you've done. I want to see the first time you ever created conditions close to what we're doing now. The more data we have, the more we can refine the process. Maybe." Josh shook his head in response to a raised eyebrow from Min-Jun. "I don't know, I just need to see it. And I want to review my firewalls for the lab as a whole; I don't know if I trust the men that set them up. Or that was me, wasn't it? But not the me that set them up when we started this. Damn it…"

Min-Jun quietly reached across the table and laid his hand on Josh's arm. It was unexpected, and Josh jumped as if it had carried an electric shock. Min-Jun waited to speak, fixing his eyes on Josh's in a request that Josh steady not just his body, but his whole person for a moment.

"Josh, you are my very good friend. I have this theory that no matter what we change, we remain very good friends. You might not see any basis for that, but I would call it a faith of mine. I think it has a purpose. I believe that, if we ever created a time in which we were not friends, I would spend that lifetime lonely in ways I would feel but never understand."

"Min-Jun, you've got a husband already."

"Do *not* joke right now." Min-Jun's hand tightened on Josh's arm, and his tone was more vehement than Josh had ever heard it. Josh instantly felt guilty for having undercut the gesture. He nodded apologetically and tightened his lips.

Min-Jun breathed deeply, with commanding force. After a few seconds of this he spoke again. "I have never understood the relationship American culture has with suffering. You do not trust any lesson or growth that comes without pain. You see self-torture as the most effective way to accomplish a task. And in any moment of crisis, you revert to that attitude no matter what you may have learned to the contrary in life. It pains me to see you do this to yourself, Josh."

"Min-Jun, what else can I do? This isn't about philosophy. People are dying because of the code I wrote."

"And if you said to me that you were going to run through the streets, trying to find every man or woman who wants to install a Beetle so you could persuade them against it, I would tell you that you were just one man, that you were tilting against impossible numbers, and you cannot change the minds you seek to change by even the most fevered and sincere arguments. And I believe you would listen to me.

"So I ask you to listen to me now: you are just one man, you are tilting against impossible numbers, and you cannot change time to how it suits you even with the greatest desire and the most finely-honed manipulation. Do you hear me?"

Josh realized that he had never met anyone who could make pessimism sound like more of a relief. No, not pessimism, acceptance. Min-Jun was still gripping his arm, and Josh placed a hand on top of his friend's. He nodded to show that he did hear, that he did understand.

"Most of my biggest accomplishments happened because someone told me I couldn't do something and I was willing to stay awake and ticked off until I proved them wrong. To me it's been a successful habit."

"Forgive me for contradicting your self-image, Josh, but you told me that your first major success came to you in an inspiration while you were out walking, and that the breakthrough which created the virus you are even now trying to combat happened in a moment of idle and excessively-relaxed mental play. Your greatest strengths may not be what you think they are."

Finally Min-Jun withdrew his arm, and his smile broadened. "I have decided to buy you a gift. I will not let you refuse it."

***

They came in obedience to all of Josh's paranoias: without any network devices or implants of any kind, all screened for the smallest sign of Ketron-Garry hiding in their brains. One of the four had a small level, although a certain latent amount of it was becoming terrifyingly common. They weren't yet symptomatic, and if they were afraid, they didn't show it. Dressed in simple, soft fabrics, they escorted a wheeled cart full of sloshing barrels. Min-Jun led the way.

The lab had an on-site fitness center. "It is a noble but futile effort to try and convince scientists to tend to their bodies," Min-Jun joked, and indeed the place seemed neglected. There was a hot tub standing empty, and it was by this that the four men with the barrels stopped.

"Go take a shower," Min-Jun instructed. "Take your time. These gentlemen have work to do." One of them handed Josh a sealed package containing a robe. Josh took it and made for the showers, which seemed equally neglected.

When he returned, they were filling the empty tub. "Water," Josh exclaimed. "All these barrels are full of water?"

"Not just any water," Min-Jun replied. "It is *onsen* water."

"Is this a Korean tradition?"

"Japanese. Koreans take baths too, of course, but I must admit I enjoy the Japanese way more. This is mineral water from a Japanese volcanic hot spring. It may or may not have medical benefits, but what cannot be denied is that it feels wonderful."

"Your gift is a bath?" Josh marveled at it. Factoring in the transport and drastic increase in the value of water over the past few decades, the notion that Josh was about to bathe in gold was not far enough away to be hyperbole.

"Yes, that is why you had to wash first. That is why the tub needed to be drained and scrubbed to remove as much of the chlorine and mineral deposits as possible. Because this experience should just be you and the water."

Josh had been holding on to a small sliver of refusal from the very beginning. Maybe it came from false humility, or maybe his intrinsic inability to relate to Min-Jun's view of things was manifesting as distrust. Either way, he had prepared a plan to weasel out of whatever the gift was going to turn out to be. There was really no refusing now, though. The only thing worse than indulging in this much water would be disposing of it without indulging in it.

He prepared to step in, but Min-Jun stopped him. "No no, it must reach the proper temperature first."

"It feels like it could cook me already."

"Yes, we are close."

***

The first contact shocked his flesh, and it took all his conscious willpower to overrule the senses that were very sure this would kill or at least torture him. But, bit by bit, he acclimated, and did not die, and gradually sunk his body into the steaming water. It tingled lightly on his skin.

Min-Jun and the attendants left, and he was under strict instructions to remain in for at least fifteen minutes. Waiting was something Josh knew how to do, but it had always been reward-based. The idea that the reward came not after the waiting but *inside* it was one of those wisdoms he paid more lip service to than actual attention.

He thought of the chaos he was entrusting his body to. If Josh had been put to the task of designing the ideal bath, he would have wanted to devise a process for creating the purest water possible, ideally containing absolutely nothing but hydrogen and oxygen. No mineral of any kind would be allowed in until its effects could be recorded and proven. The spectrum of therapeutic efficacy of heat on the human populace would need to be established amongst a sufficiently large sample size.

This was entirely opposite, a mixture produced by...what, the "design" of geology and nature? Tectonics and heat? It had bubbled up through the ground, someone had stepped in it out of faith or just blissful unconcern, and before they had the means to know, decided that it was good and got others to try. And it seemed like it was good. Sometimes, he thought, science had to play catch-up with some other sort of awareness.

His hearing concentrated around the low burbling of the tub. His sight seemed to extend, as if the other end of the tub was receding. His body was limp.

Problems surged into his head fitfully, like muscle spasms. Josh realized that he had not been master of his own mind for a long time now, but rather had been letting it drag him like a big dog on a leash. You couldn't let the dog do all the steering on the walk; not until you'd trained it to come home.

Home. Where was Josh's home? He had made the lab suit his work, and he slept here, but as a result here he was: undergoing emergency therapeutic boiling. He had begun to think of himself as a kind of walled nomad, taking his excessive security with him wherever he went, surrounded by luxury and fortune but never caring about them so much as what their weaknesses were.

Weakness. Josh had a temper. He had filtered this out of his self-awareness. Now echoes came from his memory of irritable snaps, impatient barks at employees who didn't move as quickly in their thoughts as he did. The water felt hotter as these memories surfaced, as if they were being leeched out of his brain in a fever. And he understood that when he had abused others, he was only echoing the whip he had always put to his own back. But the others hadn't volunteered for it.

Maria. Their voluntary partner. What did it take to not only believe in their insane story, but to willingly agree to take part in it, even to commit crimes for a higher good she would probably never see? It was the faith of religions and fanatics and armies. No surprise she had been military. Josh wondered if the majority of people who found their way into the military had an in-born susceptibility to this type of programming. Suddenly Josh saw it as a kind of moral programming bypass, a sub-routine installed to make the bad in front of you acceptable for a promised good. It was powerful, and, in Josh's parlance, infinitely exploitable to anyone who only cared about benefiting from the bad.

You would need to get by a lot of defenses to install a sub-routine like that. In every way, it was like implanting a virus. Instead of calming strokes before they happened, instead of trying to play whack-a-mole with the degeneracy that brought on Parkinson's and dementia, what if, instead, Josh had come up with a way to firewall the human soul against manipulative promises? To identify the neural pathways that made it possible to fool people in such savage ways and fortify them, give them the ability to check the intentions and credentials of anyone who sought access? Would fewer people get talked into going to war?

But then they wouldn't have Maria working for them.

Maybe it wasn't a weakness or a strength of humanity, but just a fact. Fundamental. Josh had been breaking some fundamental laws since this project began, it was becoming a habit to think of it as possible.

The water. He barely felt his body anymore. His mind had responded by going into overdrive. This was a sobering discovery; maybe all Josh had ever wanted was to leave his body behind and plug his mind into a computer so it could work and work. But if this were possible, would his mind hold onto its integrity, or be absorbed into the great traffic, breaking up and replicating and being rewritten by everything around it? This was too like life. Virtual perfection was an illusion; because it had been made by men, it would always be like men. Inside such a system he would not be advancing, not evolving, but just trading environments while bringing the same flaws and troubles with him.

And so the question: would Josh rather find himself changed by interfacing with great problems in the network, or by seeing his daughter?

How did this help them? *How did this help them?*

***

"You may talk about the experience when you are ready." This was as close to *Out with it, man!* as Min-Jun's vocabulary allowed. Josh was on a reclining couch in the robe, resting and drinking a great deal of cool water. Min-Jun was in a robe as well, looking thoroughly satisfied. He had been unwilling to let the *onsen* water go without taking his own turn in it. The attendants who brought it were currently rotating in and out of the tub as a kind of end-of-job gratuity.

Josh heard his voice emerge more slowly than normal. It wasn't that he was speaking with a different cadence, but that he had a strangely enlightened perspective on how his brain normally processed the words and behavior around him. That very awareness seemed to make the passing present fuller. "I didn't have a breakthrough, if that's what you're asking."

Min-Jun shrugged. "Results are not guaranteed. Never guaranteed. But learning something: we can guarantee that, if we choose."

"We can't fight against the desires that drive people without changing people. People will always want an advantage. I created two: the Beetle and the virus. I started all this."

He looked at the comfortable robe and the soothing water, with its little slice of cucumber. They seemed like perverse dressing for the dark thoughts now emerging. "I admit I've considered this before. That we can't stop this anywhere further down the road. It has to be me. Younger me."

"Josh, no."

"I'm not talking about killing me, I promise, nothing like that. But maybe we tell me, just...tell me where this is leading, convince me to care about more than just solving an interesting problem. Show me where that attitude leads."

Min-Jun thought for a long time before he answered. "The person you are now came from that person."

Josh exhaled, seeing where this argument was going.

"I think you are right," Min-Jun said. "We cannot change the nature of people. Whatever our solution is must work within that. But it must also work within ourselves. You cannot help by trying to be anyone but who you are."

"This is who I am. I'm a meddler. I tinker with no respect for boundaries or consequences. If an obstacle's in my way I get around it if I have to undermine everything other people take for granted."

"But is this your nature, or simply a stage you passed through in your life, as we all do going from child to man? You are a father now. The love and respect I have seen you show to your daughter has no resemblance to the brilliant hooligan you describe. Perhaps your sense of what your true nature is needs further exploration. It may have evolved while you weren't looking."

"What is that, a Zen paradox? A true and unchanging nature that is constantly evolving?"

"If it makes you think, then it is, isn't it?"

The relaxation he'd felt before was fading fast.

***

Josh scanned through newspaper archives. He wasn't on a particular mission; just absorbing the world that was, hoping to find the right tweak to make. He had been a teenager back then, and in the grips of that contradictory feeling of caring very little about the world at large while simultaneously being convinced he understood it all. Most teenagers think that grown-ups are idiots, and young Josh Scribner had had even more cause than most to subscribe to that belief.

Dates connected themselves to his own experiences as he read. The beginning of an overseas military engagement was two days after a disastrous attempt to invite a girl to the junior prom. She had said no, and Josh remembered spending weeks after insulting and belittling her to his friends, then finding a way to switch on and monitor the webcam on her laptop. He had hoped for a salacious show; instead, after watching her bored face for a half-hour as she surfed the web, he had broken the connection and never gone back, consumed by some black, spiky feeling he hadn't wanted to put words to.

"God, what a turd I was," he thought to himself, for lack of a worthier word.

His monitor locked up: momentary processor overload, an almost unprecedented error. His security monitor showed a surge of activity; his net had managed to catch one of the fastest, heaviest brute force attacks he had ever seen. He watched – just for a moment, only able to witness – before his tablet resumed activity. He quickly went to check the logs and run a full precautionary sweep. And suddenly a file appeared: a tiny, plain-text editor file only a few letters long. It was one of the smallest files possible to send; something a thousand orders below a metaphorical sheet of paper slid under the door. This had been the purpose of the assault, but it was peculiar. Letters couldn't harm him, could they?

After sweeping the file twice, he opened it, not with the standard reader but with his own raw code reader, with which he could filter out the invisible language and see the message he was meant to see. Whoever it was had been efficient: they hadn't even put spaces between the words.

WEAREEVOLVINGNOTDYING

Who was this? Khaslik? Certainly very few people would even know how to find Josh, and it had taken resources, persistence, and genius to get to him like this. But this didn't seem like his style. Then Josh was forced to reflect that despite the image he had constructed of Khaslik through research and rumination, they had neither met nor spoken, ever. So who was to say what his style truly was?

We are evolving, not dying. Did it mean the Beetles and Ketron-Garry? Likely. It was, at the least, a provocative proposition. And very efficiently delivered. Josh could imagine spending long hours exploring the ramifications of this idea.

So he deleted the message. Then he severed the network connection in his tablet and permanently disabled it.

***

"An encryption, that's how we'll do it."

"Do what?" Min-Jun was watching the control arm etch instructions into the next marker with elegant exactitude.

"We put the information about our future into a code, and then ask them to copy the code and send it back to the new us. I decode it on this end, I understand what's going on."

"The new you will not have the key."

"That's why it has to be a code that any version of me could break, but only me."

Min-Jun turned to his friend and smiled. "A true and unchanging nature. Then the bath did help."

"It made me susceptible to crazy ideas, how about that?"

They watched the control arm work in silence. "It's funny," Josh said. "I feel like I should say good-bye to you. As soon as we send this thing out, you and I will be replaced by another version of us."

Morbid humor seemed like the only way to cope with the idea. Min-Jun nodded, then offered his hand to shake. "Yes, farewell, Josh. It has been a privilege and a pleasure."

Josh shook his hand.

***

-13-

Wealth was a peculiar thing. With Dr. Qualls's help Maria divvied up the money into a mix of index funds and bonds, leaving her normal checking account and any bank blissfully unaware of her new comfort other than a once-a-month transfer. She had always known of the existence of these fancy investment drawers that privileged people could stuff their money into, but she had never thought she would need to know the pros or cons of them. They made right with Uncle IRS, and then paid off some old hospital bills Lia had been carrying. What a cruel joke it had been that Lia got the bill for her own beatings, and the collectors would just harass and harass her about it. Never again.

She paid cash for a used pickup direct from the owner. As she looked at the truck bed she pictured a big, chunky lump of future metal riding in it.

Maria had turned her motorcycle over to her landlord in exchange for a few days' grace with the rent. She reclaimed it, and promptly sold it to a mechanic/hobbyist who intended to strip it for parts. That one was harder to part with than the car.

She didn't quit her training job. She just told Albert to book her less. Part of her wasn't ready to give up seeing his weird old face, and she definitely wasn't ready to give up flying.

Then, after a week or so where being rich was, strangely, all she had time to do, it relaxed. She was cruising home, thinking about where to stop to pick up dinner, and suddenly splurged on the seafood place. It was the most exotic thing a desert girl could think to do. Lia liked it.

As they crunched on fried calamari out of a Styrofoam box at the kitchen table, Maria reflected aloud. "I remember talking in school with some of the better-off girls. Not even rich ones, just the ones who'd never seen the inside of a food bank. They had these fantasies of what they'd do with money. They had it all planned out in ridiculous detail; they were like eleven and they knew what brands of shoes, purses, dresses, whatever they would buy. They knew if they wanted to live in Beverly Hills or Miami or Paris." It was such an incomprehensible activity to Maria; only now as a grown-up did she understand the way that her kind of poor could stop you from even having fantasies. "The best future I'd seen for me was having a stable job and pigging out on pizza."

"You can do both now. You can have all the pizza you want."

"Yeah, unless I screw up my job and the world blows up or whatever." Maria caught herself chuckling at the absurdity of it.

"I know we need to be careful, but...um..." Lia hesitated. Maria gave her room to work up to it. "Do you think we could go buy some clothes? I don't mean fancy, but I'd like some new things."

"Yeah, kid. Let's do that."

***

Maria had never really done a girl's day out. And she realized pretty quickly how uncomfortable it made her. It took all of about ten minutes for every item on every rack to blur together. Did it look good? Bad? Was it what people were wearing these days? Who even knew? She bought a jacket with a good lining, and then tried her best to keep her restlessness leashed while Lia picked out a few things, mostly light sweaters.

"Do you think we could go together to meet your friend? The one in the wheelchair?" Lia asked in an idle tone as she studied herself in a head-to-toe mirror wearing a long brown skirt and a simple blouse.

"We're trying not to have too much contact when there isn't a job."

"Oh," Lia looked down. "That's too bad. He sounds nice."

"Nice? He's irritating as hell. Can't stop grinning about how he guessed right about the future and how they came looking for him. I think he'd go on TV and tell everybody about it if his wife didn't keep him sensible."

"She sounds funny. I think I'd like her."

Maria shook her head and snorted. "I need some new boots. I'll be back."

By the time she had found and bought them, Lia was still looking in that mirror.

* * *

Maria took extra time to stretch. She hadn't gone jogging since the experience with the fire; she was sure she'd been kicking her legs in her sleep like a dreaming dog. The nights were much colder and some families were starting to put holiday lights up. Some flakes had fallen, but no one in New Hampshire was willing to call it the first snow of the season.

She felt the shock from the first impacts of foot on asphalt. It was a very welcome pain. Her running shoes slapped the road and she fell into the rhythm. It occurred to her that she could train up to a half-marathon in not too much time if she stayed on the treadmill through winter. And while it was completely reasonable it was also a startling thought; to consider any plans beyond the next week hadn't been in her nature for a long time.

Maria hadn't thought about the future. Maybe it had always been a luxury, one she hadn't been able to afford while she'd clawed and gnashed through the draining days. Maybe that was the first thing you bought after you cleared your food and your heat and the roof over your head. Maybe you bought into the future.

Who's that guy behind you? the Voice prodded.

Maria chilled, but didn't change her stride, didn't turn her head. She had just come around a bend, and as she cycled back in her thoughts she realized there had been another jogger back there, clopping along at an unhurried pace. She tuned her ears past the autumn wind and found his steps; light and even, slower than hers, but probably just meaning long legs.

They were nearing the graveyard. She impulsively turned ninety degrees and jogged through the open gate, giving her a better look at him. - He had yuppie jogging gear on: thin thermal stuff, one of those little wrist computers to track his run, hip-hop branded headphones. But something about him didn't click; whether it was his stride or his build, he just didn't seem like a regular jogger. But what did that mean? Maybe it was just the jerkoff's first night out. Plenty of people with means did it backwards like that, spending a thousand bucks on a hobby they didn't know if they liked yet.

He turned and followed her into the graveyard.

It was an easy place to get a chill, but Maria told herself that the newbie argument was still plausible. If he didn't know where to go, maybe he'd decided that she knew where she was going and was just going to ride her route for a while. And maybe, just maybe, he was following her ass because that's just what some guys did. She kicked up her pace.

The graveyard curved over a hill, and she followed the path around. The front line of stones flowed by her peripheral vision. She couldn't help flicking her eyes over them, seeing so many old white names. Miller, Gardner, Johnson. No Kerrigans, no Caines, no O'Hallorans, no McMillans: the Irish hadn't counted as white yet when the Millers, Gardners, and Johnsons were staking their claims to the area.

Maria grinned, distracted for a moment. She really only liked being half-Irish when it served the chip on her shoulder.

The path came to a dead stop at a tree line. She hadn't planned for this, but really, how many people took circular tours of graveyards? Her muscles tightened up, and when she reached the end, she spun around and struck right back in the other direction, heading straight for the guy, fists in a ball but eyes looking far, far ahead. Adrenaline surged through her and her breath went shallow. It had been a long time since she'd been in a fight. She realized that if that's what he was bringing, she didn't even mind that much.

Instead, she blew right by him as he was making some kind of goofy, wheezy attempt at a smile and a greeting. Guy was so out of shape that he probably would have just fallen over and puked if he even tried to cause her trouble.

Her muscles relaxed back into running mode. She felt a swell of contempt for that jogger, and left him there with the dead.

**

Once she was back and had showered off, she sat down in the living room and stared out the front window for a long time. She shut her eyes and cursed herself for spilling the beans to Lia. If she hadn't been such a bull in a china shop she would never have had to leave Albany. If she hadn't been such a barely-employable screw-up, she wouldn't have needed a roommate. If she had been one ounce less of a rattlesnake to be around for all her years out of the Air Force, she might have found someone else willing to be her roommate other than Lia.

Not that there was anything wrong with the Princess. Once you got to know her you saw how swell she was. But Dr. Qualls and those geniuses in the future can't have wanted someone in Maria's state. Someone who would get that anxious around some fat jogger. Who would drag a civilian like Lia into an important mission just because she couldn't keep her mouth shut.

She heard Lia shuffle into the room, and didn't turn. After some silent seconds, Lia turned and left again.

***

"I sent the letter yesterday. So the wheels, such as they are, are in motion. The marker should be at the coordinates already."

Maria felt a bit of real excitement at putting the new truck through its first camping trip. "Doc, not that it changes anything for me, but do you send these letters to the same place every time?"

"Yes and no. They go to the same address, which is a post office. However, the P.O. boxes are sequentially numbered. They have a whole block of them, and every letter I send has to go to the next one on the list."

"How the hell did they manage that?"

"I did it!" Dr. Qualls couldn't hide the impish pride in his voice. "After the first marker reached me years ago, they provided some...assistance, financially, and in return I set up the boxes now, in our present. The very first box held the keys to all the rest."

"Why does every letter have to go to a different box?"

"I imagine it helps keep things straight on their end. Every time we send a letter, it affects their actions there. That way they can choose to be affected by one letter at the time, and the rest of the boxes are rather like the one with Schrödinger's cat."

"What? Whose cat?"

"Never mind."

"Huh. But like, the stuff you're doing with the stock market numbers, isn't that so they can track what's changed so far?"

"Yes."

"So why wouldn't we just keep writing everything?"

"We don't have to be reporters: they have the media archives of the world at their fingertips. Also, I suspect that, because they're scientists, they like to keep things tidy."

"You're like the sloppiest guy I know, Dr. Qualls."

"Oh, I just do that to annoy Willie. But don't tell her that."

***

Maria took Lia shopping again, and this was a trip more Maria's speed. Just camping gear, thermals and thick socks. If it was functional and fit, it went in the basket. It had taken a week for her arms to stop aching after carrying the marker back by herself last time, so this time she was going in with help. And it wasn't as deep in this time, so this was going to go easier all around.

They loaded all the gear in the night before they left. It was a ritual Maria enjoyed, being able to get out of bed in the morning, coffee up, and just go.

Lia hardly knew how to help as Maria efficiently puzzle-pieced the gear in and tied it all down. Generally she would just pick up something from the pile and hold it out near Maria with a soft smile on her face.

"What do you think your job will be this time?"

"Well, I asked Qualls to mention that they need to prep us a little better if I'm going to be breaking any laws. That fire was a nasty surprise and I think it happened because they didn't do their homework well enough."

"It would be nice if it were more like the painting. Telling those people about it, I mean. I think that was a really nice thing."

"Yeah, and for all I know being rich is going to turn those people into assholes. They might just buy a bunch of tacky shit and guns and then spend the rest of their lives farting around town about how great they are."

Maria heard a sniffle behind her and looked over her shoulder. Lia was just standing there, but somehow she seemed to have shrunk. She looked down and her body drew in close to itself. Maria let go of the strap she was tightening and turned. "Ah shit, kid, what did I say?"

Lia shook her head. "It's not you. I was just thinking about all those people, the ones you said...in the future. Everyone everywhere getting sick, whether they're good or bad. Some of them are probably terrible people. Maybe some of them are better off dead."

And then she looked up, and Maria saw something ferocious in Lia's eyes. "But I don't care. I want to help them. All of them."

Maria didn't know how to answer her friend.

**

They were headed back to the White Mountain Forest, where Maria had found the first marker. It was near enough to Laconia that they probably didn't even need to camp to get the job done, but they had the gear and Lia seemed to be anticipating another crack at the outdoor experience.

The weather wasn't great. Autumn wind had been slapping at the car the whole drive, and now the skies were clouding over in ominous gray. By the time the first rain drops started to dance on the windshield, it felt like they were arriving long after their announcement.

Lia looked over at Maria as the rain picked up, maybe wondering if this meant they were continuing on to the campsite. Maria looked back and smiled. "Welcome to roughing it for no good reason, Princess."

The rain became a storm, like a test.

Maria drove on, confident in her new truck.

**

The campsite manager laughed with good-humored surprise when they knocked at his door to register amidst a storm that was knocking at the door of downpour. "S'pposed to last all night," he bellowed as the drops battered his fishing cap and he gave them their pass. "If you need to warm up proper, come around and knock. I think the wife might let me crack the good whiskey with guests like you."

Maria's throat burned from an imaginary pull of bourbon. "Thanks. But if we come around, don't let my friend here talk you into cards. We'll end up owning the joint."

"That a promise? Been wanting to retire."

"Retire from what? Sitting on your ass in a trailer?"

They both grinned, as if daring one another to keeping shooting the shit until they all drowned.

***

Maria drove the spikes in deep through the mud. Lia sat on the unlifted tent to keep it all from blowing away. Every so often in the middle of her work, Maria would look over. Lia was cross-legged, obviously soaked and freezing, but solid and determined nonetheless. If sitting was the thing she could do that helped most, she did it with an absolute sense of mission, and to hell with the wind and the water.

Finally they were pitched and inside, where it was 99% dry. They left most of their gear in the car, keeping only their sleeping bags, a change of clothes, and every towel they had. "The minute this lets up I'll race you to the piss shack," Maria said.

"What do we do now?" Lia asked.

"I don't know," Maria answered. "I haven't been weathered in like this in a while. It happened to me and my brother once, only we were just in the backyard."

"It rained on you?"

"Yeah, we didn't get drizzles out in the desert. We'd get floods. When the rain picked up, Ma came out and tried to talk us in. She talked real quiet, like that way we wouldn't be embarrassed to give up on the tent or something. But we bawled and cranked and she let us be for a while. Who cared if it was just the backyard; it felt a little like freedom."

"What would you do?"

"Wrestle and shit. He would tell these stories that he'd heard from his buddy at school, who'd heard them from his older brother who'd heard them from his drunk uncle who'd been all over the place, or at least said he had. So they were at least 90% fish story by the time they got to us, but I loved 'em. Stories about foreign countries and ghosts and, like, mumbo-jumbo Eastern philosophies. We had this deal: we divided up the places in the stories, and when we were grown up we were each going to go to our half of them and then come back and tell the other if they were true or not." Maria let that hang, a path to unanswerable grief that was there and needed acknowledging, but not following.

"I have a sister," Lia said after a minute. "We haven't talked in like four years. She was jealous of me getting married. I think she always liked Jarrod and wanted him herself."

"Well she can have the dickhead now if she wants him so bad."

"It's funny, right?" Lia stared at her toes in their big thick socks and flexed them, her voice taking on a distant air. "She was the first person I ran to, you know? And she just got even more pissed, saying I must have done something and how could I blow it like this and marriage is supposed to be sacred. Like she cared about that; she kind of slutted around town."

Suddenly Lia giggled and looked around the tent, shocked at herself. Maria smiled.

The rain didn't stop. And between their bladders and stories to tell, they ended up not sleeping too much.

***

"So, should I stand watch or something?" Lia was enjoying the hiking trail, especially the dirty rainbow of leaves that crunched under their feet. They'd reached Maria's best guess at where they needed to go off-trail to find the marker. The rain had relented in the morning, but the forest still dripped from water taking the long way down along trunks and branches.

"Nah, just standing there will look even more suspicious. If we're together, at least we can claim we got lost together."

And so they stepped off the trail, which in its current state didn't look too much different from the rest of the ground, save for the lack of trees.

The trees weren't fully-bare yet, but they were getting there. As they walked slowly, searching the ground, a leaf would sometimes twirl through the air past them, finally able to join its brothers down below.

Maria couldn't help but shake her head at Lia's determination and seriousness. Of course, if you took a hard look, it was the right attitude to have. Maria was the one being all smart-assed about their mission. She hadn't been this way in uniform. Sure, she'd always had something to prove, always been the type to jaw back, but she'd also bought in completely to the mindset. The Air Force had been her tribe, and she'd been willing to take that chair when they asked her to. Bombing bad guys into the ground had seemed like a good idea at the time.

Only she'd stopped, and more bad guys had sprouted out of the ground, so some kid coming up behind her took over her chair and dropped more bombs. She didn't know who that was, her successor, but sometimes she wondered if she would have warned him.

She thought back on that crazy night hike she'd taken months ago that started all this. She'd gone out to sit on a rock and listen to the water in the night. Now she realized that it was because of one of those stories her brother had shared in their tent years ago; some many-times-repeated tale about how it would be a way to tune out the world and find yourself again.

When you're a kid, finding yourself sounds like either nonsense or some fascinating adult activity, like smoking. Now Maria realized it was just one more job that sucked but that you had to do.

"Maria!" Lia pointed excitedly. "I think...is that it?"

Maria turned and saw it, unnatural and black as ever, sitting atop an eight-foot high boulder slick with rainwater.

"Ah, shit," she answered. "Yeah, looks like it."

She tried bracing herself between rocks to climb up, but it was too slippery. And it was too heavy to poke down with a stick.

Lia bent over. "You should get on my shoulders."

"Are you kidding? I'd snap those legs of yours in half." Maria sighed, placed herself at the base of the rock and squatted. "Here; climb on, Princess."

Lia awkwardly straddled Maria's shoulders and tried to balance herself. Maria, complaining and grousing commands for Lia to stop fidgeting, pushed her legs straight and lifted her friend into the air.

She took a step or two forward, bringing their two-person tower to the rock. "Can you see it?" Maria asked.

"Take another step forward," Lia said. "I've almost got it."

Grumbling, Maria moved again. "How about now?"

"Yeah, I've got it."

Maria heard Lia sliding the marker towards her. Seconds passed, and the silence grew heavy. "What does it say, kid? Come on, your ass ain't light."

Lia answered with the sad, quiet tone Maria was long familiar with but didn't welcome back. "It says we're done. It says *Thank you, Maria, no more missions or letters are required. Enjoy your life.*"

Maria forgot the weight on her shoulders for a moment, because it was absolutely the last thing she had expected. "That's it? That's all it says?"

"That's everything."

***

-14-

Min-Jun entered the little post office in Paris. It was right around the corner from the lovely apartment he shared with his husband, and always part of his rounds, but he had allowed himself to linger in an open-air marketplace before making the daily visit. What was waiting for him would keep, after all.

This post office had been selected because he could visit it every day and still be inconspicuous. Their purchase of an entire bank of postal boxes had been done piecemeal, through a series of blandly-named LLCs created by Dr. Qualls far in the past. And Josh had since littered enough virtual bread crumbs down false network trails to make anyone lose their youth trying to determine what was going on, and that was only assuming they had reason to believe that something was going on worth investigating. Secrecy was Josh's instinctive approach to every step they took, and Min-Jun supposed it was an advantage since he would not think to do such things himself. They had real enemies out there, and Josh had tipped his hand with his speech to the world.

Of course, the speech had also convinced Min-Jun that they could, and should, do something about the dreadful situation. It fit his philosophy that both danger and grace could result from the same great act.

He gave a cheery "Bonjour!" to the clerk on-duty, and proceeded to the boxes. Stopping at the first unopened one on the list, he produced a healthy ring of keys from his pocket, and opened it.

It was empty.

Min-Jun stared at the space for a moment, perplexed. He ran his fingers around the interior, in case some paper was hiding flat against a corner, but his eyes had already told him that he would find nothing.

Cautiously, he opened the previous box. He knew this would annoy Josh because it threw off the entire system, but as Min-Jun suspected it was empty as well, since they had already claimed its contents.

This left the next box in the sequence. It could be as simple as a numbering error on the part of their compatriots in the past. It could be mail delivery sloppiness. Any number of simple possibilities could be cleared up by opening the next box. Still, Josh would like this even less. Of course, Josh also didn't want to risk an open network call, so Min-Jun made his choice, found the next key, and opened the corresponding box.

Also empty.

Min-Jun left the post office, no longer open to the bounteous pleasures of Paris as he traversed the sidewalks towards home. His thoughts heavily clouded, he didn't notice that he was being followed.

***

Josh wandered the hallways alone. He had designed it to be this way, setting up a system that reported to him when corridors in the lab were empty, and then switched off all monitors and detectors in his path.

He had told himself he was stretching his legs, trying to exercise. In truth he was brooding, inconsolable in his isolation. Until Min-Jun returned with the letter, there could be no follow-up. He couldn't speculate on the next mission until he learned the results of the previous mission; in fact, until he even learned for sure what the previous mission had been. From what he remembered, though, he and Min-Jun had sent Maria and Qualls to expose information about Khaslik that he had uncovered to Khaslik's rivals in the past.

If you could chum the water around your target, you could count on sharks to be sharks. Josh had been hesitant to so dramatically scheme to ruin the life of someone who had such a consequential impact, but it had seemed like the only way to counteract the drastic damage he saw happening to the world.

Khaslik, though, was decidedly unruined in their present. Maria and Qualls could have failed. Or it could be they had succeeded at some other mission given them by a previous Josh. So would the success or failure of that mission fall to some other, yet unforged version of Josh? Had it already? Maybe it had, meaning the true universe was somewhere else and Josh was tromping along, alone, in the blind alley of a dead now. He was having more and more thoughts like this, and he couldn't walk them off.

His footsteps echoed. The sun gleamed off the Alps, but Josh ignored it. He had ceased to care about that orb as anything but a damnably heavy gravitational influence on their time launches.

He sensed movement out of the corner of his eye and turned around. A shadow was rising; no, the distorted shape of a man, featureless and dark from head to toe, was standing from underneath the shadow of a bench in the hallway. He looked like a ninja, a hunchbacked one. But if he was a ninja, he was a foolish one, because his black fabric was starkly visible against the lab-white walls.

There was more motion, and Josh turned to see another figure all in black coming to its feet. The fabric wasn't to hide from his eyes, Josh realized in a split-second, but to hide their bodies' bioelectrical signals. The hunchback must be some breathing apparatus concealed under the fabric. So that when everyone else had left the hallway, the hallway would deem itself empty and Josh would enter. Alone, and with no security monitors on him.

That's just how I would have done it, he thought as a he felt a prick on the back of his neck and darkness took him completely.

***

Min-Jun left a message in a secure packet floating
untethered inside a datastream. He and Josh had settled on
the particular stream, so Josh would know to look for it. Josh
called it beachballing. But it meant that there was no real-
time response, no reassurance or plan of action, which Min-
Jun found himself thinking would be a real comfort at this
moment.

His husband was at work. Min-Jun was usually
comfortable with silence, but even he – a man who had
made peace with the uncertainty of the world – was having
difficulty with the uncertainty of this situation. For all he
teased Josh, his friend was a man of action in so many ways
that Min-Jun was not. And even when they didn't know
what to do, his action-oriented thoughts augmented Min-
Jun's own and somehow they always found their way to
more solid ground.

There was a knock at his door. That was peculiar:
certainly recognizable, but startlingly anachronistic. The
ritual for over a decade had involved a notification chime, a
facial recognition check, usually a courteous exchange of a
few sentences on the monitor followed by a brief silence
while the person on the inside did some useless tidying up.
However, even though doors no longer had to withstand
daily beatings, they hadn't grown thinner as Min-Jun had
rather hoped. People seemed to like the illusion of security
in a really sturdy door, and he admitted, in the moment
that his heart jumped at the sound of the knock, that he
couldn't entirely condemn them.

A home pad was within arm's reach, and he could easily
have activated the monitor to see who it was, but he felt a
signal of conspiracy in the knock and was compelled to
cooperate with it. He stood straight up, made peace with
whatever would come, and approached the door.

It was a middle-aged Western woman, wispily built, with gray hair tied in an anxious knot. Her eyes were surrounded by deep, compassionate wrinkles, telling the story of a woman who might never sleep out of worrying for the whole human race.

She quickly put her finger to her lips to silence him, and then hustled past him into the apartment. The door closed behind her and Min-Jun watched, agog but unwilling to break the silence she had enforced, as she flitted around the apartment like a flying bug exploring the space by its own haphazard radar. She was searching for something, opening cabinets, digging through drawers. At last she found what she sought and held it up, triumph turning the creases in her face upwards. A pencil. With no paper near, she took rapid little steps back to where Min-Jun stood and started scribbling words on the walls near them.

You are being watched, she scribbled.

He is after us all, she wrote beneath that.

Couldn't go near the lab without being discovered, so I waited for you at the post office.

I helped you in the past, and I have to help you now.

My name is Lia Carty.

* * *

Josh saw blurs and blobs. He was in a blurry space, with some blobs in it that might be sort of human-shaped. He might be sitting up, but his own body felt like little more than a blurry blob itself. Sounds were slow and thick.

One sound seemed to come from beneath him, and was steady and static enough for his wobbly mind to concentrate on. He stuck himself to it to see where it would pull his consciousness.

A plane. Was he in a plane? A blurry aircraft? He had just been on a plane not long ago. When was that? A man had been flying it, right? That sounded right. Where had he gone? His daughter had been with him. He had taken her somewhere. Where was Cierra?

Maybe that's all they all were: blobs in a blur. As a theory of the universe it beat the snot out of string theory. It explained everything, and if you zoomed out far enough, the blur itself was just one big blob.

Josh thought he should tell Stephen Hawking about this. Was Hawking still alive? Was Josh still alive? All of these questions were too difficult. He needed to relax. He needed a bath.

And a warm bath was just what the next sensation felt like. A warm bath in absolute blackness.

***

Min-Jun discovered some paper and left an apologetic note for his husband. Then, he and Lia left and made their way, wordlessly, to the train station.

Min-Jun brought some gizmos with him that Josh had created: pocket static throwers that could block or muffle conversations within a small bubble. He booked a private compartment on the train, and, once there, he disabled the attendant pad and turned on the thrower.

"It's safe to talk now."

Lia still didn't speak. She let off the quiet, desperate vibrations of a person feeling more than she could deal with. Min-Jun reflected that in most cases, this would be when he reached for his teapot. Instead, he simply waited.

"Who are you?" she asked.

This was a startling question, but easily answered. "My name is Dr. Min-Jun Dan. You may call me Min-Jun. Are you truly Lia?"

"I am." Her eyes darted around the compartment. "You work at the lab, with Josh Scribner?"

"We run the project together. He plots the destination and I execute the launch."

"Who else knows about what you're doing?"

"A few at the lab have an inkling that I stumbled upon an exceedingly wasteful, impractical use for a particle accelerator that achieves something resembling time travel on the subatomic level. This is the limit of their knowledge."

"But they know that the doors are slammed and locked, and you and a rich super-genius have bought the place out and are doing something they're not allowed to ask about, right?"

Min-Jun nodded.

Lia sighed. "Secrets. Sometimes just acting like you've got one is all people need to know exactly what it is."

She leaned forward, putting her head in her hands. She shut her eyes and rubbed her temples, and the words came out with wrenching slowness. "You're the first person I've ever been able to tell this that will understand. You know those nightmares where you can see the monster coming and your feet are stuck to the spot? A long time ago I lived in a version of that nightmare; knowing something horrible was coming, not knowing when or how it would reach me, but just knowing that, every day, the monster was around.

"I got out of it; my marriage, I mean. For a long time, leaving was the hardest thing I had ever done, or thought I would ever have to do. But that all changed when I found out about the future.

"I spent over twenty years knowing what was supposed to happen, wanting to stop it, thinking I had helped to stop it, and then watching it happen in slow-motion all around me. Twenty years. And nothing I could do could stop it."

She looked up at Min-Jun, her face agonized. "Why did you tell us we were done?"

It was finally Min-Jun's turn to talk, but now he was too confused to answer. "Done? But we never...we sent you another mission at the location in the White Mountains. What happened? Where's Maria?"

Lia looked up, and said the words with a cold croak. "Maria's dead."

* * *

Josh awoke on an undistinguished couch in an undistinguished room. This was fine; he felt in bad enough shape without needing to absorb anything strange.

He had the dead-limb feeling of having slept on his arm, only it covered every inch of him. His brain had the similar sense of evolving from nothingness to a kind of overwhelming static. He wondered if this was coincidence or not. People generally had entirely different words for describing the experiences of the brain and body, and yet in most of the fundamentals they were the same: wakeful or fatigued, focused or confused, trained or atrophied. Under natural conditions, the mind and body were more often than not aligned.

Thinking was Josh's way to revive. As he thought, he became more aware of both his surroundings and his own condition. His body felt excessively heavy, like the paralysis you wake to when you're not quite out of a dream. He couldn't move, but he knew he was there, and that, as the philosophers said, was what counted.

He groaned: with greater awareness came greater pain. That tidbit was popular with philosophers too. His head was filled with burning, itchy sand. He had to change his situation as soon as possible. Summoning all his strength, he rolled off the couch.

The change, he realized, was cosmetic.

Still, more and more of his mind was coming online. Two plus two was definitely four, and he remembered his name, his hometown, and the first girl he'd ever kissed. Did he remember why he was here? Did he remember where here was? The facts returned before their accompanying emotions, and for a brief second he was fascinated, not panicked, that kidnappers in custom-made body concealment suits had abducted him via a private jet. That took care of *what* and *how*. *Where* and *when* he didn't know, but that wasn't his fault.

As far as *who* and *why* were concerned, he only had a guess... but it was a guess he had a hell of a lot of confidence in. More confidence than in most of what he'd done lately.

He found enough muscle to push off the floor and sit leaning back against the couch. Standing would come thrillingly soon. He started to look around the dark room. He couldn't see a lamp, and yet there was enough ambient light in the room for him to perceive the walls and a door.

His mind shifted up a gear. Was there a pad? A screen? A device of any kind? If so, all plans began with that. No one could match what he could do with just a few minutes alone with a networked device.

He rolled his head around, searching. There, to the side: a large pad, one of the coffee table-sized ones marketed as creative meeting spaces and for family game time. At last the excitement in his brain bled down into his muscles, and he managed to rise and take the three wobbly steps he needed.

Hello, Josh, the screen pad read.

His heart sank. Leaving him alone in a room with a pad hadn't been an oversight; it was mockery. Still, Josh had plenty of experience hanging people on their own mockery. He tried to trigger a restore sequence to access a root menu. The screen went black, then flicked back on again, still reading *Hello, Josh,* only this time the letters danced, chintzy colors blinking around them like Christmas lights.

He flipped the pad over, seeing if he could pry it open and divert network access to a different drive partition so he could slip in, target it manually and boot the whole device off a remote cloud server.

When the screen turned towards the floor, tinkling music played and a male voice gleefully boomed "Hello Josh!" Then a female voice repeated the words. Then a child's voice. Then one after another in mocking chorus until Josh hurled the thing across the room.

With a hiss, the door slid open a bit. A tray was pushed in through the crack with an apple, a nutrient bar and a half-glass of water. Just as quickly, the door closed again.

Josh came within microseconds of pouring the water on the pad to try to shut it up, but his brain had woken up enough to remember two things: that technology was better than that these days, and that he was monstrously thirsty.

**

Min-Jun Dan lived in a world where it wasn't uncommon to mourn people you'd never met. It was common to have a significant relationship with someone without ever occupying nearby physical space, and everybody died. Technology hadn't changed that about life yet.

But Maria. How did you mourn someone you had not only never met, but who had never actually been alive for all the time you had known and interacted with her? When they had accepted her as their agent in the past, Josh had been adamant about not investigating her in the present, and it seemed sensible. And yet, because she was still relatively young twenty-three years ago, and in a prosperous America with her finances settled, the odds had favored her still being around in their world. Min-Jun realized that this assumption had been a comfort to him, a small faith driven by an unconscious need. It was only now, with it gone, that he realized how important it had been to him that they'd done at least one solid good thing in all their meddling.

It had been different with Dr. Qualls. He, they knew, would not last until 2038. Learning this had been an unavoidable consequence of studying his credentials to ensure he was the sort of scientific collaborator they needed. Naturally they had never shared this knowledge with him, but his letters had always communicated a sense that his whole life had been validated by their work together, and through that Min-Jun had found the balance to carry on.

He had no similar road out of this sadness. But of course, it had been mere minutes since Lia had shared the news. Minutes for him, but many long, hard years for her, forced to carry the true import of her friend's death in silence.

"How did it happen?" he finally asked.

"Not in a moment," Lia shook her head. "Maria died slowly. It started when the mission ended." Lia's words didn't come across crisply, but rather with an intense evenness. Her head tilted to the side and she tugged at her hair; an echo of sadness passed across her face as she did, as if the gesture itself was a sort of nostalgic act.

"I wonder, sometimes, if she would have lived longer if you had never found her. She was miserable, eating herself alive day by day, but she was surviving in her way. This mission gave her something she hadn't had for a long time; it changed her. Then, suddenly, it was all gone. Even the idea that we'd succeeded wasn't enough; she didn't believe that we'd really done it."

"She was correct. Someone has interfered. I wonder how. Our launch went as planned; errors are always possible but we..." Min-Jun's voice caught for a moment, then deepened with new humility. "We had become very confident in our procedures, our security, our fail-safes. Arrogant, even."

He told her about Khaslik, his role going back to the very beginning, and Josh's perpetual anxiety that Khaslik would interfere. "We must go back to Switzerland, but I fear what we will find. He has gone from being unaware of us to having over two decades' head start."

He reached out to this woman he had never met and took her hands in his. Her hands moved to accept the gesture, simply and comfortably. Min-Jun felt great strength in her, the kind that went unseen but was needed to power so big a heart. They sat there quietly in the train for a long time, connected by things they did not want to put into words.

***

-15-

Chocolate cake. Store mix and store icing, but who cared? It was chocolate cake. Lia spread the icing while Maria looked at the marker on the kitchen table. Despite its finality they had hauled it back rather than leave it for someone else to discover.

Maria kept re-reading the words and searching for the elation she should be feeling. They had fulfilled their mission. Millions and millions of lives had been saved or bettered. Evildoers had been thwarted. The lottery money was theirs to keep. It all sounded wonderful...it just didn't feel that way.

Maybe the problem was the medium. Those cold, laser-chiseled letters on an unappealing black lump. Every sense memory Maria had of the markers was unpleasant: sore muscles and joints, strained fingers, so many scuffs and scrapes. Honestly, she hated the sight of them.

Maybe the problem was that they couldn't see it. If there had been breaking news on television about the future of the human race suddenly being better, then at least they would probably feel some thrill at seeing their pictures there. It wasn't so much that Maria wanted public attention – pretty much everything about that pushed the wrong buttons in her – but it would have been nice to have more confirmation than a single sentence.

Lia shoved the message marker aside and set the cake down in front of them. She had written a message in awkward, sugary cursive on top: *Maria & Lia! We Saved the Future!*

"What piece do you want?" she asked, setting out plates.

"Corner," Maria answered in a faraway mumble.

"That's my favorite too. We'll both get corners. And then there will be two more corners left for us. Or, should we take the rest to the Doctor and Willie? I didn't even put their names on it; maybe we should make another one."

Maria pushed back from the table and stood to go to the fridge. "Milk. Gotta have milk with cake."

"Good idea! Let me get glasses."

Maria poured herself and Lia some milk. The cake slice sat in front of her, looking moist and sweet.

Oh yes, congratulations, the Voice said. Maria jerked in her chair, startled.

"What is it?" Lia asked.

"Nothing," Maria said. "Sudden chill."

Why are you hesitating to enjoy your reward? it continued. It looks so good. I never ate anything so good in my life.

Maria rubbed at her temples as Lia, smiling as she made sure there were no objections, slipped her fork through the cake and brought it to her mouth. She chewed contentedly.

Honey, a few drops of honey; that was the closest I ever came to dessert in my life. Of course, I didn't have much time, did I?

Maria picked up her fork and speared the cake slice. Tugging loose a giant bite, she shoved it in her mouth and chewed.

Lia smiled even wider at what she thought was Maria's voracious enjoyment.

Maria did nothing to contradict her. She kept eating, and the Voice kept talking. Later, she threw up, and it still smelled a little like chocolate.

***

Dr. Qualls and Willie wanted to celebrate too. Maria kept reminding herself that they were in the right and she was the crazy one. They met Lia at last, and the three of them chattered for a long time about nothing earth-shattering. Lia seemed engaged in a way Maria barely recognized; she wondered if she was catching a glimpse of the woman Lia had been before.

The Doc cooked a disaster of a homemade chili in a giant pot, and they all made a good show of pretending it wasn't bad at all. Everyone but Maria split a bottle of red wine, though only after she promised it was okay for them to drink in front of her. She couldn't ever remember seeing Lia drink; then again, Lia never went anywhere. She sipped forever at a single small glass, but a little relaxation seemed to go a long way with her.

"It's funny, isn't it?" Qualls pontificated, obviously pleased to have the floor for the occasion. "That a warning from the future also brings with it some optimism. No nuclear war, no epidemic or mass starvation in the next twenty years. You wouldn't believe that from the news, would you? And technology: such advances! These brain implants really do sound extraordinary, although, there are clearly still some kinks to work out."

"Uh, Doc, what if they're wrong?" Maria managed to ask the question as if she were only curious, but she felt restless, aggressive in the face of everyone else's happiness.

"How do you mean?"

"Let's say in the future – like six months after they told us it was all done – that they figured out it wasn't really done and they still needed us. Can we even still talk with each other?"

Dr. Qualls looked at her sympathetically, and Maria felt the hairs on her neck prickle. He answered soothingly. "There's always been coordinates for an emergency pickup. If a marker failed to arrive, or if anything else happened, they promised to send instructions to that location and we could resume communications that way. And we can always reach out to them via the post office boxes."

"What if we did that? I mean, just asked to double-check that it's okay?"

Dr. Qualls smiled. "What you must understand about time travel is that it's best that we do it as little as possible. All the limits our friends put in place are there to limit pollution, the spread of future knowledge. We can't let our anxieties lead us to abuse a power this awesome."

"Okay, well how about you tell me where the emergency pickup spot is? I can take the new truck out there; I've got nothing but free time now."

Qualls giggled loosely in response to Maria using the word "time" in that way. His laugh passed around the table to the others, and Maria became more irritated. "It's no problem, right?"

Finally his laughter settled and he waved and nodded at her. "Of course, of course. It's written down somewhere in my study. I'll dig it up for you later." Then he chuckled again, this time at himself.

The bottle of wine on the table was empty. Maria stared at it, pretty sure she would have grabbed it otherwise. She didn't even like wine.

* * *

It was late and everyone was tired and happy. Qualls and Willie were putting on a display of tipsy flirting between longtime lovers that was so charming that even Maria had to grin. But now they were headed for bed, and Lia and Maria had been invited to stay. Maria had agreed instantly, letting Lia have the guest room.

"Going to jog," she told Lia.

"Now? In that?"

"I've got gear in the truck; I'll just change quick and go do a few miles."

"I mean, you don't even know your way around here."

Maria tapped her skull with a smirk. "Pilot brain. Even when I'm on the ground I picture what a place looks like from above. I can navigate a neighborhood."

Lia let it go with obvious resignation. "Be safe, okay?"

Be safe, okay? The words echoed in Maria's mind, and she wasn't sure if it was just her memory underlining what she saw as a pointless caution in this cozy white neighborhood, or the Voice seizing Lia's words and bouncing them back mockingly. The Voice was showing off too many new tricks.

***

It was intensely cold. After loosening up, Maria got up to pace; as she'd boasted to Lia, the neighborhood wasn't complicated despite the way its old streets looped across the local hills. By staying off the main road, she could explore the cul-de-sacs in different orders and combinations for a few miles at least.

Don't run, the voice said.

"You don't tell me what to do." Alone and with her feet thumping the road, Maria felt safe enough to answer.

Don't run, it repeated, harder and with a firmer edge than she was accustomed to.

"You can't make me, little boy." Finally, she had something she could direct the evening's anger at. Whether or not this choice was healthy could wait.

DON'T RUN.

Maria stopped. She couldn't understand it. She had been jogging, getting her heart-rate up, pushing steam out of her lungs, doing everything like normal. Her limbs were warmed up, loose enough to go. It had nothing to do with stamina, or the cold, or blisters on her feet, because there weren't any. She had just stopped, regardless of her own will.

She leaned forward, sucked in some wind, shook out her legs. Nothing was wrong with her body at all. She was in prime health. But she couldn't run.

"What the hell are you doing?" she asked. The voice didn't answer.

She went through her ritual stretches all over again, right there by the curb in front of some stranger's house.

She put herself in race start position, rocked back and forth on her ankles a bit. Then she burst forward.

After a few hard, fast steps, she pulled up again and stopped.

Now she stalked around in a circle, fury growing inside her. "You can't do this," she said in a quiet growl. "Not this, don't take this."

But her body wouldn't. Not couldn't. Just wouldn't. She started walking. Not willingly. Just because it was cold and it was time to lie down.

She felt guided as she walked, steered by something else. Her mind tuned out, and without the energy to sustain her anger she felt something far worse emerging; an old feeling that she had believed she could weed out permanently.

It was despair. It was helplessness. She walked because she couldn't make herself run. The voice wouldn't tell her why, and for once she actually wished she would hear from it.

A horn screamed, and she turned to see a car rolling towards her, headlights pinning her. How could it be coming right at her? Had she drifted into the middle of the street? She didn't know, and she couldn't move. Was she dying right now? *I'm a deer,* she thought to herself with lethal irony. *A deer in the headlights.*

The car swerved and stopped, missing her by less than a foot. She stared dumbly at it. The driver was mouthing something, maybe at Maria, maybe just to himself. She couldn't hear anything. Her brother was dead.

She ran at the car. She kicked the doors, punched at the window, bruising her knuckles and screaming uselessly. The driver's face turned to terror and he floored the gas.

The son of a bitching car was getting away. It had killed her brother and it was getting away.

And she couldn't run after it.

Maria sat down in the road and bowed her head. If another car came, it could take her.

No cars came. It was a quiet neighborhood, and not many people went out at night.

***

She didn't know what time it was when she returned to the house; she wasn't moving of her own volition anymore. The voice, or inertia, or whatever the hell was keeping her going just made her kick off her shoes and socks, lay down on the couch, and pull a blanket that didn't fully cover even her short frame over as much of her as possible.

Sleep didn't come. Her brain drifted to that place that wasn't sleep but where time and the senses were meaningless. A clock was ticking somewhere and it was impossible to tune out. All the quiet sounds of the house mocked her. Old grudges stomped through her thoughts: against high school classmates; a fellow pilot who had gotten a little too handsy one day; Brian's wife Jennifer, who was totally justified in hating Maria but had gotten unbearably smug about it.

She breathed slowly and steadily. No sleep. She squeezed her eyes shut. No sleep. The clock kept tick-ticking, and it was louder than all the noises of nature. She wished she was out in a tent. She wished a bear would come by; she wanted to see if she could scare it off.

She imagined future people in sci-fi clothing with weird scars on their foreheads, dropping dead from a techno brain plague. She imagined FBI agents kicking down the door, arresting her in her jogging gear, and throwing her into a dark hole for daring to interfere in the efforts of the super-rich to make themselves even richer.

She imagined a bomb. A bomb somewhere far overhead, attached to a little drone cruising serenely in the night sky. She imagined it waiting for its moment to cut loose from its ride, to drift, to aim itself, and then to plummet silently through the air, down, down, down onto the home of Dr. Weldon Qualls, scientific meddler; his collaborator wife; and the notorious anarchist, drunk, and loser Maria Kerrigan. And Lia.

What was it waiting for? What in the goddamned hell was that cruel bomb waiting for?

No sleep.

* * *

Maria let Lia do most of the driving on the way home. Lia was very serious and careful about driving, enough so that more than once Maria cracked: "It's got an engine in it, you're allowed to use it."

"I've never driven a truck before, I don't think," Lia grinned. "The other cars look really small when you're up off the ground like this."

"Well, you're a truck driver now," Maria answered. "That makes you at least one-quarter country."

"What would be next? A hat?"

"Nah, you don't want to be too country," Maria answered, looking off at the horizon. "A little keeps your feet on the ground. Too much stops you from ever going anywhere."

"Were there a lot of country people in Arizona? I mean, it's not the South."

"There are country people everywhere. We had our share. There was this one; oh he thought he was a stud. Wore a big hat, big boots, big belt buckle. Meanwhile he's about as wide as a pencil and he's got acne all over his face. When I was fifteen I thought it was kind of cute, and we did some tonguing by the school pool a few times. He didn't want to be seen with me, though. Said his friends were teasing him, calling him a bean eater. Usual shit: thinks he's tough, but can't even take a little name-calling from his precious buddies."

Lia looked over with a smile. "So what did you do? Smack him around?"

Maria finally looked over. "No, kid. I cried. I felt like I was the smallest little turd of an insect in the world, and he'd just stepped on me. Back then, I didn't fight. There was no point."

Lia's face creased with sadness. "That doesn't sound like you at all. I'm glad you started fighting."

Maria shrugged resignedly. "Yeah."

"Can I tell you something?"

"Sure, fire away."

"You're my hero. You were my hero even before you saved the future."

Maria squirmed in her seat. "Ah, shit, Princess, why do you have to say that?"

"Really. I'm not sure if I can even describe what life was like for me before we met. I was like...like a pinhole. There was only that much of me, and all this nothingness around it. Breathing through a straw, isn't that what they say it's like for people with asthma? I think I know what that's like; only for me it wasn't just breathing, it was everything.

"It really scares me. Like, really, really scares me. To think about how little of me was in there and that I was okay with that. You changed that, because you just fight so much and do so much and don't let anything stop you. I don't know how I got so lucky. But you're my hero."

Maria slumped down and stared at the road ahead. All she could think about was how incredibly wrong Lia was, and how lousy it was that the kid wouldn't be able to handle a truth like that. It wasn't fair.

***

They made it to their little house, but Maria didn't want to go in. She felt like she might never come back out. She saw herself old and grey in there, playing cards with a wrinkly Lia who wouldn't stop telling her how amazing she was.

Lia was already tugging her sad little suitcase up to the porch; she looked back at Maria expectantly. Maria jumped back in the truck. "You go on in. I'm going to head into town for a bit."

"Oh. Okay...have fun."

Maria drove away, not sure what counted as fun anymore, but determined to find out.

***

She smelled cigarette smoke. She heard the jukebox and the clack-rattle of pool balls. It was a real hole of a place to be, which made it perfect. She took the keys out the ignition and went inside.

The atmosphere hit her all at once: a dizzying cloud of sawdust and cheap beer and sad mumbles and lonely assholes biding their time until the desperate hours. Walk into it once and you'd wonder why anyone would ever want to be there. Stay in long enough and you'd forget there was any other place to be. The brightest light in the place was from a grimy antique popcorn machine, with a little clown turning a cylinder of kernels. The poor bastard had probably been at that job for fifty years or more. The woman at the register had leathery skin and tits to the floor.

Maria went for a bowl of popcorn, but didn't sit at the bar yet. She swept back and forth past it in slow steps, like a pacing cat. She had the weirdest feeling, like she should ask them if there was a cot. She felt like she could sleep all night in this place without even asking anyone to quiet down.

She turned and walked to the pool table. The two men playing checked her out with no shyness. She pulled out a twenty and slapped it down on the rail. One of the players, the tall one – he was six-four at least, with a grass patch of gray hair, a big mustache, and a delicate old creak in all his movements – circled around, put down a twenty of his own on top of hers, then dropped the little cube of chalk on top of it to seal the deal. Then he silently nudged her aside with his cue and resumed the previous game.

Maria leaned against the wall and watched, a buzz that drowned out everything else filling her mind. She didn't even need a beer; just being there felt good.

The tall man made short work of his opponent and then stood up straight and silent, waiting. His head was so much higher than the table light, it looked like he didn't even have one: it was just this tall, masculine body gripping a pool cue and fading into nothingness at the neck.

She re-racked the balls. The weight of them in her hands made them feel like weapons. The tall man still didn't move. So she lined up to break, and the game was on.

Maria was rusty, and even when she hadn't been rusty she had always kind of sucked. He took her to pieces, cool and slow. She had only sunk two before he put the eight ball away, stretched up tall again, and folded both twenties into his shirt pocket.

He'd never said a word. Given the girth of his mustache, she couldn't even say for certain he had a mouth. He put his cue back on the wall and strode slowly towards the bar.

She pulled out another twenty and slapped it down. He didn't take the bait. But another guy did, a jagoff with a permanent smirk on his wide, stupid face.

Maria felt a rush of satisfaction, because she knew that on this night it wouldn't take ten minutes before she punched this guy, and that if she was really lucky she'd spend the night in jail over it.

**

-16-

Josh pounded on the walls. He yelled. He sulked. He indulged in silly fantasies of brawling his way to freedom like a game hero punching out A.I. hooligans. Eventually he ate the apple and the nutrient bar. And napped. And peed in a little trash can. None of it changed his circumstances.

He wished he had something to work with. His kingdom for a pencil. A long time later, the door slid open again, and another tray with another glass of water and another nutrient bar was pushed in. This time there was a banana.

Josh had been on exotic holidays to resorts with no network signal. It was now a luxury adventure to find silence, and his fellow travelers had experienced it with all the bemused obtuseness of tourists in a slum. They played at privacy in a world they had assured would have none. But those trips were coordinated, scheduled. There was perpetual activity to drag you away from the gnawing knowledge of silence. This was different; this was absolute lack of stimulus, access, and distraction. Getting punished with this as a kid had nurtured and sharpened Josh's teenage resentment. How dare his parents – how dare anybody – leave him alone with his thoughts?

He imagined Min-Jun sitting in the lotus position in a corner, smiling and relaxed. He didn't think he had ever seen Min-Jun in the lotus position, but that posture – along with big Buddha statues and all that damned tea – lived in the same corner of Josh's brain that Min-Jun did, and sometimes they made strange associations. It was at least a little racist; and that was never fun to know. Maybe it was racist of him, but all stereotypes came from somewhere.

It had been a day or two since his kidnapping, depending on how long he had been unconscious (the phrase "solve for x" floated through his mind, where x represented the time he'd spent drugged). There was no mirror, but his nose told him he smelled ugly. Although he'd never been obsessed with hygiene, he had to admit that a shower and shave would have been amazing right then.

He kept his thoughts light. It was better to be shallow and focus on comforts – to think about one of Min-Jun's miracle baths, or of the indignity of the toilet situation, or the way that couch made his back ache – than think about Cierra. There's no more destructive mental loop than the one inside a parent that says your child may or may not be in danger and there's nothing you can do about it. Those thoughts were horrible, and they would do nothing for him. It felt dangerous to even think his daughter's name, as if that might be all that was necessary for someone to hack the knowledge of her location right out of his brain.

That truth, his share of the responsibility for it, his turn of fortune...no, it was far better to fixate on a bruised banana and the rudeness of his hosts. Since they weren't killing him, why be rude?

**

When Min-Jun and Lia finally made it to the lab, they didn't find Josh. Instead, they were met with blacked-out monitors and halls swept clean of any evidence pointing to where he might of gone...or been taken. The longer they walked the sparkling clean corridors asking other scientists if they'd seen Josh and searching both the obvious and not-so-obvious places where he might have left a message, the sick ball of dread in Min-Jun's stomach grew. Without a way to contact his daughter, work was all Josh had; there was literally no other place in the world Min-Jun could think of where his friend might be. And the painful irony of it all was that the very measures Josh had implemented to keep them safe made it impossible to find out what had really happened while Min-Jun had been in Paris.

For lack of better action to take, Min-Jun showed Lia their section of the lab, with the combination particle accelerator that launched their messages into the past. The block that said *Hello, my friend Josh* was still sitting on the shelf between two orchids where Min-Jun had sent it many months ago. It had been his most sophisticated launch working alone, and he was proud of that no matter how much more radical the work with Josh had become. It also memorialized a moment that he valued greatly: the start of their partnership.

Lia ran her hands over the engraved metal of the original slab, fascinated. "I shouldn't have trusted that marker we found. Maria didn't. Looking back, I can see why. The language just didn't feel right. So curt and dismissive. You and Josh were different: thorough in one way, but very vague in another. Almost poetic. But we rationalized away our doubts because we wanted it to be true."

"Our instincts often yield to our desires," Min-Jun admitted.

"Memory yields," Lia turned and looked at him. "Josh said that, in his speech. The one that lit everyone's hair on fire. 'At last, memory yields.'"

"Wise words."

"A dumb opening," Lia replied. "Josh told everyone in that room up front that they were venal and stupid, himself included. Nobody wants to hear what you say after that. But it's how I first guessed he might be the one behind the messages. He was smart enough, rich enough, he'd had this flash of conscience, and the timing seemed right, what with the Ketron-Garry stuff happening. I did whatever homework I could, but it was still a miracle I turned out to be right. I'm not good at that stuff, and I didn't want to poke around so much that it would look suspicious. Not that there was any reason people would be watching me specifically."

Uncomfortable, Lia turned and fidgeted with the orchid, moving the simple glass vase one way and then the other. "It's weird and I feel like a jerk for even thinking about it, but I wondered if I was...you know...important? I didn't know if any of the people in the future knew that I was helping Maria. Looking back, I'm not sure if I really helped at all. I was trying, but I was pretty messed up back then."

Min-Jun gently moved the orchid aside. "We first just heard about you as the roommate, when Dr. Qualls was giving us general information about Maria to determine if she was reliable. None of us were really sure how to judge, and it seemed as though we were running out of options. So we took her, knowing only that you existed.

"Later, when we were trying to work out a means to alleviate Maria's financial worries, we concocted a method for her to unobtrusively win a million dollars with a lottery ticket. She insisted that it be two million, and said that it wasn't just to take care of her, but to take care of you as well.

"She said she couldn't do this without you."

**

The person on the other side of the door was not who Josh expected to see. He thought he might see Khaslik, or some anonymous flunky. But there she was: Analuiza Gil, one of his former allies and the business partner he'd worked with not only the most, but the longest. While he'd often proven temperamental and mercurial in managing others, she'd been brilliant at managing him, which had probably kept him from bankruptcy at least three times.

He had distanced himself from her the moment he made the speech. He tried to remember the look on her face as he'd bustled off the stage, before she had uttered what he thought would be her last words to him: *good luck.* There had been shock, yes, and confusion too, but those had been on every face in the room. On Analuiza's face, though, he'd thought he'd seen - or maybe he'd just imagined - a flash of a smile. As if to say, *finally, you made a mess bigger than I can keep you out of.*

Josh had prepared a menu of responses and strategies for what might happen when the door finally opened for longer than it took to slip in a meal. They were neatly arranged on a sort of blackboard in his mind, like a flowchart. Analuiza might as well have chucked eggs at his blackboard. The only response he could manage was "What the hell?"

"Oh Josh," she replied. "You should see yourself." The worry on her face scrambled Josh's assumption that he was in the middle of some sinister scenario. This frustrated him, as problems which turned out to have hidden extra layers always did.

"The smell isn't me," he insisted. "Well, not entirely. There wasn't a toilet, so I had to use the trash can. Technically, I guess, it is all me. Are you evil now?"

Analuiza rounded her lips and blew out a column of air. "You made yourself impossible to get a hold of, Josh."

"For good reason."

"I had to take some drastic steps. And when you work with people like the ones I hired to bring you here, they don't always respect schedules...or people. I only just arrived an hour ago. Please, come with me; there's a suite waiting for you where you can clean up."

"A suite? Where am I?"

Analuiza's face tightened. "I'm not going to tell you. Right now, I know you want to escape. I hope; well, I hope if we have time to talk that you'll change your mind."

"About what?"

"About just about everything." She turned and started walking down the corridor. The door stayed open, so Josh followed. She was right, of course. He did want to escape, and walking out the door increased the odds of that.

***

"Can you do it yourself?"

Min-Jun had known the question was coming. As they sat without solace, without a plan, naturally Lia would ask if the one weapon they had could be used.

He looked plaintively at the control panel. "Yes and no. Before Josh arrived, sending that plate over there from the accelerator to that shelf was the height of my abilities. With the algorithms he programmed in, and from my experience watching him on other launches, I'm sure I could do better now. But to send a full message that far back? The odds are infinitesimal."

"Why?"

It was a simple enough question, but took so much answering. Min-Jun did the best he could to explain the restrictions of their process in layman's terms without digging too far into the physics.

"That's why it was always these slabs of metal? So the weight would be precise?"

"Precise, and predictable. Ink evaporates. Wood rots. No organic processes are happening in the metal at a rate that will significantly change its mass before we send it. Also, bacteria won't live on its surface, and even its capacity to hold a static charge has been reduced as far as possible; even a mote of dust won't stick to it."

"But what if we prepared something, and...I don't know, quickly weighed it, and then just sent it off before it could change too much. Clean rooms, right? That's what you call them? Don't you have clean rooms and robot arms? Whatever the coordinates are, you could put rough estimates in, then get the final weight, make your adjustments, and then...then...*bang*, you know?" Lia was becoming excited, pantomiming the process as she imagined it.

"In theory, everything you say could work. But when we're talking about that much time into the past, an error on the level of a millionth of a percent will ensure that the object will never land in this solar system. You have just asked if I can do something many times more difficult than I have ever done before, and now you have asked if, in addition, I can do it while blindfolded and standing on my head. As Josh would say, we need to control the variables."

"Josh isn't here. It's only us. And Maria. Saving her might be the only way to save Josh."

Min-Jun leaned forward, face intensely grave. "Do you know what happens when you change the past? Beyond the security we had to keep, it is one of the strongest reasons Josh and I never solicited help here in our time. When you change the past, whatever life you've lived after that moment, including all the memories of the experiences you would have had after that, is wiped out. We live new lives all the way from the moment of change up until now, and that change cannot be undone. I have never known how to ask someone what I ask you now. If we send something back to your roommate when the stakes are this high, you might not survive until now at all. Are you willing to sacrifice the life you have had since then, entirely, with no knowledge of what life you might live instead, and no promise that you will improve Maria's life at all?"

Lia was quiet for a long time. She seemed to be looking inward. Her lips moved subtly, as if she were talking to herself and making the movement out of instinct. Then her head tilted, she clasped her hands together in her lap, and a vast grief took over her face.

"Some things in the universe make you feel small because they aren't fair, or they have nothing to do with you but you're stuck with the consequences. Things suck and we automatically think, *why is this happening to me?* I guess that's ego. Everybody feels it."

Her face hardened. "This is different, though. It's wrong that she's dead. If we're changing history, going back and forth between that time and now, making it different each time, whatever this is here is wrong. If she's dead, it...it can't be right. This can't be where it all stops. And it's not just my ego talking here. Something is wrong with everything if she dies back then. Does that make any sense at all to you?"

Slowly, Min-Jun nodded. "I have never heard it put in words so well. I am convinced." He sighed and looked back at the control panel. "We must try."

***

Power dinners were Analuiza's forte. Josh had seen her move a half-billion dollars from someone else's column to theirs just through the way she worked a meal. In the same way that some people were seemingly born to throw a football, Analuiza was born to conjure up equal parts charm and power in the way she savored a glass of wine and carved into a fine cut of meat. She could conduct a meal like a battle campaign. Disarming chitchat over salad came first; she saved her cannons of confidence for the first course, a strategy which always shook loose details the other party had sworn they would hold in reserve. The inexorable lean of grave concerns over the other party's demands pressed them out of their trenches during the second course, and, finally, victory came during dessert, followed by a warm celebration of harmony with the newly-conquered over coffee.

So when Josh entered an antique-styled study with a table set for two and saw her seated opposite an empty chair, he knew what was in store for him. He was no longer an ally: he was a battle objective. He had no doubt she would leave the meal with something. His only chance was to figure out what she wanted in advance, and figure out a way to surrender a facsimile she would accept.

"It's good to see you cleaned up, Josh. You cut a dynamic figure when you want to."

Josh wondered if he should simply act insane: start combing his hair with the fork and gibbering about Nazis on the moon. The rules of social custom tilted every contest in the favor of masters like Analuiza: just a few unrefusable requests could cost you everything. Playing the lunatic would certainly disable a few assumptions.

Of course, the time to play crazy would have been before he'd bathed. And Josh still fancied that he could play it straight. He didn't want Analuiza to shut down; he wanted her to tell him what was really going on. So the fork stayed where it belonged and he sat.

"I can see you packed your closer wardrobe. Didn't you wear that bracelet when we landed the North Sea deal?"

She smiled. "It's funny. I rarely remember what I wear, but I always remember what I eat. It was salmon that night, very fresh."

"What's on the menu tonight?"

Her smile grew even wider, and Josh felt like that conveyed the true answer long before she could start talking about food.

***

"In this case, time is not as important as space. It rarely creates a problem if we miss time by a minute or so in either direction. But if the deviation takes us too far away spatially, the whole endeavor is useless. So we must find a space which is as large as possible, but isolated enough that only Maria will find what we send."

Lia had changed into some white, disposable lab clothing that almost caused her to fade into the paint behind them. She was occupying Josh's seat in the cafeteria, but unlike Josh, she was transfixed by the mountains outside.

"I used to be afraid of the outdoors," she said. "I didn't even realize it. The first time Maria took me camping I acted really weird and finally just lost it. I lost it a lot back then. It wasn't the outdoors' fault though, it was the asshole I had been married to.

"I never went skiing. Always kind of wanted to; I think I would have been good at it. Now I've got old bones, and any snow-covered mountain costs more money to get to than I've got."

Min-Jun was patient. In very little time he had sensed both awareness and great intelligence in Lia. She had absolutely heard everything he had said, and understood its importance. Her roundabout path to verbalizing her thoughts was obviously the result of some crucial emotional failsafes she had built. Every person had their own unique, moated fortresses they put between themselves and others. For her to come out to speak at all, he recognized, had not always been possible.

Sure enough, without even looking away from the mountains, she answered him. "I think I know a place. And the message can be small, the smallest message you've ever sent. That will make it easier. Then you'll send another."

"Will I?"

"Yes, the first message only needs to get her off her ass. I already have that one. The second one, the one you'll send to the failsafe location, that's the one you can put details in."

Min-Jun didn't know for sure if it was his contemplative nature which drew out the decisive qualities in others. He could, after all, only live in his own skin. But it did seem that whenever he needed someone around to say what was going to be done, whomever he was with found it within themselves to do it. It had been harder for Lia to make this move than almost anyone he'd met, and Min-Jun took her resolve as a compliment. Her faith in him did a great deal to soothe the sudden terror of the challenge he was about to face.

* * *

-17-

"**I** thought you might like to take a walk. I was going to anyway, and you know, you could come along."

Lia's voice was muffled, partly by the bedroom door and even more by grating uncertainty. Maria was in bed, just dandy where she was, and all Lia's unsubtle concern accomplished was to make her want to burrow further in.

This was a hangover. You think you can remember what they feel like, but then one actually gets you again and you realize that you'd only logged a pale copy of the experience. The night before, it had taken all her time and willpower to hold herself back from buying a beer. She had resisted thoughts of how good the bottle would feel in her hand. She had felt the anticipation of a nice buzz making something like a preview of a real buzz in her mind, and fought it back. She had done so well, and then she had been sitting at a tall table by the jukebox, just working a soda, when someone had sent a shot over. Not a handsome someone, and probably not a nice someone either; just someone. And without even thinking she made up her mind that she was going to take his shot and give him nothing the hell else. That was what led to her first drink in two years.

After that there had been more. She didn't remember where her truck was: she was pretty sure she hadn't driven herself home. All she knew now was that the house was too loud and the sun was an asshole.

"Maybe later, I didn't sleep well," she managed to croak. The bed seemed to be pitching and yawing under her.

"Okay. I can make you something, so let me know if you want anything." Maria kept silent, and, after a few seconds, Lia's feet shuffled away.

Maria groaned. A war was brewing inside her between her need to never move again and her need to drain what felt like a gallon of piss. Lying still was winning so hard right then, and it might keep winning for a truly disgusting amount of time.

**

She tried walking in the snow. The cold air slapped her face red, and after about a quarter-mile she just stopped and heaved. She still couldn't jog. She sat in a snowbank by the roadside for awhile, her head still squeezing like it might pop her eyeballs out from the inside.

She wasn't hearing the Voice. That was a blessing. It hadn't spoken to her since it stopped her from running. She remembered what it said, its claim to be that boy. It was horseshit, clearly; whatever it called itself it was still just a cuckoo Voice in her cuckoo skull and she needed to get rid of it. She had to admit, though, that she would learn to live with it if she could just run again.

She tried calling it out. "Hey there, asshole. Yeah, I'm talking to you."

Silence.

"What, nothing to say? That's funny, you've never been shy before. You've always been a talkative little a-hole." Silence and wind.

"Come on; you can laugh it the hell up now. Maria's off the wagon. Maria's a rich bitch and she's as sad as all the other rich bitches. Come on!" Silence and wind and a car driving by, with the driver throwing a funny look Maria's way.

"Don't tell me you don't hear me!" She stood up now and stamped around in the snow. "Yeah, it's me! I killed you. Me! I don't know who you were. I didn't give a shit. You think I give a shit now? I'm a hero!"

Silence, and wind, and a cop car slowing to a halt. And a boyish young officer with a very concerned look on his face. He even drove her home; a whole quarter-mile.

**

The next time she came out of her room there was a Styrofoam box on the floor outside her door with a whole order of fried calamari in it just for her. If she had seen it a half-hour earlier it would have been puke city. She took it and dragged her feet into the living room.

Lia was bundled up on the couch. The TV lit the room in flickers, playing some channel that was on a pledge break: all people with terrifying grins enthusing in smooth tones about all the wonderful programming they had to offer. Lia was turned away from the screen; she probably just wanted the company of the voices.

Maria fell into the old chair and stared at the screen. She tried to munch on the calamari but it didn't feel so good in her mouth. She reached out to put it on the side table and missed, and it fell onto the floor.

She thought about doing something about that for a minute. Then she just settled back. It was black outside the window, with only a few white flakes dancing by. The voices on TV promised to get back to the show in just a few moments, just a few moments.

* * *

The next day, Maria still felt remote and disconnected.

"Yoush flight here." Albert turned and teetered out of the room, expecting that was all the conversation that needed to happen. When Maria didn't answer, or move, he re-appeared in the doorway and saw her sitting in a chair, looking at the wall and checked way the hell out.

"Hey M'ria," he urged. "'Eysh waiting. You pre-flight?"

Maria stood and marched out, brushing around him, feeling like a sullen kid called to the principal's office. "Yeah, I'm on it, Jesus."

"You, uh, okay?" he asked after her, the almost articulated words sounding alien coming out of his salty old mouth.

"Peachy keen!" she shouted, throwing back a mocking middle finger as she kept walking.

* * *

She conducted most of the lesson in grunts. Whenever her student asked about a component or term, Maria would answer with only the absolute necessary words, usually followed by "steady."

She wanted a bigger plane. She could buy a ticket and ride on one. Fly to every island in Hawaii if she wanted, get a bikini and sit out there with all the other motherhumpers in bikinis. For some reason the idea of riding in a big plane was even more intolerable. She could already feel the useless little seatbelt choking her, could imagine crying kids and stupid movies on a tiny screen, and all on a two-drink limit.

A big plane she could have all to herself and fly; that sounded like the ticket. A 737 started at about eighty million these days. Maria didn't have that, but maybe she would after a weekend in Atlantic City. Maybe she could write to her future friends for some help at roulette. Hey, if they just gave her enough money she could put all the assholes of the world out of business

The sky was lopsided. Maria didn't mind that; it felt appropriate. She was just sliding, sliding along down, a kid going *whee!* on the playground, down the slide towards that little brown patch where what once was grass had been stomped dead forever by thousands of small feet hitting bottom.

She heard a weird noise like choking and saw her passenger with a death grip on the stick, paralyzed with fear, gulping and swallowing and unable to speak as the plane came degree after degree closer to a roll.

Maria took her own stick and righted the plane. Hooray, she'd saved another life. Somehow the boost wore off a little each time she did it.

***

"What are you looking at?" Lia couldn't see the laptop screen from where Maria was seated at the table, but Maria still got irritated and shut her browser window.

"Nothing. Just surfing."

"You weren't clicking the mouse, it looked like you were just staring for a long time."

"You spying on me?"

Sadness took over Lia's face. She wavered where she stood for a moment, engaged in a suddenly fierce struggle over whether to step forwards or backwards. Maria was more than happy to vote for backwards, and Lia seemed to feel that.

Finally, though, she managed to walk forward and sit down opposite Maria. She couldn't say anything, but when Maria looked up to try to glare her away from the table, she was struck by the resolve that had replaced the sadness on her friend's face. Maria realized that Lia would probably let her slit her throat if that's what it took, but she wasn't leaving the table.

Maria lost track of the moment, astonished at her friend, and, for just that moment, aware of how her actions had been affecting those around her.

Outmatched, she relented. "I was looking at the hole in the ground. Where the pipe used to be. The satellite maps changed a couple of days ago; they used to show the construction site, now they show the hole."

Lia made no acknowledgment of the way she had just matador side-stepped Maria's anger. She just answered Maria's admission. "Do you think that might be dangerous? One of my shows says that they always watch the scene of the crime because sometimes criminals are drawn back to it. They might be doing the same thing now, not just in person but online too."

"From everything I've read, they're not even sure it was a crime. I could probably drive down there and write *Maria did it* in the snow and nobody would care."

"I wonder if this house is still here in the future."

"Bet you in a hundred years it isn't."

Lia almost sort of smiled. "Bet in ten years it is."

"Fifty years it isn't."

"Twenty-five it is."

"No way. No way in hell twenty-five."

"Is that the bet? Twenty-five?" There is was: that almost-smile teetering right on the brink of a grin.

"Sure, fine, what the hell. How much?" Maria stuck out her hand to shake.

"How about a million dollars?"

"I don't have a million. Uncle Sam took half of my million and half of yours."

"Okay, I bet you a half-million dollars that this house is still here in twenty-five years."

And just like that, Lia shook Maria's hand. Then, she smiled completely.

***

Maria got fired. Albert looked pretty sad to be doing it; it wasn't as though there were a lot of certified flight instructors among the 16,000-odd souls in Laconia, New Hampshire. But she was drunk enough that he couldn't pretend otherwise. And then there was the matter of the open beer she was drinking from when he confronted her about it.

He didn't say much as she took her last pay in cash and stalked out. He seemed to know that whatever he had to say, it needed to be heard by a healthier her later, or just never spoken.

***

She went home with a guy. His name was Ken or Kyle or some other honky bullshit. She'd never seen him in Finnegan's before, but then she hadn't been in Finnegan's for a while. When he turned on his lamp, she caught a glimpse of his shitpile living room and turned the lamp back off. When he kissed her she bit his lip, laughed at his cry of surprise and then slapped him in the face.

Turned out he didn't have a lot of rough in him. Which was so his loss. She left him sleeping in the bed and stole the lamp on her way out. She rode home in a cab with it, then left it in the middle of the road in front of the house, where it looked goddamned hilarious to her.

＊

Her knuckles abused the door. There was a doorbell, and a little brass knocker too, but she was in a mood, and fist-on-door was the way to express that mood.

Willie opened the door, imperious and grumpy. "Hey. Didn't know you were coming."

"Yeah. Is he here?"

Willie's demeanor changed. Even under her worn out lounge-around-the-house clothes, a bit of professional steel suddenly, visibly, straightened. "He's at work. Because it's daytime."

"Hey, no need for attitude."

"Is that right?" This Willie wasn't friendly, and Maria suddenly felt like a little dog jumping and yipping at a great big dog that was only just tolerating her.

"Look, uh, it's okay he isn't here. I just need to get something."

Willie put a long, conspicuous arm across the door frame. "Something I can find for you?"

"What is this? I've been in there before. I even ate his dumbass chili, am I right?"

Willie raised her eyebrows and chuckled. "I see sick people all the time, and I've got no problem saying things other people won't say. You're drunk, Maria. It's 9:30 in the morning and you're drunk."

"Haven't you heard? I'm part of the leisure class now."

Willie sighed. "Jesus, you drove here, didn't you?"

"Yeah, well, I did most of it yesterday. Stayed at a hotel last night. Did you know that I don't think I've ever stayed in a hotel that wasn't a motel? They gave me a newspaper. And I kind of did an around the world with what they had in the mini-fridge. That was probably expensive, but you only die once, right?"

"I could kick your ass off the curb right from where I'm standing, but now I'm double-sure you shouldn't be driving around." Willie shook her head, fuming. "I'm going to put you in our bedroom, and you don't come out of there for six hours, you understand? Then I'm going to look you in the eyes, and if you've got your brain back you can talk to my husband when he gets home. But if you don't, then I'm going to kick your ass with interest."

Maria snorted and saluted Willie, who practically dragged her into the house and shut the door. Two hours into Maria's six-hour assignment, she broke the bedroom window and left.

***

She didn't know much about New Jersey, but little towns were the same everywhere. She killed some time at a gas station, burning through a pile of lottery scratchers and glaring at anyone who approached. She bought some cheap but gaudy sunglasses that didn't do anything against the pounding in her head.

Wandering the sidewalks, she found a park with a little frozen-over pond and a couple of kids practicing their ice hockey skills. She was overcome with the urge to coach them, and stumbled out onto the ice, waving and shouting something incomprehensible. The little assholes ran, and pretty soon she fell on her fat butt and lay there, looking up at the gathering clouds.

The dirty orange of a winter afternoon sky was disappearing into a deep, sad gray that seemed to cover the land and every person she passed. She tried to tell one of them a joke and it didn't go well; she wasn't good at jokes even when she was dry. A guy offered her a ride somewhere and told her he could help her with some money. She threw a rock at him and shouted that she was a millionaire from the future. He drove away, shouting back at her that she was a crazy bitch.

Crazy Bitch, she thought to herself. That's my superhero name. *Look! Up in the sky! It's Crazy Bitch!*

She found an empty lot with a useless, beat-up fence around it and snuck in. All this piss in her and not a bush around. What the hell, it was dark. She shimmied down her jeans and squatted in the dirt.

A big, bright, stupid light hit her in the face. She squinted at it, more confused than surprised. "What's up?" she called out to it.

A smaller light joined the big one, a bobbing little light that danced up and down. Then she heard feet on the dirt. And a voice. "Excuse me, ma'am?"

Maria chuckled at being called ma'am with her drawers down. The last person who did that was probably the doc who did her Air Force physical. "Call me sir, cadet!" she barked, laughing and aiming her middle finger at the little light.

The voice mumbled something and she heard a squawk of static. Then it piped up again for her to hear. "Ma'am, this is private property, and you're trespassing."

"Doesn't that mean you're trespassing too?"

"Ma'am, I'm a police officer. You look like you could use some help."

"Help? No, no, you got it backward. I help. People say 'Maria, help,' and I do it. I help. 's my job. Not anymore, though. I retired."

She finished her piss just as the cop loomed over her. "Enjoying the show?" she asked.

"Ma'am, I'd like to see some I.D."

She scrambled to her feet and punched him. Suddenly there were more footsteps and a lot more lights. Swirling, colored ones. Maria was in no mood for colors and swirls.

They shouted at her and threw her on the ground. She shouted back, just a dung salad of everything she'd ever heard back at Lackland.

As they hoisted her and carried her towards the car, she saw the vacant lot illuminated. She saw a line of dead and blackened trees. She saw the giant hole in the ground. Her head lolled deliriously as she looked around further. Oh yes, she had been here before.

She stopped shouting and started cackling. She got her mighty legs under her and started jumping off the ground, straining against their grip, bloodying her wrist on the cuffs. "The scene of the crime!" she bellowed hysterically. "Take her away, boys! She's at the scene of the crime!"

They stuffed her in the back of a police car. It was nice to lie down.

**

There was a blurry night in lockup and then a blurry arraignment. Maria was dry but she wasn't sober. Words spoken to her came in and out of focus, usually failing to pierce the hot red buzz banging inside her skull. She didn't use her phone call. They told her that in light of a first offense and in light of her meritorious service to her country and in light of her willingness to plead and in light of whole lot of other blah-blah-blah she was going to get ninety days plus rehab, and that sounded okay once the dweeb in a suit finished suggesting it to her. Dweebs in suits tended to know more about this stuff than she did. She was suddenly paranoid about anybody learning she was rich. If she was lucid for longer than a few minutes, she usually just said "I don't have any money."

About three days in, sealed into a boring-as-shit white room that made her think of a walk-in fridge – the faker didn't even have the decency to have bars – real quiet started to take hold. That's when she started kicking at the walls, puking into the little cold toilet, and raising hell. Not with the guards; her respect for the uniform was coming back. But when she was alone Maria would howl for lost moons. Her cellmate requested a transfer PDQ.

From the moment her cellmate left and they didn't give her another, she didn't sleep at all, and each night felt like a year. She imagined she could feel her hair growing while she lay there. She tried scratching herself with her nails, trying to draw blood over nothing but cold-ass boredom. She fantasized about turning into a wolf, loping through the woods and mauling anything that looked cross-eyed at her.

About sixty hours into sleeplessness she was crying about the future. She hadn't asked anything about it, and at first had decided that was because she'd see it when it came around. But then, in the hold of the darkness, she realized that it was just the opposite. She hadn't asked because it wouldn't matter. There was no way she would ever live to see it.

She wondered how long she'd been expecting to die. Ever since Lackland, maybe. Maybe even before, when she'd heard about her brother. You couldn't forget about Death after something like that. In her teenage years she'd tried running away from Death: hiding from shame and confrontation, being extra cautious about everything. Then when she got in, she'd expected it to come for her any given day of Texas sweat and delirium. Maybe she'd excelled there because she truly didn't expect to live through it anyway.

Suddenly she knew something; understood it in a way that neither she nor any Air Force shrink nor priest ever had. And she had nobody to tell about it. The one she wanted to tell most was the Voice, but it still hadn't returned.

***

At ninety hours of no sleep, she was pacing her cell. Maybe she'd tunnel her way out this way. She laughed aloud at the thought, and the sound echoed bloodlessly back at her.

Suddenly her toe hit something that skidded away from her foot. She knelt on the ground and groped around in the dark, confused. She'd paced her cell a few hundred times without kicking anything at all. There wasn't anything to kick.

Her hands found a small wooden box that hadn't been there the moment before. A box that couldn't possibly have slipped into the room through any vent or crack in the door.

They'd found her. The bastards had found her.

The lights were out, so she couldn't see any details on it. So she set it on the bed, sat cross-legged by it, and stared until the guards ordered the lights on.

There were no words on it, no code, and it wasn't made of the strange future metal. It was just a featureless little hinged box. Maria opened it.

Inside was a small piece of colored cloth and ribbon. The ribbon was red, with two sets of vertical stripes, dark blue inside light blue. The medal itself was in the shape of a compass rose, elaborately etched, with two overlapping triangle shapes imitating a six-pointed star.

In those details it could belong to any of tens of thousands of officers. It wasn't a particularly special medal. But Maria knew it. She knew the place where it had frayed, knew the stain spot that marred the light blue stripe on the left side. What's more, she knew the effort that had gone into earning it: an honor few other drone pilots received. It had involved extra workouts, extra training, repeated petitions. This one had mattered to Maria. This was her medal. The one that said *Combat Readiness*.

One she had sold to help them make rent.

They'd found it. Of course they could do that: they could do all sorts of things in the future. Things like know she was going to be here in jail, alone in a cell; a place where they could send a message that no one could see.

But it had to be a secret message all the same, impossible for anyone to understand. Anyone but Maria.

She had her orders, loud and clear.

***

-18-

Analuiza's greatest asset was her confidence. *With my business savvy and success,* it said, *would I ever back a losing horse?* As the meal wore on, though, Josh began to sense a trend behind her smooth delivery: she was sticking strictly to the surface of the issue, avoiding technical details as much as possible.

In other words, Analuiza wasn't making her own pitch.

So Josh waited for the rudest moment to interrupt her, and then redirected the conversation as bluntly as possible. "This is Khaslik, isn't it? You're working for him?"

Analuiza cleared her throat slightly. It was a heck of a poker tell, but one she covered so quickly that only someone as familiar with her mannerisms as Josh would have caught it. Off-balance, she slipped into one of her strongest modes: calculated candor. "That was obvious, wasn't it? Look at it from my perspective. There's something happening here that I really believe in. I believe it's important, that it will help people, and that the only person who can get it done is you.

"Do you know how long you've been railing about Khaslik?" Analuiza cast her eyes up at the ceiling and sighed, which was a lovely detail. "As long as I've known you. I don't know if it's some kind of projected guilt, but nothing puts your walls up faster than the mention of his name, and it was just too important that I at least get you into a conversation before that happened."

"Okay, so you've fed me and you've flattered me. Do I have to wait until dessert to find out what you two want with me?"

"Josh," she paused before a bite, letting something on the end of her fork drip as she regarded him, "you really do look different. We worked together for so long that I didn't notice all the little changes, but now that you've been away, I can see it all over you. You're an adult now, Josh, not a child genius anymore, so negotiating with little tantrums just doesn't suit you. Not at all." And then she crunched back into her food.

Josh didn't reply. He felt the pressure in the room, the way she had preemptively cast this move on his part as its own sort of tantrum. There was no question she was better at this game than he was. But so far, that fact hadn't been a problem.

"Josh," Analuiza continued, "you've known me to been tenacious, and sometimes secretive. But have I ever told you an out-and-out lie?"

"No, no you haven't," Josh said, dutifully providing the answer in her sales script.

"Then know this: Mr. Khaslik's organization did approach me, after your speech. They showed me some proprietary data, stuff that could cost them billions. It was a great gesture of trust. And the conclusions they've come to are every bit as startling and urgent as what you're proclaiming, only they show something completely different.

"Ketron-Garry is not a plague: it's an awakening."

Josh nodded; the attack on his network had given him a sneak preview of this argument already, one that may have been designed to soften him up for this very moment through a kind of implanted confirmation bias. "Evolving, not dying. That was you guys, right?"

Analuiza nodded, candor still fully engaged. "Yes, we hoped you might do your own research into the idea, but you stayed committed to your insane mission."

"It's a theory. A rhetorically appealing one. Certainly a convenient one for Khaslik. How comfortable are you with the murders he's committed using this," Josh mimed air-quotes, "'great awakening'?"

Analuiza shook her head and used her best look of disappointment. Then she went back to darting her fork around her plate. "I asked him about that the first time we met. Your assassination virus is a theory, too, isn't it? I mean, you've tied together a whole lot of stories from the news in a very thrilling way, but you've never proven anything beyond your own paranoia.

"But he took the accusation seriously when I put it to him. So he showed me something." With impeccable timing – Josh didn't even know how she'd signaled for it – an underling brought in a pad and presented it to Josh.

"The room is network-shielded," she continued, "but everything you'll want to see is on the in-drive."

Josh expected the worst. A picture of Min-Jun lashed to a torture table. Cierra...anything involving Cierra. What he found instead were equations. The surprise was so disabling that he found himself absorbed despite himself. He scrolled through pages and pages of numbers and symbols and lines of code. Even someone of his expertise couldn't see the intent of the language just from looking at it from this perspective, and yet it fascinated him, the way an art connoisseur might enjoy just ignoring the whole picture to concentrate on the brush strokes for a little while.

His finger started to trace interesting bits. "Can I...?"

Analuiza finished his thought. "A simulator is loaded on the pad. Play with it any way you like." The same underling came back with a luxurious old coffee pot. He filled Analuiza's cup, and she settled back, sipping with deadly patience.

After who knew how long – two cups of coffee, drunk slowly – Josh looked up with a face scrunched in frustration. "It's nothing. It's a dead end. You can push it any which way and nothing coherent comes out. What the hell is it? You want me to try to fix it? Because I'll tell you right now I can't. It's a mutant kludge-baby descended from three generations of kludges before it, masquerading as some kind of obsolete delivery protocol. It's sprawling, Swiss cheese, totally useless."

"That's what you see?" she asked. Her cup was poised near her lips, and every part of her radiated anticipation.

"Is there something else I should be seeing?"

"Funny, they say a parent can always recognize their child. Josh, that kludge you describe is your virus."

Josh's eyes locked back down on the pad, and he zoomed out so no individual piece of code could be read by human eyes. He looked at the thing as a whole, as if he might recognize its shape like a portrait in silhouette. This would never work, but no rational reaction had occurred to him in the shock of the moment.

"I'll make it easy for you. There's an option to swipe it back one generation at a time. Try that."

Gradually, Josh stripped away layers of code, detached routine patches, searching for something that he hadn't seen since he first crafted it in an intoxicated haze. Several steps before he reached 1.0, he started to recognize it as his own: gawky; wildly ambitious; built on great, gaping presumptions and unresolved conflicts...but revolutionary in potential. Here was a better portrait of Josh's adolescent self than any school photo could hope to present, all bounding ambition and wild, egoist vision.

Analuiza continued. "That's the great, killer mind virus that the brilliant young Josh Scribner created, which was then stolen by a young Spartak Khaslik. I gather he wanted to buy it from you but he had suffered a financial setback. But even if he didn't give you money, you robbed him blind, as it turned out. This is your concept plotted and permuted out as far as the best minds on Earth, besides your own, could take it. He made a very expensive industry out of trying to develop this concept, because he believed in you and in his younger days he thought it could be useful. I'm under no illusions that he's ever been a saint, but he's been legitimate for a long time, and it has softened him.

"Of course, I don't understand any of the technical side, but Khaslik told me that I wouldn't need to; that once you saw it you would understand. It doesn't work. It never did."

Josh stood awkwardly. "I think I'd like to lie down. I haven't been sleeping well."

Analuiza showed perfect concern and compassion. "Of course. Thank you for coming this far with me, for being willing to participate. I know how difficult it must have been for you. Take the pad with you, if you like."

***

He was lost, without bearings. The dinner had been a rout: Analuiza had given nothing away, and had dismantled all his mighty assumptions along the way. Despite his fatigue he spent three more hours examining the extrapolation of his virus, checking the work every step of the way, looking for unexplored paths or signs of fakery. He couldn't find any. There was no way to know for certain – he would have needed months of time and massive computing power to simulate it all from scratch – but it certainly seemed that the assertions Analuiza had puppeted were true: that Josh had never created a virus at all.

It was a strange thing to reconcile. On one hand, a great burden of guilt had been lifted from his shoulders, one he had carried so long that he'd forgotten what it was like to live without it. On the other, he couldn't deny there was a strange element of wounded pride. Coming up with a world-changing idea on a stoned whim was part of the private legend Josh lived with, an anecdote that helped him define his greatness. Although the use of such a power made him recoil, the God-like nature of the power was too alluring to not take credit for.

Had that been what drove him in his crusade? The need for the great conspiracy to be true because at the heart of it was a confirmation of Josh's own genius? What other surprises did they have for him?

He realized the danger of his position a little better now. He had never been good at taking comfort or reassurance from other people, and now he felt more exposed than ever, and had no one around he truly trusted. He, Josh Scribner, was in the midst of being hacked, and on one level of consciousness he could see it all happening. He was vulnerable now: to new suggestions, new frameworks, new instructions. What he had known before was, in the coldest language, no longer operative.

Finally he slept, and he dreamed. He saw a city emerging from a rip in space, a scar among the stars. That wound was the foundation, and skyscrapers extruded from it as though invading. They pushed further and further into the universe. Josh's vision zoomed in and around them, glimpsing people moving at blinding speed, flowing around the city system like electrons through wires. Up to the tops of buildings, down again, and all around the floating city.

Lamps switched on and off in windows, whole buildings flickered bright and dark on cycles, days seeming to pass in seconds. *The people make the lights,* Josh thought. It was an obvious observation, and yet it thudded at him, refusing easy dismissal, suggesting deeper meaning. The people make the lights. The speeding, luminescent cycles rippled; the lights were a traveling pulse, in some ways predictable but infinitely variable in the details, and always evolving. The second cycle was very much like the first. Ten cycles along, you could barely recognize how the initial pattern was connected.

The buildings grew further and further. They strained their dimensions, becoming strangely fat, obscenities against architecture. They twisted, bent, crashed through each other; incredible progress was becoming incredible obliteration. And yet in that black vacuum it looked silent and serene, no more shocking than any other natural inevitability.

The lights kept flashing on and off, but faster now, brighter. They made a frantic visual music as the great metropolis moved towards its final collapse.

Josh tried to take control of his movements. If he could circle the city, he could swoop amongst its towers. He could catch the fallen like a superhero, wrench the towers out of each other's way. But he had no command. He hovered in the blackness, just watching; the whole industrious endeavor was being sucked back into the place it had emerged from.

Josh strained to feel fear for the people he had glimpsed inside the system, but he couldn't find it. And yet he did have *a* fear, one that was familiar, but that he'd never acknowledged. A feeling he'd never considered to be a feeling at all because it had fused itself so deep in his core that he'd never seen it as separable from his essential self.

The fear was not what would happen to everyone else, but that he wasn't a part of it. He wanted to be sucked in, even to be destroyed if that's where humanity was headed. If the choice were put to him, he knew what he wanted: death, death over being a lonely observer in the void. But he couldn't go, and he was doomed to be apart.

He woke up from the nightmare feeling better rested than he had in months.

***

A man and a woman sat in separate rooms, divided by a wall. They wore identical medical scrubs, and their heads had recently been shaved. Each room had sparse but quality furnishings, books, puzzles, and controls to play music. There were also supplies of food and water, and a private area for toilet needs. Both rooms could be observed through a single, wide pane of one-way glass.

The man and woman didn't utilize any of the provided entertainment. Instead, they made faces. The woman paced her room while the man just sat in a chair, but both appeared to be going through the same process of spontaneous reactions to...what?

"They look like they're in a conversation," Josh muttered in the dim observation room. The exit door was unguarded;

an unnecessary courtesy. Part of Josh still wanted to escape, but he was curious to know whether the situation called for escape, or sabotage from within. For that, he needed more information. And, if he was honest with himself, he also wanted to know what the hell was going on.

Analuiza smiled. "They are. They're talking to each other." This snapped all the behavior into focus. The reactions on the subjects' faces were playing off each other: a disarming smile producing a warm softening of the facial muscles; perplexed interest turning into mutual delight. It moved faster than a normal conversation would, and seemed far more intense, judging by the shameless gyrations of expression they were each displaying.

It was mesmerizing. For a few minutes, Josh could do nothing but take it in, insatiably curious about how the conversation might be translated into words, if that were even possible. Another part of him was envious of the experience, of this new form of intimacy. Conversation fully-consummated, mentally.

Josh leaned in closer to the glass, studying their faces. "I see a scar on him. They've both got Beetles implanted?"

The glass was powered for display. Analuiza summoned patient profiles for both the man and the woman, and then slid them towards Josh with a flick of her finger. "Have a look for yourself."

Josh paged through the records. Some of it was medical jargon, but he understood the broad strokes. "They were Ketron-Garry patients."

"Yes, both in middle-phase, when the medications can't tamp things down anymore. They were unable to work, and looking at a short and horrendous downward spiral. They sought out Beetles because of the...folkloric belief that they could help."

Josh threw a dark look at her. She continued: "They do, you know. They provide stability, a slowing of symptoms, increased quality of life. But then something else happened with these two, and only these two. They started talking with one another, Beetle to Beetle, mind to mind. You're looking at living proof of your wildest theories, right here."

The man made a playfully stern look. The woman stopped pacing and her mouth rounded and expanded in a silent, joyous laugh.

"What are they saying to each other?" he wondered aloud.

"We ask them to keep journals and report on the conversations. What we get back is always vague, cursory."

"Words can't capture it."

"Naturally. Or it's possible they can't even recall the ins and outs of these conversations via normal memory. We're talking about very, very new uses for neurons here."

"It's funny," Josh mused. "I think when people speculate on telepathy, there's always this fear that the other person will see your dirty secrets, your darkest impulses...that any true glimpse of another person would be repulsive."

Analuiza shrugged. "If two people get naked in a room, they're tense, they fear judgment. Fifty people naked in a room are just people, flaws and quirks and all. None of us are totally free of darkness in our natures, but our minds are alive, we can drive them; that creates our personalities. I think they're getting a much richer version of what we already sense from gestures, humor, style, etcetera. Pure personality."

"Minds want to connect." Josh remembered the words he'd used to sum up both his speech and the perils and possibilities of it all. "So is the spigot open all the time? Are they just linked for life now?"

"We don't believe so; or rather, they seem to have ways to withdraw from each other. Watch." She brought up a command menu on the glass and pressed something. A chime rang in the woman's cell and she responded to it. A look flashed across her face, which the man answered with a nod. Josh realized how quickly he could find analogues for these looks. The woman's was uncannily like *sorry, I have a call.*

She approached an intercom, and said "*Oui?*" Her voice was pleasant but flat, and her face had ceased its delirious show of feelings.

Analuiza spoke a bit with her in French, then bid her a pleasant day. The woman stretched out her arms, looked around the room, and then tilted her neck in a particular way. The man decidedly "heard" it, and, with a relieved grin, resumed their "conversation."

"She's French?" Josh asked.

"From Africa, actually," Analuiza answered. "And he's from Germany." She smiled at the chance to share a truly killer detail. "They don't speak a word of each other's language."

Josh's voice was quiet with captivation. "Of course: linguistic forms are culturally imposed. They shape thoughts but can't fully define them. How many others have you found like this?"

"These two are the only ones we know of. They could be one in ten thousand, could be one in a million. Their brains just...found each other. They were separated by two floors in the medical clinic, had never seen each other face to face as far as we can tell. And they started talking anyway.

"And the more they talked, the healthier they got. Look at the records."

Josh obeyed and paged through report after report, including video supplements. The patients in the videos were miserable, plagued with tremors, without equilibrium; nothing like the joyous pair in front of him.

"Ketron-Garry is the adaptation process," he said, finally accepting the idea but putting it in his own words. "It's cultivated by signals put out by the Beetles, but it's not...my God, the capacity this suggests..."

"With the Beetles to regulate the process, these two have made a leap. All the data in the brain of one is available to the other: images, sensations, even things like if the other's heart is beating too quickly. And, it does appear that some privacy and concealment is possible; something that could be developed further, with practice.

"And you want to know the really stupefying thing?" She dangled the question just at the moment Josh found the answer in the records. He scanned the page twice, and then stared at the subjects in front of him, absolutely agog.

"You took them out?"

"Yes. We deactivated hers for diagnostics: as you can imagine, we were seeing whole new categories of signals and we couldn't tell if it was malfunctioning. Sometimes it seemed like it was spontaneously switching itself off, letting go like something vestigial. And nothing changed, they carried right on conversing. He even helped us monitor the surgery; he could report what her body and brain were experiencing even while she was under anesthesia.

"Once we found that they could converse without hers, we deactivated his as well, purely for experimental purposes. They never needed them again. We took them out, the connection remained, and they haven't shown a trace of Ketron-Garry since. Their evolution finished."

"So the process is underway. All over the world it's underway." For a few moments, all thoughts of time travel were ejected from Josh's mind. They were like an old car he'd used for so long that he could only see its flaws and difficulties, whereas this new circumstance – this new mountain of revolutionary, powerful data that so few people in the world would know how to climb – it stimulated everything in him, including (most dangerously, he knew) his pride.

Could the process be refined? Disciplined? How could people be screened for compatibility? Was his Brain Alphabet truly universal, or did it differ along the genetic spectrum?

He was seduced for longer than he was proud of. And then he spoke a number. "Five million. We passed that...casualty milestone with Ketron-Garry last month, I think. So at best, at *best*, right now you've got two miracles and five million dead bodies. It isn't like you to rationalize something like that, Analuiza. Not at all."

"Nobody knew what was happening at first, Josh. Not even you. But you said it yourself: the process is underway. Like when the oceans started to rise...you can't put it back. People are dying, and they will keep dying. But this is the real answer as to why. And with this answer, we can save more lives. Guide the process. Steer the human race towards connection and healing.

"Or, we can try to buy back and deactivate every Beetle, stop the signal in its tracks, and treat every Ketron-Garry case conventionally. I assume you've seen the mortality figures on that approach?

"You know people, Josh. We don't move back. We move forward. The only question is where are we going, and how will we get there? With you, we'll get somewhere better, and more of us will reach that destination. And that – in answer to the question that's been on your lips since you saw me here – is the message I am here to convey."

Josh wiped away all the files and formulae that had littered the glass since they had begun talking. Instead, he watched the German man and the African woman in their respective rooms, making a mockery of the drywall that separated them. The man had a jigsaw puzzle open and was just running his fingers around the cardboard edges of one piece. Her fingers were rubbing together in the adjoining room, but doing what? Experiencing the touch with him? "Seeing" the shape of the piece and assisting him to find its place in the big picture? No one but these two would ever know.

***

Josh tried the door to his quarters. It was unlocked. A guard stood outside but didn't react. Why would he need to? In essence, he was a prop, a display of authority, like the guards outside Buckingham Palace. Josh had other eyes on him, and if he did something prohibited, more people than that single guard would probably get involved.

The guard didn't move as Josh tentatively stepped out into the hallway. He had some real freedom, then. The door to the outside would be another matter, but it wasn't his immediate goal. If they intended to make him feel free and comfortable, he would take their hospitality.

He paced the hallways, looking for anything useful. The complex was clearly enormous, well equipped, and technologically advanced. Josh knew a few things about Khaslik's business holdings, enough to guess at two sites this might be. Of course, Khaslik did have a gift for hiding things. He had kept something very big hidden, and perhaps even Analuiza didn't know about it.

He started to build a map in his mind; the building was hardly maze-like with dedicated attention. Josh counted every footfall and didn't try a single door, not yet. If he had hallway access, he was going to get the most out of it before trying anything else.

On the "west" side of the compound – Josh had set his first direction as "north" and oriented from there – he found the longest hallway, nearly a quarter-mile from end to end. One end of it had a door set in the narrow face, suggesting passage into another corridor or area of the compound. At the other end, a door was set off the side, suggesting a room within that compound.

Josh knocked on this door. No one answered. The door was code-sealed, but not sealed enough. He convinced it to open, entered and found exactly what he'd expected to find.

Now the alarms sounded.

* * *

The meal this time was breakfast, in Josh's quarters. Analuiza looked less carefully assembled. It had a funny resemblance to intimacy, the two of them sharing a meal here. Josh knew by her appearance, though, that he had upset the agenda.

"Did you know?" he asked, "That Khaslik reproduced the accelerator setup from Villigen?"

"How did you find it?" she countered.

"The first accelerator, the one that initiates the process, is linear. I just looked for a long hallway. Still a bit of a lucky guess, since you could have run it perpendicular between labs over open ground, but Khaslik's not much of an "open ground" kind of guy. Plus, I knew there was something to find. How much mucking around has he done in the past?"

"You're talking about something I'm not privy to now. I was just briefed on it."

"You were briefed? So he doesn't want to talk to me?"

"Josh, I'm here as the best qualified person on the planet to broker an understanding between the two of you. I'm trying to save lives too, while you still seem to be treating this as some chess match between continent-sized egos."

"I'm still waiting to know what the job is. I've heard a lot of vague appeals to compassion for the human race, and not a lot of specifics."

"I wasn't going to be the one to give you specifics, but you've changed the timetable."

"Cute expression." Josh watched as Alauiza, flustered, knocked over the salt shaker. "That's bad luck, you know."

"Five million dead. You spit that number at me yesterday when you were throwing over a decade's worth of trust and partnership between us under the bus and accusing me of turning overnight into some genocidal ice queen. My understanding was always that Khaslik was seeking you out to reduce the number of future dead. But that's not it anymore.

"From five million dead to zero. That's the job only you can do." Analuiza straightened up and smoothed away a strand of hair, sensing her recovery. "In the world we're living in now, the human race is taking this journey, but no one knows how many of us will make it. Maybe a billion will die. Maybe more. Maybe the two we have here are the new Adam and Eve. The first human trial of a Beetle happened in

2020. Imagine if they knew then what we know now? Imagine if you, when you were developing the Brain Alphabet, knew that the brain was going to respond in this way. You could refine the device, increase its field-amplifying potential. Shepherd people to the end without Ketron-Garry clipping short so many lives.

"Khaslik has been able to send things back, yes, but with nowhere near your precision and sophistication. Only you can summarize the data and figure out how to get it into the right hands: your own."

Josh looked down, feeling heavy. Her argument held together impeccably. Here was the ultimate Josh Scribner problem, more complex and potentially miraculous than any she had ever brought him in their business career. And yet he still thought he could pull it off. He thought about that phrase she had thrown at him: continent-sized ego. It wasn't a lie, and she'd just given that ego the precise stroke it most longed for in the world.

"It will be the single greatest thing anyone has ever done for the human race," she said quietly. Josh looked up and saw hints of desperate urgency all over her; in the way she gripped her fork, in the way her breath was held waiting for his response. But in the end, it was the fact that she'd said anything at all that gave it away. It wasn't her style to make an extra push.

So he went with his gut.

"No."

Analuiza shed the first tear he had ever seen grace her eyeball. "Don't, Josh, don't. Think about everything I said, the opportunity..."

"I'm not arguing, Analuiza, I am telling you my decision."

The door hissed open. Analuiza jumped to her feet, throwing up her arms. "No, don't, give me time...please!"

It was the last thing Josh heard before the guards reached him, and he felt that prick at his neck again. Whatever they used, it worked quickly.

***

Josh woke up in a strange delirium, one both familiar and totally new. Fatigue pressed him into whatever bed he was resting on: he felt three times as heavy as usual. And yet, with the limited awareness he had, he seemed to be taking in a vast and overwhelming spectrum of sensations. The regular air, to his nostrils, tasted like the crisp and heady air on a mountaintop. It was more than a little like what THC had done to him back in his pre-parenting days; amplifying everything while taking the tiny but fierce limits of consciousness off-line.

His heart beat, and he felt it intensely – *BOOM* – like his whole left side might jerk forward from the concussive force of it. Had he thought all that in one heartbeat's time? How fast was time moving right now?

He had the strangest sense that he might even be moving backwards in time. Memories that had been stuffed in old drawers were coming back, cycling past his mind's eye like flash cards. This rain of recollections rushed like new water into an old dry bed of land, remaking a river as it went.

This was no way to wake up from being drugged. Josh thought – *I should be groggier than this.* Then, with that thought, he dialed into the weight of his limbs, their sluggish response, and then realized – *I am groggy. Something else is happening.*

One of his hands was hooked up to an I.V. drip. He let that one lie. The other arm he lifted, and even that motion had subtleties he had never noticed: skin stretching and sliding at the knuckles of his fingers, fabric brushing the hairs on his arm.

He touched his leg, his chest, his neck, his cheek. Everything felt, for lack of a better description, exaggeratedly normal. There was a painful throb in his forehead; when he'd first woken up, he'd assumed it was from the knockout concoction Khaslik's men had stuck him with once again, but when his fingers touched the skin above his nose, the pain nearly shut him down completely.

His head was injured. He'd been cut there. He felt a rough, fibrous bandage covering something.

He probed more carefully, wincing from the pain. It wasn't a wound, it was an incision. There was only one procedure Josh knew of that involved an incision in that spot.

The door opened, and there was Spartak Khaslik. Josh knew the face: the neat, flat brown hair combed down conservatively; the round and perpetually-youthful face that seemed at rest to take the shape of a smile that made you want to back away. For over a decade Josh had seen that face from a thousand angles: watched it grin in triumph, or furrow with sorrowful thought while giving testimony, or simply look disdainfully down and away while tromping off to some new conquest. In all that time, though, he had never been in the same room as the man. Khaslik looked taller than Josh had imagined, but with the way his senses were spiking like a speaker about to blow out, who knew what that meant. The man might be four feet tall but just look like a giant to Josh's new, forcibly enhanced brain.

"You know what I have done to you?" Spartak whispered, perversely affirming Josh's new sensitivity even in this detail. He could hear the man as clearly as if he'd been right next to his ear. Josh slowly nodded.

"Good. Analuiza did persuade me that she could win you over, but really, I was never comfortable with her approach. This...this is what has always worked for me."

He raised his voice, giving it a timbre that echoed through Josh's mind as if he were inside a piano. "Josh Scribner, I dare say you are about to be the most brilliant man in human history. And you work for me, or you will die."

***

-19-

It was day sixty-three. She was getting out tomorrow. Sixty-three plus one didn't equal ninety, but they had credited her time for good behavior. Maria laughed at the insane definition of good behavior they must have needed to concoct to get her the hell out of their prison.

She paced the perimeter of the exercise yard. She didn't have any companions; the few women she'd come to know weren't people she ever wanted to know past tomorrow. They had given her perspective on what crazy really was. All she had was an imaginary voice. That was kindergarten stuff. One woman had told her that Wolverine lived in her garage. Not the actor who played him in the movies: the actual comic book character Wolverine. She had stolen a whole lot of prescription drugs and was, appropriately, a cutter.

Every day since the medal had appeared Maria had walked the yard. Regardless of the winter weather, she marched around that rough square watching other women pump weights, play basketball, or just loiter on their chosen turf. Everyone knew she was just a tourist, so no one was too invested in her solitude; it didn't threaten anybody.

She was fifteen pounds lighter than when she'd come in, by her guess. She bundled on every layer of clothing she was allowed, and would walk until her whole body steamed. She felt the poison oozing out her pores, felt her mind sharpening and re-awakening.

She had time to feel shame, and anger. Sleep still came with difficulty as she brooded on the pain she had sown among the few people in the world she called friends. Every time her temper swelled thinking about it, she did pushups until she collapsed.

She had sent Lia a postcard so the kid didn't explode from anxiety. Lia had written back every day since. She shared news about the weather, and the Christmas lights on their street, and about how much she liked her new heavy coat. She talked about the squirrels fattening themselves against the winter, and about how proud she was at shoveling snow off the porch all by herself. At the end of every letter, she closed by saying that she would be there the day Maria was out. The poor Princess even apologized for not visiting sooner, saying that the place made her too nervous.

At night in her cell, Maria found that the Voice had rejoined her, and was less of a jerk than it had been. It would visit, they would talk, it would leave, she would sleep.

"I wanted to tell you something," she said one night.

Is that right?

"I never thought it was fair. Deep down. Getting to just kill with a button like that. Which is weird, because the Air Force doesn't fight a lot of fair fights. But a pilot at least, she's out there in the air. You tag the plane, you get the pilot. From where I was sitting, no one was ever going to get me, never. Part of me wanted the other side to just get a free shot at me. I'd stand up on a hill somewhere waving Old Glory and they could throw a bomb and we'd just let God decide what happened then.

"I get it; I get why it's not fair. Unfair fights mean more of us come home alive. That's how officers are supposed to think. Generals, presidents. I never had the knack for that, though; I just became an officer because that's what it took to fly."

Are you saying it's their fault for giving the order? That all you did was mindlessly pull a trigger?

"No. I know what I did. But you know, your parents put you in that house. They were making bombs and strapping them to people and blowing up my brothers and sisters, and yours too, and they thought putting themselves in a house with kids around made them safe. That's about as much as they valued you, kid: as a symbol to make other people look bad."

Lot of blame to go around.

"You're not kidding. We made a lousy world and you didn't get to stay in it long. I'm part of the reason for that, and I'm never going to forget it, so if you think you need to come around for that reason, trust me, you don't."

I know. I'm not really here for that anymore. But there aren't a lot of people in your life you can talk about it with, are there?

"Yeah, not since I gave the big 'screw you' to group therapy."

You've always been a fighter.

"That's it, isn't it? I was looking for a fight, and the Air Force gave me one. I guess I should be a little pickier about the fights I take, huh?"

We only live once.

"I don't know which way you mean that."

It's not for one side or the other. It's just a fact.

"Yeah," Maria answered, and at that moment she was just talking to herself, lying on her back in her bunk in the dark. "Yeah."

***

Lia was there, with coffee and a whole box of doughnuts. With awkward enthusiasm she tried to throw her arms around Maria while still holding them, which led to starts and stops and setting things down and hugging and stooping to pick things up, then stopping and hugging again.

"You're okay," she whispered over and over, as if afraid to speak any louder. "You're okay you're okay you're okay."

The sight of the doughnuts almost put Maria flat on her back from desire and gratitude. "Put those in the car and follow me, will you?" she asked Lia.

"Follow you?" Lia fell in step next to Maria as she started walking.

"No, get in the car and follow me just a bit at a time."

"What are we doing?"

Maria planted one foot in front of her, breathed deep, rocked back, and ran. For the first time since the Voice stopped her, she got up to speed and it was glorious. She expected to go until she puked, that was the deal she had made with herself for the moment she got out, but after about four miles, she pulled up, walked it out for a few circles, and then waved at Lia, parked a hundred feet back and watching with a glow in her eyes.

"Alright," she said, "I'm good."

Then she tasted one bite of every different flavor of doughnut in the box.

***

Within two hours they were at Dr. Qualls and Willie's place, and this time Willie measured Maria's stare for three seconds and then nodded welcome into the house. The four of them gathered in the living room, where Maria presented the medal as well as the box it had arrived in.

Qualls turned the box over and over, keen to make some added discovery about it. "This is a new layer of sophistication. Do you think time has passed in their future? That they've advanced their techniques? I wonder what year this came from."

Maria answered: "I think we're only going to get that answer from whatever else they send. I need that emergency pickup spot. My guess is that the mission is waiting for us there."

Qualls waved absently, still staring at the box. "Yes, yes, I'll get it. But why would they cancel the mission and then revive it? Or is this a new party? Or someone from a parallel future? I think we ought to take this to the lab; there might be a radiation signature on it that..."

"Doc." The force in Maria's voice stopped him. "It came to me. I'm sorry if that bothers you, but it's my mission and I don't want to wait to get started."

Qualls sputtered, his head shaking, trying to deny her implication, but eventually he withered and nodded. "Yes, yes, of course. I'll get you the information." He wheeled out of the room and could be heard rummaging in his study.

"Killed your screwaround in there, huh?" Willie asked. When Maria nodded, Willie continued. "Guess jail actually does work for some people. Don't worry, I won't tell."

***

This time there was no question whether Lia was coming along on the expedition. She started assembling gear for two as soon as they got back to the house. Maria needed time to walk around the place again anyways. It still had the stink of guilt in its rooms, and she was wary.

She took a long, hot shower, scrubbing herself head to toe. The soap perfumed her, made her smell like orange blossoms or something; it felt like a lie compared to the prison soap, and that, more than anything, made her realize that she still hadn't adjusted into anything like life. Maybe she never had.

They ate a mostly silent dinner, Lia respectfully avoiding chatter and just watching as Maria gradually settled back into the stillness of domesticity.

Then out of nowhere, Maria just started talking. "Before I met you, which would be the last time I was a drunken mess, I started hooking up with this guy Brian in Albany. Don't even know why I was in Albany, really; I'd heard maybe I had a cousin up there on the Irish side and thought I'd hit them up for a job. Mostly I just hadn't had a straight head in two years and was grasping at straws just to keep moving.

"There wasn't a cousin, but there were enough bars. I met Brian at one of them. He was out because he'd been fighting with his wife, and man was I the wrong solution for all his problems. I could go like a hellcat, probably about as exciting as he ever had it; we'd screw in motels and I'd drink him to blackout and I thought it was just funny as anything, me dragging this guy along into my tornado.

"I got ugly, though. I asked him for money and that put a wall up real fast. And of course because I was savage and stupid I took it personally, started coming around to his house. I knew when his wife would be gone and he wasn't good at saying no."

Maria stopped for a moment, shook her head and laughed darkly before sharing the next bit. "I lit their lawn on fire. Like it was nothing. Poured a gas can out, lit it up and laughed like a motherhumper. House didn't catch, thank God. But they ran out and called 911 and by this point she knew about me so I was getting it from both barrels and I thought, 'Jesus, has this all gotten boring,' and then I rode off on my bike and crashed into a tree.

"An ambulance came from the 911 call and they told it to take me to the hospital. Can you believe that? Such nice assholes."

The hums and ticks and creaks of the house got oppressively loud after Maria told her story. She felt relieved, so maybe the discomfort wasn't about what she'd just said, but what had always been there. She'd gotten too good at distracting herself from her own thoughts. Her foot tapped on the ground while Lia absorbed it all.

"I'm sorry if this is rude," she finally said, "because you're still my hero. But if you drink again I'm leaving."

Maria nodded at the ground. "Good for you, kid. That's absolutely right."

***

It was a terrible time to camp; so terrible that the roads were blocked into the park where the drop site was located. They spent a whole day driving the park perimeter, searching for the gate closest to the coordinates. Then, first thing in the morning after a night in a motel, they parked the car a couple of miles back along the road from the gate in order to avoid suspicion.

"This is hardcore now," Maria said to Lia as they cinched on their packs. "It's going to be as cold as the moon tonight and we won't be able to start a fire because they'll catch us. It's just us and the little gas heater and every layer we can throw on."

Lia's pale complexion looked almost translucent against the snow, a little like glass. She tightened up her mittens, gave a resigned half grin, and started walking even before Maria took her own first step.

Admiringly, Maria followed, letting Lia lead for a bit.

The road was still mostly clear, and they stayed on it as long as no vehicles came by in order to keep their feet as dry as possible. No way that would last, but it was important while they had the choice.

Nobody seemed to be around. Little animals scurried and foraged, but the thick forest at large was in a healthy sleep.

Conversation slipped to nothing; they just tuned in to each other's breathing, picked their path with their eyes. Finally, they turned off the road and pressed into the woods.

Maria tried to think about the desert; the days when she'd lain out in a coating of sweat by the community pool, a kid with early curves in an awkward one-piece. All that tough, heavy heat; was any of it still inside her? Or those dusty marches at Lackland; was she still part baked by them? Could she turn old heat out from inside her to last longer against this deadening freeze?

The sun was already on its way down when they got to the drop site. The snow had piled up deep but soft, and they were crunching a column of it down every time they swung their legs up in the big, marching steps necessary to make any progress. "Careful," Maria said. "If we step on this damn thing we're likely to twist an ankle and then it's going to get ugly out here."

Before they started searching for the marker, they swept away a campsite, pitched the tent, and started the heater up. With no means to cook dinner they munched on beef jerky, which Lia treated as a novelty that might have made her smile more if her face could still move.

They hung their packs to dry outside and then, finally, started to search their immediate surroundings. They only had maybe twenty minutes of good light left, and Maria didn't like their chances. Depending on when it had arrived and how much snow had fallen since, they might walk by it a dozen times before uncovering it.

The last sunlight got swallowed up by the horizon with no success on their part, so they zipped up in the tent, cocooned themselves in their sleeping bags, and pressed their faces as near to the heater as they could stand.

"Congratulations, Princess," Maria said, quietly shuddering. "You've turned into one tough-ass camper."

"Can I ask," Lia gulped. "What jail was like?"

"Jail was like...boring. Mostly, really boring. At first it was horrible, but then it was just what I needed."

"There have been times I thought it might be nice to go to jail," Lia said. "Is that weird? Like, it would just be women around, and the meals would all be set. I'd miss getting to dress nice though, sometimes. Just sometimes I like to dress nice."

"What would you do to get thrown in jail?"

Lia pressed her lips together and thought. "I guess shoplift something, although that would make me really nervous; I don't think I'd be able to keep straight how to get caught without looking like I was trying to get caught."

"I got an idea: why don't you smash something?"

"Like what?"

Maria shrugged. "Anything; doesn't matter. You're a pretty careful kid, and that's good I think. But you ought to know what it feels like to be not careful once, just wreck something for the sheer hell of it and laugh because none of it matters."

Lia was quiet for a moment. "I'll think about it," she answered. And Maria laughed, because that was exactly the sort of thing Lia would say.

***

At first light they shared some fruit leather and peanuts, with an unspoken agreement that neither would say out loud how hungry they were. Lia found a couple of long branches, and suggested they poke them into the snow to probe around. "As long as what they sent isn't really tiny, we should find it."

This proved to be just the trick – it took over two hours, during which time Maria thought she breathed out enough steam to send up a balloon – but finally, she struck something with her branch, and wiped away enough of the snow to confirm the find.

"Kid, I got it!" she called out, and dropped to her knees to push off the rest of the snow and see the message.

Lia moved at a hasty trudge and was soon behind Maria's shoulder. "What does it say?" she asked.

Maria, agog, just answered, "I don't know." Which was true, because she hadn't made it past the first two sentences:

Maria, it's Lia. It's 2039 here.

***

They were wordless for most of the time it took to break camp and lug the marker out of the woods. As with their hunger, they had silently agreed that they wouldn't start this conversation until they could be assured that they wouldn't be so distracted by it that they froze to death.

The sun was setting as they reached the truck, and Maria's appetite was ferocious. She wanted a steak, then a lobster, then appetizers, and then dessert. It was some kind of hunger to make any headway at all against the mind-warping idea that a future version of her best friend had just sent them a message.

"I hope you're okay," Lia finally said.

"What?"

"I guess the marker means I'm alive, but it doesn't say where you are in the future. I hope you're okay."

"That's sweet, kid."

Very quietly, Lia said, "I have a confession." She looked up at Maria. "I was the one who bought your medals on eBay. Well, I got my friend at work to do it, like a loan; it was really hard to explain, but she bought them, and then when we got our money I paid her back and held onto the medals so I could give them back to you at some point. Christmas, maybe. I guess I hold onto them for a long time, though, so that's why I worry that you're not okay in the future."

Maria smiled, laughed under her breath, and realized that more than ever she had a sense that she was, indeed, okay in the future. Provided they got some dinner soon.

Her phone beeped: a voicemail that must have come in while they were up in the woods and out of range. "Check that for me, will you, Princess? I've got to keep my eyes on the road in this weather."

Obligingly, Lia picked up the phone, touched the screen and listened to the voicemail.

Then she screamed.

***

They found Willie in the hospital's waiting room, silent and numb. A cop was with her, standing by the door in uniform, not guarding her but just being present. Out in the hallway was the perpetual noise of life and death and joy and grief.

Initially Willie stared at them without recognition, but after a few seconds she began to look around the room and rub her hands together, as if the familiar sounds and rhythms of the hospital made her feel like she ought to be working.

Lia approached first, and barely needed to bend over to hug Willie's large frame. Willie put her arms around Lia in return, patting her back and nodding. Then she looked past Lia's shoulder and made eye contact with Maria. Maria subtly nodded in the direction of the cop; Willie nodded; and Maria got the message.

She walked over to the cop, who was young, with a nearly-shaved head and baby smooth cheeks; he probably had less than two years in uniform under his belt.

Maria spoke low. "What happened?"

The cop leaned in and matched her discreet volume. "My uh, understanding ma'am is that it was a home invasion. Intruder broke in, there was a confrontation, and then the intruder uh, shot the victim before fleeing the scene."

Something dark flowed out of Maria's heart and through her veins. This was wrong; this shouldn't be happening. "He got away?"

"The suspect fled the scene. Detectives already got the description from Mrs., uh...well, your friend here."

She saw his jaw working back and forth uncomfortably, knowing that he was trying to do his job to project confidence and control in the situation; but here he was, alone, probably on his first homicide, with no superior to defer to and real ugly human pain in front of him that he couldn't boss around or taser.

She threw him a lifeline. "Listen, I hate to ask, but could you do us a huge favor? She could use some coffee and I think we could too. I can give you money."

He straightened visibly and some stress rolled off his shoulders at the prospect of something concrete to do. "No ma'am, don't worry about that. They uh, we get free coffee around here." And he skedaddled out of the room.

"I bet you do," she said to the door. Then she turned and joined Willie and Lia on the chairs.

"Willie, I..." she tried to start, and was grateful when Willie shook her head, because honestly she had no idea what words could possibly come after that. Lia hadn't stopped hugging.

"He was after him," Willie whispered. "The man came for Weldon. He wasn't a *burglar.*" The last word came out with a venomous pop.

Lia pulled back in shock. "Someone's after us?"

Willie reached into her coat pocket and pulled out a book. "After all of you." She handed the book over to Maria.

Maria leafed through it. There was her address. Her old work address at the airport. Lia's name. Dr. Qualls' home and office. Other names, too, that they didn't recognize. And dates as well, with instructions. Dr. Weldon Qualls was highlighted on this day.

"What the hell is this?" Maria hissed. "This is everything, where did it come from?"

"It has to be someone else," Willie answered. "Weldon would joke about it; that if we were working for the good guys, that there might be bad guys out there trying to stop us. He joked about it." Her voice broke the second time she said "joke," a sudden heaving breath making her throat shudder.

Maria realized the dumb fog of naiveté she'd operated in: it was so obvious that whomever was on the other side in the future might be trying to stop them. She reflected on all their previous efforts with fresh paranoia.

"He didn't know I'd be there; we never married, legally. We threw a party but we just hadn't bothered with the paperwork yet. I always said we should for, for visitation and...anyway, I think that's why they didn't know about me." Willie shook her head at the irony.

"I jumped him. Gave him some good knocks. He got me once..." she peeled open her coat and Maria and Lia both stifled a gasp at a red bandage on her side. "It'll be okay, the bullet just took some meat. That," she pointed at the book, "fell out of his pocket when he ran; I think I freaked him out.

"I can't tell the cops about this. But that book says where he's supposed to go next."

Maria nodded. "I'll go."

Willie nodded. "Yeah, and I'll stay, in case the son of a bitch comes back looking for it."

Lia looked from one woman to the other. "What...what are you talking about?"

Maria answered for them both. "Whoever this is, I'm killing him."

***

-20-

"I wonder how much I even need to explain to you," Khaslik said, his voice still quiet, and cruelly fascinated.

Josh had been moved to a cozier, less antiseptic room as he continued to regain his strength. His brain was still getting accustomed to the furious influx of sensations, the new awareness of thought processes that had always happened *sub rosa*. He imagined his conscious thoughts as a little boat tilting and lurching at the mercy of storm waves. Was this what it was like in those first moments of life, when there is no experience with control and no familiar things? If so, he concluded, it was a good thing we forget that time.

Khaslik was still speaking. "Perhaps you already know my entire plan. Perhaps you have already solved the dilemma for which I need your abilities. It's quite a mystery. I am looking forward to the moment you have something to say."

Josh stayed quiet, hoping that the Beetle inside him might deliver him to freedom in time. But so far it hadn't given him any better knowledge of where on Earth he was, or even how to get through the walls. And would escape even matter? Hiding no longer seemed to be an option.

"Are you going to speak?" Khaslik waited, then sniffed, and raised his wrist to tap at a small padwatch. "Pardon me, I'm impatient sometimes. Perhaps it is the secret to my success."

Suddenly, Josh roared in agony. His heart surged, and all thought shattered into fragments; in one moment he lost all language, memory, and consciousness, and was reduced to a naked organ flooded with a pain it could not comprehend or describe.

He had no way to know how long it lasted. When it finally ended, the split-second he needed to recognize a world without that pain – to even recognize himself as human – was the most truly frightening after-effect. Struggling for breath, he looked at Khaslik, whose finger still hovered over his padwatch. Josh's pulse doubled at the sight: an instant Pavlovian response with just a single punishment.

"What Analuiza showed you was real; your virus never worked. The *idea* of a virus, though: that was tantalizing. That was a dream worth searching every road to reach. Perhaps it wounds you to know that others succeeded where you failed; then again, you quit somewhat early, didn't you?"

He walked up to the bed, gently lifted Josh's head from the pillow, and held a glass of water to his lips. "Go ahead, drink," he urged. "There's plenty of water here. All you need."

The water soothed, it cooled, and most importantly, it gave Josh something new to perceive other than the screaming memory of what Khaslik had done to him. Josh knew that he would never be free of that memory. It had been a glimpse of a truly human hell: pure, soulless suffering without limit, reason, or escape.

Josh didn't want to admit what he would gladly give to never experience it again. His eyes flitted with helpless panic to Khaslik's wrist.

"Look at you," Khaslik said with unmasked delight. "You are impressed."

With exaggerated care, he unstrapped the padwatch and set it on a table, then took a few steps away. "There. More comfortable now?

"I can, of course, trigger such a response from any device. You and I share a fascination with raw data, so I will happily share: I can trigger a natural-seeming, relatively painless death, as you surmised. Or, I can do what I just did:

cause pain. There is a setting for pain at which the average person will die after about ten seconds. What you just experienced was roughly twenty percent of that setting. For three seconds. Not knowing what it feels like, I leave it to you to extrapolate."

Josh couldn't know if he was lying or not. There didn't seem any reason to lie; Khaslik could have said that he'd spent an hour in that torment and he would have found it believable. There was no calculus as to whether he could bear another dose at that level, a higher level, a lower level. His personal willpower simply wasn't part of the equation: the virus disabled everything before it even set to work.

"I can see you are fatigued, so I am happy to leave so you can rest. As I said, though, I am impatient to hear a word or two from you to whet my appetite for when we get to real business."

Josh searched for something to say. This was an entirely new battle for him. He didn't even have it in him to fake defiance. So all he said was, "Thank you for the water."

Khaslik's grin widened to predatory dimensions and he switched off the light, leaving Josh in a windowless, lonely dark.

***

Min-Jun. Josh's thoughts about him were strong. Their first meeting had been a conversation of mutual fascination and delight which, essentially, had never stopped in the fifteen years since. He had always been brilliant, Min-Jun, but his refusal to admit to ambition was something that had irritated Josh right up until the moment when that irritation had turned to admiration. Min-Jun presented himself as a happy wanderer through advanced knowledge, relishing mysteries regardless of whether he found answers to them or not. Josh couldn't believe such a person existed in their field. Besides being wonderful to commiserate with,

Min-Jun's presence always comforted Josh precisely because he was the opposite of what Josh knew himself to be.

Perhaps Josh thought of him now because his best friend – who was always willing to look at things from a spiritual angle – might have been the only person equipped to hear what he'd just been through, and to guide him to calmer waters.

Once, late at night in the days before Min-Jun met his husband, he and Josh had gotten gloriously drunk at a conference in Brazil. Min-Jun had asked, in a gentle voice that somehow carried over the raucous music of the street, "What is the purpose of the human race?"

Josh had laughed, and then, as Min-Jun waited for him to answer, become annoyed at the persistence of the question in the air. "What do you mean?"

"I mean, so many of the choices we make – how long do we try to sustain life, how much effort do we expend on the most unfortunate, what qualities should we value most in individuals and call moral – they must be based on something, right? There is a premise underneath, operating instructions, and this must be the question those instructions answer: what do we believe is our purpose?

"It's funny to consider, because in all the ways we subdivide our philosophies and thoughts and politics, it seems as if not one person out of eight billion has the same answer to that question. And yet, as we all push together with our own ideas, a consensus emerges that leads us into the future."

"Leads?" Josh seized on the word, delighted to play devil's advocate in such a dialogue. "What you call leading I call blind stumbling, chaos, savage competition. You know why ants can't build a better ant hill? Because they're stupid ants. That's what we're living in; a kludgy, short-sighted, perpetually crumbling ant hill that doesn't adequately protect or feed 80% of us on a good day, and which we've only barely managed to keep from collapsing on our heads for a few thousand years."

"Yet look where it has taken us," Min-Jun replied. "Just over a hundred years ago it would have been impossible to have this conference here because air travel was not yet pervasive enough. Forty years ago this building we're standing in would have been science fiction."

"You?" Josh snorted with delight. "Now you're arguing the merits of pure technological progress?"

"I am simply pointing to what is easy to see with drunken eyes," Min-Jun said, as his own eyes twinkled. "We have built a world. Ants also build an entire world for themselves; by their perspectives they are masters of a universe."

"Yeah, and if a foot squashes them they start a religion about it because otherwise there's no explaining it."

"A-ha! You have hit on an insight. The ant does not pursue the question of the foot; it is always building, building, building. Think of what we have learned about the universe outside of our hill. We have developed the ability to learn, to question; even better, to record and share our knowledge so we can answer questions that would be beyond any one person. And though some use it only selfishly, greater and greater numbers of us are using it to decode our existence."

"And some of us are just using it to grow a better tomato."

"Think how much richer a life is when you count up the number of meals that can be improved by a better tomato!"

Josh had laughed. Back then, he couldn't remember how the conversation had started. Now it returned vividly to his upgraded brain, bringing with it that simple but infuriating question: what is the purpose of the human race?

Now that he was on the precipice of being used to enslave the entire human race to a madman, the question seemed important.

***

He didn't see Analuiza again. Her purpose had apparently been exhausted. Instead, Khaslik doted on Josh like an old provincial uncle: bringing in an extra blanket, watching as he ate. He didn't wear the padwatch anymore.

"All this will heal," he said. "Your swelling, your fever. Even the effects of the virus. Oh yes, those memories will be eradicated completely."

"You can do that?" Josh asked, despite himself. To target and delete memories opened up whole new alarming categories of possibility.

"No, no, not like that; although I would love to explore the idea with you. The memory will be gone because you will cease to have lived it!

He pulled a book from his pocket; a small, weathered journal, and he leaned in as he read from it, making Josh think of kindergarten story time. "You will re-educate yourself, you will change your own future. Your younger self will stop, mid-stride, in the road where he now walks, and turn down a better one; one where this never happens to you, where you will be smarter, wealthier, and gifted with the knowledge that you have saved countless lives and brightened humanity's prospects."

"While giving you godlike powers."

"God?" Khaslik's eyes widened, bemused. Then he gave a fussy little laugh, "Not at all. Gods are worshipped, and gods are immortal. I have no need for anyone to know my name; not the masses, in any event. No, Josh, I am the quintessential human: I simply want the fullest life I can achieve. Full of experience, full of acquisition, full of triumph."

"And you do want to live forever," Josh blurted.

Khaslik didn't answer, only smiled that hunter's smile.

"Conspicuous, that you didn't say you didn't want to be immortal. That's where this is leading, right? You want a form of the Brain Alphabet that can work in reverse; that can bring your whole mind pattern into the network, right?"

"You do make such astounding leaps of insight now, don't you? Had you ever thought your invention could be inverted in such a way before? It's true, the sort of appetites I have can so inconveniently destroy a body."

"Or a planet."

Khaslik ignored the remark. "I don't think I would like to be a ghost in the machine, if that is the expression. I don't think I've evolved beyond the flesh. Of course, once I am in the system, my feelings may change. No, I think I'd simply like to...and it's funny because I've never spoken these words aloud to anyone...I'd like to copy all my personal data, and transfer it to a newer, more secure drive."

"A blank?"

"Reformatted, let's say."

"So you'll find some healthy young person, wipe their brain, and carry on."

"Yes. I think I'd like to be taller next time!" Khaslik took a deep, satisfied breath. "You are valuable to me, Josh, because I can talk with you about these things. You can discuss implications without being disabled by devolved moral shock. It is a rare trait."

"What's the book?" Josh asked, eager to move off the topic.

"This?" Khaslik held it up with mock innocence. "This is the greatest book in the history of humanity. Demonstrably better than the Bible, because it is clearer, truer, and its advice actually works."

"Who wrote it?" Josh asked, already suspecting the answer.

"I did!" Khaslik grinned. "In a manner of speaking, I wrote every word, though I remember none of it. It is the story of my life, and what a thrilling success the story is. I often wonder how wealthy I was the first time I wrote it. Far less so than I am now, certainly."

"You send it back through time?"

"I did. I have an associate there. Actually, I have you to thank for that. Apparently he found one of your markers, and was very eager to help, but your man Dr. Qualls rejected him; didn't think he had the appropriate character. So Qualls told him some lie about it being a sociological experiment, which he didn't believe. He posted in a number of Internet forums about his experience, including pictures of the marker. From what I understand from this book, another version of me found these references in this time, brilliantly concluded what it represented, and was able to reach out to this man in the past, posing as you.

"So, I send him this book, he does what I ask, he returns it to me in the past where the younger me holds it for safekeeping. In this version of my life, he has returned the book to me eight times. I have eight copies of this book! But of course, they are not copies; I have the same book eight times, each one slightly more complete. Only in the most recent do I write what is consequential: what has transpired since his last mission, what he needs to do now. The others I destroy. It seems safer this way, don't you think?

"It's remarkable: he really does believe he is doing good, even when I ask him to kill. But I do think it's very human to see someone else's death as less important than having a properly large sense of self.

"So every life I live is better than the last, and better still, it is the only one I remember. And now in this life I have the chance to thwart you just at the moment when you were making bold to expose my younger self to my enemies."

Josh's mind was in the highest gear it could reach, searching for some useful angle in the story Khaslik was revealing to him, but it was fruitless. No insight did him any good while he was a prisoner. All he hoped was to see how much Khaslik could be encouraged to reveal.

"We saw Qualls was killed. Didn't know that was you."

"Yes! One of my more recent gambits. I suppose we are in the phase now where I sweep the rest of your pieces off the board. You and your partner Dan must be protected, of course; without your combined efforts I won't have this wonderful tool to use. But you are, I must say, running out of friends."

Josh thought of Maria and Lia, who had volunteered to help them on such a giant leap of trust. Who had risked so much. He was helpless to reach them in the past. In the present, though, that was different. "You'll never find them all," he said.

Khaslik chuckled "And who do you think is safe?"

"My daughter. All your fancy technology can't get her."

Khaslik, fascinated, leafed back through the diary, muttering to himself as he re-read some passages, and then finally stabbed a page. "Oh, no, you don't have a daughter."

Josh's blood froze in its veins. "What?"

"You never had a daughter. Well, this version of you didn't. Yet you think you do? That is astonishing. We should explore this. Do, tell me more."

Josh sputtered, frantically searched his memories. "Cierra, her name's Cierra. She's sick, I didn't want to put a Beetle in her so you couldn't get her."

"A very wise move. What does she look like?"

Josh was dumbstruck. He scrambled for details: "Well her...her hair, and...her eyes..."

"And her mother...what was she like? What did she do? When was the last time you saw her? What was her name?"

Josh had no answers.

"Do you even recall the last time you thought about your daughter's mother? It's a curious gap, isn't it, to be so fixated on a child and forget the mother?" He was right; Josh couldn't summon any image of Cierra's mother at all. Couldn't even remember the last time he had thought about her.

"You see, Josh, that was my doing. You put such effort and ingenuity into protecting your daughter now. So I simply had the mother killed back then. It just happened this time around. So fascinating that you remember a child that never was. I'm sure there's a lesson about the workings of time in it. Of course, as with your swelling and fever, I think those false memories will fade. It may take only a day, or a year, or perhaps until the next time I send back this wonderful little book, but you will forget her. You will forget there was ever anything to forget. Time will take care of it."

Josh was still struggling to picture Cierra. He had left her somewhere, somewhere out of reach. He couldn't picture it: the place had vanished in fog, and she had vanished with it. All that remained was the sureness that she had been real, and that he loved her.

He didn't know how, but he knew now he would do whatever it took to get his hands on the accelerator again, and it had to be before her memory departed his world.

***

He cooperated. He updated all the leading research on the Brain Alphabet, incorporating the discovery of the bonded pair in the lab Analuiza had revealed to him. He walked it backwards to a 2015 state of understanding, shortened the path to the breakthrough, made the breakthrough itself healthier and smoother. Khaslik and Analuiza had both been correct about him – pride gave him a sometimes horrific capacity for focus – and the more he became accustomed to leveraging the Beetle inside him, the more often he found himself swept up in the horrific joy of pure achievement without moral consideration. The thought of Cierra brought him back to himself, but only with increasing difficulty.

He didn't know yet what he was going to do. He wished he could see the book in order to know which things were real in the past and which had already been erased. Of course, he could always go further back...or could he? They had never attempted it out of caution, so he didn't know. Was it possible to reach beyond the very manipulation that had created this version of him? Or had Time slammed the past beyond their meddling behind a gate, only allowing him to deal with the world they had already made? More and more Josh was beginning to envision Time as having its own will, its own design, even its own kind of life. And he was slicing into it, no surgeon but the most savage battlefield sawbones, making life-and-death guesses with a primitive's knowledge.

He asked Khaslik's permission to view the record of every launch that had ever occurred, which Khaslik still had stored after successfully hacking into Josh's network. The motive was pure appetite, but it undeniably increased the chances for success, and therefore Khaslik understood it. Josh had proposed he could make his past self an unwitting conspirator, placing bread crumbs of discovery in his path rather than just a box of impossibles from the future. Khaslik seemed indifferent to the dangers of the latter, but Josh argued his adolescent self might reject the offer out of sheer rebellion, so Khaslik allowed the amended plan. Maybe it amused him.

Josh scarcely rested. He took the data to his quarters at night and explored it more abstractly. Equations danced inside his eyelids. He didn't like sleep now: his dreams had become a hectic blur. He seemed to have ten thousand of them a night.

At Josh's request, Khaslik had provided a pad of paper, and every night, Josh wrote on it: "Your daughter's name is Cierra." Every morning he woke and the words were still familiar, he cried with relief.

Reviewing one of Khaslik's earliest launches, he plotted its trajectory, going through the process as routinely as he had hundreds of times already, and suddenly dropped his pad in shock. He picked it up to recalculate the trajectory, but found his own brain already reaching the same conclusion.

"You seem surprised, my friend." Khaslik's voice echoed through the room, reminding Josh how often the villain watched him from afar.

"It landed on Earth. This test object. You actually landed it."

"A happy accident."

"No...it's *where* you landed it. New Mexico, 1993."

"Further back than any of your launches, yes?"

"It would have landed in the middle of a highway. Maria...Maria Kerrigan's brother was killed when a car swerved off the highway to avoid something. You started this, didn't you? Her whole life...her whole stinking life: joining the Air Force, drinking, moving to New Hampshire where she found our marker, All of it started with that accident. And you caused it."

"No, Josh, it remains an accident. Just a much, much bigger one."

It was an impossible coincidence. No, it was the precipitating event, which made Maria's discovery of the later marker the coincidence. But hadn't that marker gone out before Khaslik's? Josh felt his mind exploding with new questions about whether their own forward march in time made them naively assume that cause and effect all flowed in the same direction; that the very question of when it all began might be based on a false premise.

Now Josh experienced something entirely new; his mind, his enlivened mind, going blank with anger, like the light of a bloody red sun blinding everything.

"Josh, can you hear me? Something interesting is happening in your mind. But I guess you know that."

Josh smashed the pad into the ground. Kicked it against the wall with his foot. Hurled his chair. Screamed with a grieving guilt that they had ever opened this door; that they had allowed for the ruination of lives, the taking of lives, before they even had a clue what they were doing. He hated himself, Khaslik, Min-Jun. He hated discovery. Hated Time. He hated the whole human race.

And then the shrieking, wretched torture erased it all and sent him to the floor, howling.

Khaslik didn't keep him there long, though the only way Josh knew that is that he was still alive when it stopped. The first thing he was able to feel was his chest, heaving air in and out of his lungs. He hadn't experienced Khaslik's punishment since that first demonstration. There was no measuring if he had become acclimated to it. It existed beyond such things.

"Calmer now? Good." Khaslik clucked his tongue over the intercom. "Anger is such a distraction."

Khaslik didn't speak again. He left Josh alone in the dark. Anger was indeed gone, and now despair had taken over. Did Josh even deserve all his awards and triumphs, all the luxuries and sins they had bought? Did he even deserve his daughter?

What was he even doing? He had already lost it all. He was a prisoner, broke and broken. All he had left was his mind, and even that he didn't wholly own anymore. For how long had he maintained the illusion that he was engaged in some noble, mighty duel with the whole human race his chess pieces? Even the metaphor flattered his ego.

He thought about death all night long.

**

There was one piece of information he needed, and two places he could get it from. One place was Khaslik's book, which he couldn't imagine the man ever parting with until it was time to send it back to his associate in the past. Even showing curiosity about it would be fatal. The other place was on the rWeb; if the information existed, it would be there. There was only one day, though, on which he would be allowed even monitored access to the network at large.

For both these reasons, Josh said he was ready for his first launch.

He couldn't succeed; with the very first change, he might forget his intent. He measured his life in seconds over and over again. How long would it take to learn what he needed, and how long would he have to live after?

If he failed, the world probably wouldn't get any worse. He'd meant the thought as a sarcastic comfort, but he found it wasn't one he could die peacefully with.

***

The day came, and the accelerator controls were at his fingers. Josh Scribner, master conductor of the dimensions, poised to lead his next symphony. Weary, eyes blackened by nightmares, he looked at his own hands with disgust.

Josh took the book from Khaslik into the static-free room to weigh it, and then walked it to the launch site. Cameras watched him every step of the way, and Josh suspected Khaslik was even monitoring his brain waves like an old polygraph, looking for leaps of stress that might indicate an attempt at subterfuge. So Josh stayed steady, even in the split second when he slipped a piece of paper inside the cover of the book. A piece he had privately weighed to the micron level. He added the weight of the paper to that of the book for his launch calculations without a pause. Even with his old brain, addition had been nothing for him.

He worked on several screens at once, flicking between them at the controls, command windows flashing across them at a speed few could comprehend. Weirdly, he felt more at peace than he ever had; in essence, he was working at his utmost, doing what he had been made to do at the highest peak the human race could make possible. He was probably doing about three Nobel Prizes' worth of work, and no one would ever know about it. Numbers sparkled like stars birthing and dying.

He used this speed, and Khaslik's own triumphal lack of focus, to inch himself closer to his goal. On one screen in the corner, a window hid behind another, only flashing to the front for split seconds at a time so he could type another character or two into it. He couldn't risk more time than that. Every bit of progress required a readiness to die.

Finally, the equations were settling. It was nearing time to launch. He believed he was close to making the discovery he needed, but would need to leap without looking first. His launch protocol had a new wrinkle: it would either send the book to a new destination Josh would type in the next thirty seconds, or it would trigger a cascade effect that would destroy the lab. Either way, this was the end.

He was surprised to find himself thinking about music. He hummed something he vaguely remembered from childhood, maybe getting the notes right, barely knowing the words. Music, he had been told long ago, had a secret math in its design. Child prodigies in one might well have skills in the other.

I wish I'd loved the piano, he thought to himself. Then he started the countdown.

He brought the secret window forward. He finished the search. He found what he needed: the date, time, and location of the death of Maria Kerrigan. *Oh,* he thought, scanning the details, *so you're throwing me this curve ball.* He appreciated that this final added challenge underlined that what he was attempting would have truly been impossible for the pre-Beetle Josh. Now, it was just a few extra keystrokes.

Even as his fingers flashed, programming the new sequence, he heard that voice – that drab, piggish voice – behind him, exclaiming. "Josh....JOSH!"

And then Josh felt the pop in his brain. He was on the floor, looking out sideways at tiles, table legs, Khaslik's shoes. He was dying, his body going offline one system at a time.

His last thought would have pleased his best friend: *I'm not a surgeon, I'm a white blood cell.*

He died, having done what, to his ultimate surprise, was truly in his nature.

***

-21-

Andrew Swanner had always wanted to be a hero. He'd read about heroes in comic books, then novels, then newspapers, and finally on the Internet. He had learned that real heroes sometimes went overlooked by the masses, real heroes could be hounded and misunderstood. Other people might think heroism brought money or women or medals, but Andrew had seen that these were not unifying threads in the stories of all heroes. The one thing – the only thing – that all heroes had in common was that when their moment came, they did the heroic thing.

This gave him a faith that carried him beyond everyday setbacks. The police force in his hometown had rejected his application three times. He failed the fire department physical three times.

He pictured himself talking to kids in school, telling them about character and integrity. He remembered speakers like this from his own childhood, telling him to stay in school and stay off drugs. He had approached a couple of schools in the area, proposing that he could just speak to the class about these things. He had posters made up that he brought in to demonstrate what the talk would be like. But because he belonged to no recognized organizations, hadn't been to the Olympics or in the headlines or made a million bucks in a business, they wouldn't have him. He hated their short-sightedness, but rose above it.

He never told anyone about the unifying theme to his ambitions, though. As strongly as it guided his actions he rarely acknowledged it even to himself. Heroes weren't pretentious; in fact, he had envisioned a hundred thousand times the moment when someone would call him a hero and he would humbly shake his head and say only that he had just done what he hoped anyone would do.

And then his moment had come and he found that strange marker from the future. The idea that time travel was real hadn't shocked Andrew for long; he had read about many variations on the idea in his life, watched many movies and TV shows about it. He had found the message, delivered it as asked, and then the egghead in the wheelchair had lied to him about it.

He came to understand that the man in the wheelchair had betrayed people in the future and was now working against them. That he was trying to bury the existence of the markers so the good people in the future, the ones trying to prevent the great war that would kill so many, wouldn't be able to find allies here in Andrew's time. Allies like Andrew.

Nothing stoked Andrew's rage like betrayal. He had been betrayed by his ex-wife, and any number of times by his government. While he tried to find solace in his own personal character and the nobility of his personal ideals, it didn't always work.

When the people of the future found him, enlisted him, trained him, and told him that he needed to kill Dr. Weldon Qualls for the good of the human race, he was still reluctant, even though he knew Dr. Qualls deserved it. But this was only because no hero should be eager to kill. Set against the deaths he would prevent, Andrew was able to see the greater good. So Dr. Qualls would die. As would the others on the list: Qualls's terrorist/field agent Maria Kerrigan; her partner and probable lover Lia Carty; and his next target, a chemistry student named Sky Sebelius.

This one had been the most troubling, because the evil she was destined to cause had yet to manifest itself. Yet he had been assured it could not wait. He had been instructed to deal with her even before Dr. Qualls, but his weakness had delayed him as he struggled to hold the righteousness of his actions in his mind. "Kill one and save millions," he would repeat to himself. "Millions against one, millions against one."

He had botched his mission with Dr. Qualls. While he had succeeded in eliminating the target, he had lost his book. He had sobbed that night, smacked his own face dozens of times, screamed, drank, passed out, and woke up alone and filled with self-loathing.

They had given him instructions for this contingency. He had to shift mindsets now, from predator to prey. He had to cover his tracks, prepare to send a report to his contact in the present time, Mr. Khaslik, that he would not be able to re-deliver the book this time. He knew Mr. Khaslik would be upset, but killing Sky would surely get him back in good graces. He didn't need the book for that. He remembered exactly how to find her.

He set out along the highway, thumb pointed at the road, preparing to head west. This would cover his mistakes, put everything back on track.

Finding the marker had been a million-to-one coincidence; Andrew had known that right away. Which made it so right that it would fulfill his purpose. Millions against one, millions against one.

Cars growled by in the night. One pulled over to pick him up. Andrew rode in pleasant silence, closing in on Sky. An ironic name, he thought, because there was one other common quality to heroes. They got to ascend to heaven.

***

Maria had stolen a plane. Poor Albert. For a while he had called to her on the radio, at first in official tower-speak, but then with quieter, sadder personal appeals. "Maria, uh...don't want reports on you, but uh..." he wheezed, buzzed his lips, then fell silent.

Maria couldn't answer him. She ached to tell him that she was sober and right, that this wasn't a stunt, but she knew she couldn't start without telling him everything.

She and Lia had returned home with the strange book left behind by Dr. Qualls's killer. Much of it was in Russian, preceded by multiple warnings that this portion was not to be read by others lest it cause "pollution" in the timeline. The other half was in English, and was addressed to "Our Soldier Andrew." Maria and Lia's own names were in this section, along with another: Sky Sebelius. They had researched Sky, found her enrolled at University of Michigan-Ann Arbor, and still alive, despite the fact that she was at the top of the list of targets. But they didn't know how long they had to reach her, which to Maria was reason enough to steal a plane.

She and Lia didn't give one good damn about timeline pollution, and used their computer to try to translate the Russian half. It talked about the future; specifically about one man's future. He wasn't named in the book, but it read like a long letter to himself, mostly in Russian. It included personal details, as if whoever it was needed to prove it was himself writing. It talked of amassing wealth, conquering enemies, and a scheme to make brain implants ubiquitous in the human population. Only not for their benefit, but because of the power it would confer upon him as the master of a lethal virus that affected those implants.

It talked about mistakes, about revisions in strategy. "The son of a bitch," Maria had said. "He gets to just do this over and over again and win more and more each time." Already the future looked dark, though apparently there were people fighting back, and they were the ones who had enlisted Maria. It was a small relief to have confirmation from such a monster that she was on the right side. "I bet 'Our Soldier Andrew' never even translated this stuff, just like a good little servant." Maria said, tasting acid in her mouth.

All that was even more reason to steal a plane.

Lia had accompanied her to the airport, where Maria said she needed to get things from her locker. Lia, who had needed over a year of therapy just to face the normal world after the horrors her husband had put her through, was willing to follow Maria out to face this murderer. And that was Maria's ultimate reason to steal a plane: to leave Lia behind.

"Maria?" There was her voice, replacing Albert's on the radio. Maria's chest heaved hearing the voice. She knew the Princess so well, could recognize her uncertainty over whether it was proper to be talking into the tower microphone.

Before long she would be out of tower space, but she was staying low and plotting a course to duck in and out of the space of the towers between Laconia and Michigan. The Cessna had long-range tanks on it for training. Ann Arbor was just in range if she stayed over the lakes and flew at optimal speed. She knew the plane well; about 115 mph would be right. Six more hours, give or take, and she'd be there.

Her hand stayed steady on the stick. Surgeon steady. Top of her class. All she had to do was not answer Lia, and then nothing could stop her from this mission.

"Maria, please."

Maria begged for the voice to distract her. The drone of the sky filled her ears like a rushing ocean, and she tried to give herself over to the peace she had always told herself she would get up in the clouds. From her first dream of flying it was what she'd wanted, to be up there and away from the sounds below.

"Maria..."

Maria squinted her eyes shut, made a growling cry, and thumbed on her radio.

"Hey kid."

"I'm going to drive after you."

"Princess, I don't think that's a good idea."

"It's Lia. I want you to call me Lia."

Maria was struck by the resolve she heard; the realization of how belittling her pet names could be hit her like a punch. "Right, okay, Lia. Sorry." She mashed her teeth together to stop herself from adding "kid" to the end of that.

"Lia," Maria said, staring ahead into a setting sun that she was chasing, prolonging. "I put a brochure in your jacket pocket. It's for a little place that rents cabins in Maine. Nobody else has seen it. Only you and I know about it. You ought to get yourself there and wait this out for a few days."

"This isn't fair, I want to help. I can help."

There was a long silence. "You've been helping all the way. Rooting for me to go right. Reminding me when I'm going wrong. Being strong. Lia, I don't know anybody as strong as you." Maria's voice caught as she said this; only when the sentence was already halfway out of her mouth did she realize how true it was.

"But for what I'm probably going to have to do," Maria said, "I don't want you within a thousand miles of it. Get to the cabin. Be safe. Be a thousand miles away when I do this.

"Don't see me do this," she finished, almost begging. Dark, shameful feelings flooded her heart as she switched the radio off. The sunset was still ahead. Black waters were underneath.

***

Swanner had some emergency cash from his partners, and had never spent a penny on any personal luxury. He knew they had means, but was dutifully frugal nonetheless. It comforted him as he reviewed his performance on the previous mission. Nothing played out as perfectly as it did on paper. You needed to plan for contingencies, prepare to respond to a fluid situation. Cash made that easier. His responsibility with that cash would mean more success in the long term.

The driver who had picked him up hadn't spoken much. They had listened in silence to some podcast where writers and thinkers talked about what the future would look like, about scientists and politicians and charities and churches working to make it better. Their voices were quiet and sober, imitations of intimacy in front of some hip curtain of music.

Andrew chuckled a few times. It sounded like brainwashing to him: a comforting trance of optimism. Trust the brainiacs. Part of him wished the driver would ask what was so funny. Part of him imagined saying that he knew more about the future than any of those great people, and that he was going to do more to help.

Not that it was a big deal. Just doing what anyone would do.

***

Maria was caught. Freak luck. Maybe a Coast Guard boat patrolling the lake. Maybe even a civvie. Someone had called it in. But now the FAA was calling, and she couldn't just fake a broken radio and play for time: she had no flight plan filed, and she was obviously flying evasively. The spectrum of possibilities for what she was in their eyes probably started at drug smuggler and ended at mass-murderer-to-be.

They were going to be coming for her. She'd get warnings though. You could count on America for that. In these situations, they wanted to give you every possible chance to change your mind.

She'd be painted soon, then either escorted down and surrounded by guns, or shot out of the sky. They would know where the plane came from. Albert would be questioned.

She remembered her silence to him; remembered the last impression he'd had of her. She thought about how the government would punch her name into their computers, and what they would find: a troubled veteran, a drunk recently released from prison. The story would be a sad one. *She was a hero, and yeah she stole that plane, but she really only hurt herself, nobody else.* She might even get the military honors at her funeral because they would feel guilty about the image of another broken veteran. She wondered who would get the folded-up flag.

The solution to this situation was obvious. What would that Maria Kerrigan do? The fuck up, the drunk?

She checked her position relative to the shore. It was freezing outside. Close to the shore the surface would be frozen solid. Just what she needed.

She took a moment to psych herself up. She'd never crashed a plane. Everyone had scares – malfunctions were a mathematical fact after enough hours on the stick – but she'd never been in a real crash. She treated her planes better than she treated herself. Unconsciously, she patted the ceiling of the cabin.

Then she reached out and cut the engine.

Something caught her eye on the other seat. A book. The book. Confused, she patted her jacket pocket. The book was still there, like the end of a funny magic trick. She pulled it out and looked at it. With the engine off, the only sound was the wind.

She put her copy back in her pocket and picked up the new one. A note slipped out.

Maria, I have given everything to try to get this message to you, and you will never hear from me again. From where I am now, history says you are about to die. Whatever drove you to steal that plane, it must be secondary. You have one final mission: you must survive to take it. You do not need to kill anyone, or blow anything up. But if you succeed it can change everything.

I have a good friend who has worked so long to convince me to seek something other than the hard solution, the direct solution. His ideas were appealing, but deep down, I never trusted that they would work for anything serious, not for real problems. For real problems you needed to be cold, and relentless. That's what I believed. I was wrong.

What you need to do is both simple and difficult. It will seem to go against your nature, but we are out of time, and you are the only one who can do it.

You don't need to hurt anybody. You just need to distract someone...

It went on to describe what needed to be done. The note's author was right: the plan outlined there seemed ludicrous, not even possibly workable. She was chasing a man who was being ordered to kill and not ask questions. Although she hated death, she understood that he needed to be stopped. But this...

Her eye caught the altimeter, which was gradually dropping. She remembered what the note said about how she was about to die. The note was signed "Josh Scribner"; at last she had a name for who had set her fate along this path. Where might she have ended up if she hadn't found his first marker?

"Thanks for the heads up, Josh," she said, and tilted, letting the plane go into a spiral. It didn't take much at all. She thought of one of her stock phrases for reassuring students: *it's all stick and rudder at the end of the day.*

Calmly, the whole planet twirling around her, she reached for an emergency chute. She also took off her boots. Just in case she was wrong about that ice, she didn't want to do any more sinking than necessary. She had a mission to live for right now.

***

Andrew checked into a motel, a thrifty one near the campus. It was too late to make a useful search for his quarry.

He watched some television. Spent some time doing a blend of stretches and kicks until his breath huffed. He hadn't been in many physical confrontations, but surmised that between his strategic mind and others' natural underestimation of him, he could surprise people.

He ordered a pizza and only left the room to cross the highway to the liquor store for a six-pack of beer. He drank half the pack and ate half the pizza, humming to himself.

Finally drowsy, he slipped under the covers, taking a wad of tissues with him. He imagined college students. Pretty ones, two of them.

***

Maria wondered who Sky Sebelius even was. Would she be a great scientist? A politician? A superstar singer? Whoever she was, all her potential was ahead of her, and made her worth killing. And Maria...Maria had no idea what her future held, or if she was even alive. But she had a new mission now, and needed to forget Sky. Josh Scribner hadn't even mentioned her in his note.

Sky, Maria thought, *if you do get blessed with a new guardian angel, I promise she'll be a trade-up from me.*

Freezing and alone, she wadded up her chute and tossed it into the hole her Cessna had punched in the ice. And then she tossed in her driver's license. History said she just died, after all. The remains of her Cessna were sinking already. She started trudging away long before it slipped under the water.

Land-o-Matics, she thought. *You needed a real effort to crash them.*

***

Andrew dressed himself in a cheap suit and a poofy, mismatched coat he'd found at a secondhand store. He figured he could pass as a visiting speaker or a parent casually checking out the school. He'd been told before that he had unremarkable looks, and now this was an asset.

In the mid-afternoon, he spied Sky Sebelius as she crossed a parking lot from her dorm to the student center. He watched her through a window while she chatted with friends at the café there and studied unselfconsciously in her heavy campus sweater. She was pretty, Andrew allowed himself to notice, although he wouldn't say remarkably so. She probably wasn't even aware of the evils she would do in the future.

That made it merciful, he decided. He would save her the ravages of conscience that accompanied going down that road. Innocence would be preserved, and her life, while shorter, would be on the balance far more happy and rewarding.

There was no subtle place to do it in this parking lot. The dorms would also be well-monitored. Andrew had to hope that she would choose to go out again on this cold evening. If he was lucky, she wouldn't be a complete innocent.

He mused about how this sort of killing was easier than normal. In common murder, not only did you need to not get caught in the act or its immediate aftermath, you needed to not get tracked down after. Psychotics followed patterns, behaved according to criminal profiles that the police knew how to decode. And their impulses drove them to keep killing until they were caught.

But Andrew wasn't a criminal, and his victims had no unifying element anyone in the present would understand. Their deaths would never come together as chapters in a single book for anyone else. They would simply be isolated little tragedies involving people no one had ever heard of. In a worse future they had become infamous; thanks to Andrew, though, that future would never arrive.

**

It took Maria a few hours to find a highway on foot. As she worked her way through the trees, she remembered the camping trip that started all this: knocking herself out on the rock in the middle of that creek, and the strange, furious pursuit of calm that had driven her. At the time she believed she was on top of her troubles, and boy, had she had been wrong. She had been on her way to dying.

She walked along the road, which had no street lamps. Just two lanes and the moon. A helicopter thuddered by over her head, back into the woods towards the lake. Her crash was being investigated. But there would be no rescue effort. A minute looking at the site and they would strictly be in recovery mode.

Only if someone especially eagle-eyed found her trail in the night, and only if they searched this far and wide, was there a chance they would help her right into a prison cell. But they would be searching with the wrong assumption: that she wanted to be found.

She heard a car coming up behind her. Its headlights set the trees glowing before it appeared from around a bend.

Her skin began to crawl with anxiety. Here she was, walking a roadside alone, a car coming her way like it had for her brother. She had jogged along countless roads, passed by countless cars, day and night. The thought had never taken hold, so why now was she paralyzed in the roadside dirt, dreading the car that was coming closer?

Because it's quiet, I'm sober, and I want to live now, she decided. And with that she brushed off fear, stood tall, and stuck out her thumb.

The driver was helpful, and headed her way. East, away from Michigan, towards her next leap of faith.

***

Andrew watched Sky Sebelius exit her dorm with two girlfriends and walk north, around the corner to one of those foreign cafés students loved. There was an old arcade next door, and it tugged at him for just a moment. He smiled as he thought about the childhood things he had put away since taking on his mission. He ordered a cup of coffee and sat at a corner booth, watching.

Sky's friends came and went, chatting and studying books and checking their phones. Sky looked unremarkable among them, mostly concerned with the blast of outdoor air that accompanied every opening of the door. She had a big coat on and kept it zipped over her body the whole time.

Some boys were mixed in with the group, and she seemed friendly with a particular one, a smiling musician type with dreadlocks. Maybe they were intimate, maybe not. The boy wanted it bad either way, Andrew could tell that.

He shifted in the booth. The smugness of college kids wore on him, and he dreaded the possibility that he might need to surveil Sky from among them for several more days in order to find an opportunity. There hadn't been any quiet spots between her dorm and this place, and the campus was open and well lit.

Eventually, though, she and a smaller group got up as one to leave the café. He left as well, following at a distance.

They walked a curving road out along the perimeter of the campus, not in any particular hurry. They were passing around a couple of thermoses, probably something warm spiked with alcohol. Average decadence for a college student, Andrew thought, but a clear sign of where that kind of immorality could lead a seemingly average girl like Sky.

They passed a cemetery. Andrew reflected back on the most frightening day of his mission so far, when he'd attempted to surveil Maria Kerrigan on her jogging route and followed her into a cemetery. She'd demonstrated expert military tactics in clearing her six, luring him to a dead end and then turning on him at the last moment. The hellcat had looked ready to tear him apart right when he was most drained from the run. Whether that was simple situational instinct or she'd made his identity he had never known, but he had shifted his focus to Dr. Qualls at that point out of caution. From the way Dr. Qualls had stayed unguarded, either she had never figured it out, or she had arrogantly underestimated Andrew. She wasn't the only person who'd ever done so, and especially not the only woman.

Sky's group of students – that dreadlocked boy had his arm around her shoulder – reached the entrance of a park by an arboretum. The park had a gate marked CLOSED in front of it. They heedlessly walked around it. Just another transgression.

There were no crowds left to blend into. He waited as they disappeared into the woods on a trail, and then followed, using their laughter as a guide.

The trail turned away, but he heard their voices among the trees beyond the trail, and he chased them. He moved from tree to tree, always pausing to make sure their carefree sounds hadn't stopped for noticing him.

He got close enough to see their backs, silhouetted against the sparkling view of a river. They had paired off and were enjoying the view, tossing the occasional rock and engaging in other horseplay. As the minutes passed, each couple drifted off in their own direction to do what couples do. Why stay out in the cold when they had their dorms so close? Andrew didn't understand it, and didn't care to.

He just watched Sky and her chosen boy find privacy among the trees, kissing and laughing.

The boy was a moral wrinkle. This was the best opportunity Andrew might ever get, and yet the boy would probably have to die too for any chance at operational success. Innocents came into the crossfire all the time. Andrew was rationally comfortable with that idea, but it gave him pause. Millions, he just reminded himself. Millions against one, millions against two: it was all the same. He may have even muttered the word aloud. *Millions...*

Searching the ground, he found a heavy rock that he could swing with one arm, and wrapped a hand around it.

He heard little rustles, and giggles, and the crackle of bark. Sky and her boy, kissing among the trees. Sinners, but by the standards of what she would do someday, Sky was as innocent now as Eve in Eden. As good a time as any.

Andrew walked lightly out from his cover and approached them. She had her back against a tree while the boy kissed her neck. Her eyes were closed, and she ran her hands up and down the boy's back. A strange revulsion rose in Andrew's throat and, hardly thinking, he swung the rock.

The boy barely made a sound; he grunted and slumped forward. As he slipped to the ground out of Sky's grasp, blood from his skull wiped across her hand. She looked down at him, saw the blood, then looked up and saw Andrew.

She had a look of total horror, and Andrew found himself, to his absolute shock, wanting to cry.

She opened her mouth and made two choked sounds, as if trying to scream. Andrew stepped forward and swung again.

She ducked under his swing and ran. The rock collided with the tree and he lost his grip on it.

Andrew stumbled after Sky, and he started to curse his own stupidity aloud even as he chased her.

She was more athletic than he was, but she kept looking back, and in the dark on the uneven ground, that cost her. She twisted her foot on a branch and fell. Andrew caught up and fell awkwardly on top of her.

She squirmed and shouted and clawed at him. He saw terror and anger in her eyes. Before he could even think about what would be effective in the situation, she got hold of his ear and pulled at it, digging her nails into the soft flesh and making him howl with pain. His mind blanked out.

She was squeezing out from under him, yelling "Help!" This snapped him out of it.

"Shut up!" he shouted, slapping her. He grabbed her throat, shook her, and started squeezing. He heard his own voice rising: "Shut up! I have to save them! I have to!"

She kept scratching, grabbing, resisting. She screamed again and he clapped a hand over her mouth, as his other hand searched the ground for another rock, a branch, anything.

Pain and panic were lighting up all over him, but this was everything, this was his mission, his heroic life. She just didn't understand that she was the key to everything.

His hand found a large rock. But before he could grab it, it seemed to fly out of his grasp.

He tried to turn around.

Then, there was only a thump, and things went black.

***

Sky freed herself from underneath the man's body and scrambled back, using a tree to help herself stand.

She breathed heavily with the adrenaline of the fight, and already her cheek was swelling with a bruise; similar purpling marks were appearing on her throat. She stood poised to run or attack, depending on what she saw in the mystery person who had saved her.

A lightly-built woman, a few years older than Sky and dressed like a modest librarian, stepped forward. She was looking with absent sadness at her torn sweater, even as she still held the blood-caked rock.

Finally she spoke, but so quietly that Sky couldn't hear her.

"What?" Sky asked, even less certain what to do when being confronted by the least threatening person she could imagine.

"I said, are you okay?" The mystery woman asked, stepping forward. "I'm really sorry I didn't help sooner. I've never...hit anyone before." She smiled resignedly. "You're probably mad at him, but we shouldn't hit him anymore, trust me. We'll just call the police, okay?"

Sky, confused, finally nodded rapidly. "Who is he? What's going on?"

After a long beat, the woman answered. "All that matters is that he'll never hurt you again. And that it's so important that you be alive."

"Where did you come from?"

"My name's Lia," her savior in the librarian clothes answered. "And I came from New Hampshire."

Sky's friends arrived. Her boyfriend was treated and would be okay. Lia rode in the ambulance with Sky, holding her hand and watching her with a fiercely loving glow.

Andrew went to jail. He asked to defend himself in court, and was put in an asylum.

And Maria Kerrigan was somewhere hundreds of miles away, jogging.

***

-EPILOGUE-

Oulu, Finland, 2025

"Actually, I like scars," Josh said, feeling bold under the influence of good whiskey. "They tell us a secret about humanity."

He heard a snicker next to him. Min-Jun Dan, a brilliant physicist whose reputation had preceded him into this party, had been Josh's primary partner in conversation all night and an instant delight from their first exchange. Now Min-Jun was watching out of the corner of his eye as Josh perused a bumpy line of skin on an otherwise impeccable female arm.

The woman with the scar smiled softly and took the bait. "What secret is that?"

"We're imperfect. Our maintenance systems, I mean. We can create an arm like this, repair a certain amount, but past a certain point, patching the damage proves to be more important than perfectly recreating what came before. Your body is like a ship launched into the ocean, and your systems are designed to keep you afloat, not pull into harbor looking flawless."

"I think scars are about memories," she answered, stretching her arm out and looking at it. "With this, I have the memory of something painful, but I don't have to remember it in fear anymore."

She was a few years older than Josh, but seemed charmed by his confidence and the way he couldn't conceal that something about her dazzled him. For Josh – who at twenty-four hadn't spent much time participating in bartop social rituals – it was a rare thrill to be doing it for real, and apparently successfully, at least in the early going. She was neither aloof nor chasing him, and had spurned conversation from several others in this very impressive room, seemingly preferring silence to triviality. He didn't detect any cynicism in her sparkling eyes, though; she was vivaciously curious, and content to wait for something worth exploring. So far this conversation seemed to be working.

"In my business, we say that makes it a feature, not a bug," Josh answered.

"Yes, if I accept the scar, and the inevitability of the scar, it means I'm free of regret."

Josh chuckled and grinned. "Regret. It's uniquely human, isn't it?"

She just smiled, while her eyes revealed the strength left behind by some terrible obstacle surmounted.

"You know, I'm very lucky," he followed up.

"Are you?"

"Incredibly lucky. I've met two people tonight who have been able to show me a different way to look at the world. Have you heard of Min-Jun Dan?" Min-Jun leaned forward over the bar so the woman could see him. He waved, then went back to his pretense of not listening to them.

"I have," she answered. "Looks like I picked the fun corner to be in."

"Really? There's rock stars over there. Diplomats. Thinkers. Economists. Your standard party-whoring billionaires. But you want to hang out with the science nerds?"

"I am a science nerd," she answered. "I'm a chemist."

"Really?" Josh answered. "You should work for me."

"I do work for you," she answered with a smile.

Josh didn't hide his chagrin. "Ah. Analuiza hired you?" The woman nodded. "She's a godsend. She's taken care of me since day one."

"She knows you need it."

"So what's your name?"

"Not yet," she answered. "How often do you get to make a billionaire squirm?"

***

The conversation had happily become a three-way one. Josh loved the arrangement: they were distinct and separate, and yet very exciting when packed together. *Neapolitan ice cream,* he thought idly, enjoying the childish metaphor and the memories attached to it. It never failed that the most interesting moments at these globetrotting thought clouds, or whatever the hell buzzterm they were going by these days, were not in the lectures and symposiums but in the parties. Josh wondered if a more successful gathering could be engineered just through a system of assigning invitees to particular party rooms to mingle with a cultivated selection of minds. Surely such serendipity as what he was now enjoying could be engineered, he thought cockily.

"Min-Jun here," Josh gestured with his whiskey tumbler, "says he is going to convince me to change careers."

"Why would you want to do that?" the woman teased. "Aren't you enjoying being the savior of Earth?"

That bloody Time Magazine cover, Josh thought. *I'll never get to live that down.* "Listen, no, what I did is solve a problem before anyone else did, and it turned out to be useful."

"And by problem," Min-Jun interjected, "he means an equation, not a troubling situation."

"How do you know me so well already?" Josh laughed. "If I'm being honest, it wasn't even my idea."

"Really?" she said, brushing her hair back before settling her chin on her hand and leaning in, her interest piqued. "The genius Josh Scribner, a thief?"

Josh looked around. Their table was surrounded by security escorts, because people had a habit of trying to foist their crackpot ideas on Josh if they could get near him, and then sue him afterwards by saying he stole them. Even now, he could sense hopeful eyes around the room, casting glances at him and hoping they could somehow bridge the few feet between them, maybe even just beam a little message into his brain. But that was still science fiction: they had a discreet little island inside all this heavyweight noise, so he decided to enjoy it.

"Okay, I'm going to tell you a story," he said, dropping his voice low to up the conspiracy factor. "We're in a little club now and this is our club secret."

"Should I spit in my palm?" the woman asked.

"I would rather not," Min-Jun volunteered, waving for some fresh hot water for his tea.

"So, I'm fourteen years old," Josh said. "My parents had grounded me for something. Never mind what. And when I say grounded, I mean grounded in a way that really gets to someone like me. No network access, no devices. They took my smartphone and turned off the cable in their own house, sent requests to all my friends' parents to not let me use their networks. I was using pens and paper for my homework!"

"Torture!" the woman interjected with a perfect balance of teasing and sympathy.

"Right? Exactly. So, I got ticked off, and I took a walk towards the school. There were like six different Wi-Fi networks there, and I had borrowed a friend's tablet. I was a junkie looking for a fix, you know?

"So I hop the fence around the school and I'm on the athletic field. And there's these two women, jogging. One of them especially catches my eye, she's just plugging away around the dirt, *thump thump thump thump thump.* She had this fierce look on her face – I immediately thought that by running she was, like, fighting something. Does that make sense?"

Min-Jun nodded, and Josh continued "So, I don't know why, maybe it's just because everybody else is doing it, but I decide to run too. And I've never been an athlete. I'd rather invent a cyborg body and put my brain in it than hoist a dumbbell. Barbell? Whatever.

"I put the tablet in my little backpack and take off running, and, before I even get around the track once, I'm wheezing. Just totally useless."

"Not even once?" the woman asked.

"Like, three-quarters of once. 65% at the very least."

"But you traveled the distance from desire to action, and that is where you must be proud!" Min-Jun interjected.

"Are you serious?" Josh lost himself to giggling. "I don't pat myself on the back for getting out of bed each day, and I never jogged again, so that doesn't count as a triumph in any philosophy.

"But I'm over near the drinking fountain, doubled-over, heaving, and the weirdest thing happens. My brain starts to focus: I mean really dial in. All my frustrations, the adolescent anger, all these things are distractions and suddenly they're just evaporating. I feel like if you'd put a computer in front of me right at that moment, I could have come up with something to make me a fortune."

"And that's when you had your breakthrough?" she guessed.

"Honestly? No. I think I was working on some other breakthrough." He laughed and looked down. "I know that sounds off-the-charts arrogant, but that's where I was at. I don't even remember what it was now. Because this woman, the jogging woman, she stops at the drinking fountain next to me and she just starts talking. And I'm fourteen, so the only grown-ups who talk to me are teachers and, I don't know, store managers, so I'm totally confused.

"She's really salty, like, blue collar, and I haven't met a lot of people like that. And she takes a big drink and says 'Water. Damn. Everyone needs it and they aren't making any more. Anybody who could figure out where every drop of water is could make a trillion dollars.'"

"No!" the woman shouted with delight, reaching out to smack Josh's arm affectionately. "She didn't! Some stranger on a jogging track?"

"I was dumbstruck!" Josh answered, caught up in the delight of the story. "Because I realized she was absolutely right. It was one of those subterranean equations about all human life, right? How much water does a person need? A forest? A city? How much of it needs to be salt water to spawn the sea life needed to feed a population? Suddenly I saw the whole Earth as this closed system of water that was going to get more and more valuable, and need closer and closer management. Suddenly all I wanted to do was to go home and start modeling it."

"Well, did you thank her at least?"

"All I could do was stare! And then she walked over to me, and said something even weirder. 'My name's Maria Kerrigan,' she said, 'and you owe me two things. One, don't be a selfish asshole. And two, don't ever come looking for me. This is our last conversation, okay?'"

"That's what she said?"

"Word for word. I've never forgotten it. And okay, now, *now* we get to the weird part."

The woman shook her head incredulously. "Please, tell me the weird part!"

"After I got my first big contract writing software for a city water department, I decided I would look her up. Kick her a bonus, not be a selfish asshole, right?

"And I swear to you, Maria Kerrigan is listed as having died the night before I saw her on the track."

"What!"

"Maria Kerrigan, pilot, former Air Force, picture looked exactly like I remembered her, described by friends as an avid jogger...died, *died*...the night before I saw her, in a plane crash hundreds of miles away. I checked the dates over and over again, and she was dead."

"You're telling me a *ghost* gave you career advice?"

"The Universe must not have thought you could interpret subtle signals," Min-Jun teased.

"The Universe isn't wrong on that one. But that's where it started. Everything that went into my company, my business, my fortune."

"A much smaller fortune than others would have made once you made all your algorithms pubic."

"Trust me, the traders never stopped squealing about that. Said I wasn't just leaving a fortune for myself on the table, I was strangling a million would-be water market entrepreneurs in their cradles."

"So you decided that no one should ever die of dehydration?"

"We decided no one should die of polio if we could help it, why not this step too?"

"Some might argue," Min-Jun said, "that the purpose of the human race isn't to save everyone, but only those who earn survival."

"I guess I never asked myself what the purpose of the human race is," Josh said, "but I know I don't agree with that. Or maybe I just don't know what earning it means. Definitions are important, aren't they?"

He leaned back, suddenly reflective. "It's not even the first fortune I turned down. When I first started getting a profile, before I connected with Analuiza, this company reached out and offered me a job. This weird Russian guy ran it, he had a reputation in the hacker circles. I won't even quote you the salary he offered: it was probably the most lucrative job offer in human history. Said he wanted me to hack the brain so it could talk to computers."

"Sounds like a thrilling field."

"Sure. I mean, even now I think about it from time to time; it's an enticing problem. But water, by that time water already just felt like me. It's hard to explain. The guy got desperate – I think I turned him down ten times – and he started showing up in person."

292

"Khaslik," Min-Jun said, his head tilted and a strange look on his face.

"Yeah! Khaslik. How have you heard about him?"

Min-Jun nodded to himself as the memory confirmed the strangeness he had felt first. "Yes, Spartak Khaslik. Russian, very rich. He made me an offer too!"

"What did he want you to do?"

"He would only say it had to do with particle accelerators working in tandem, and that I would have unlimited resources. He was...exercised about it, I think is the best word."

"And you turned him down too?"

"I did! It did not feel like science. And I did not need that much money."

"Now there's a coincidence I never thought I'd see. I think you and I were meant to meet!" Josh answered.

"I think so too," Min-Jun answered, sipping at his tea with immense satisfaction.

Now Josh turned to the woman he found so fascinating. "Please tell me the mad, rich Russian also found you."

She just shook her head. "Nope, sorry. Never even heard of him."

Josh snapped his fingers in frustration.

"Do you ever regret turning down two fortunes?" she asked.

"Well," he stared into his glass, "if you go back and start changing your life, you think you're fixing something but you might find you can't put it back together the way you like."

"Because we're imperfect," Min-Jun added.

"And you end up with scars," she concluded.

"Yeah." Josh smiled. "So anytime I find myself on that road, I just think back to that night on the jogging trail and I just let those thoughts," he wiggled his hand upwards to demonstrate, "escape up into the sky."

"You got it," the woman smiled.

"What?"

"My name. Sky Sebelius."

Josh leaned forward. "Sky Sebelius. Now there's a name I can't imagine forgetting."

***

-END-